Remember Wake

Also by Teresa R. Funke

Dancing in Combat Boots
and Other Stories of American Women in World War II

For Younger Readers

The Home-Front Heroes WWII Series

Doing My Part

The No-No Boys

V for Victory

Visit www.teresafunke.com to:

• Add your stories or your family's stories about WWII.

• Learn more about women's and children's experiences in WW II.

• Download a book club guide to *Remember Wake* and learn how to schedule Teresa to speak to your group.

Remember Wake

a novel based on a true story

Teresa R. Funke

VICTORY
HOUSE
PRESS

Published by:
Victory House Press
3836 Tradition Drive
Fort Collins, Colorado 80526
www.victoryhousepress.com

Library of Congress Control Number 2009936547

Printed in Canada

ISBN 978-1-935571-08-7
(Previously published by Bailiwick Press, ISBN 978-1-934649-02-2)
(Previously published by 1st Books Library, ISBN 0-7596-7535-X)

Acknowledgments

First and foremost, I must thank the men and women who actually lived the experiences depicted in this book. Sadly, most have passed away, but their faces are etched in my mind and their stories live on in this book: Joe and Marcella Bayok; Max Boesiger; Edythe Brueck; Genevieve Donoho; Joe Goicochea; Bill Gooding; Clint and Audrey Haakonstad; Clarine Johnson; Eloise McLeod; Lloyd Nelson; Ike Wardle; and Grady Westby. Most of these fine people were members of Survivors of Wake, Guam and Cavite, and to that organization I also owe a debt of gratitude.

Authors love reference librarians. Thank you to the wonderful librarians at the Idaho State Historical Library and The Boise Public Library for all their help.

Special thanks to Susan M. Stacy, who inadvertently introduced me to this story and then thoroughly supported my efforts to write it. To Lisa Spires for first believing in this book.

And, most importantly, to the members of my writers' group, the Slow Sand Writers Society, who spent countless hours poring over these pages offering suggestions and edits, unwavering support, and a good swift kick from time to time: Jean Hanson; Karla Oceanak; Tracy Ekstrand; Paul Miller; Marilyn Colter; Kathy Hayes; Luana Heikes; Jennifer Nastu; Julia Doggart; Douglas Black; and Todd Shimoda.

I mustn't forget my three children, Brian, Lydia and Ava, who dealt so patiently with the many hours I spent working on this book.

Finally, to my husband, Roger. What can I say? I couldn't have done it without you. All my love and thanks.

This book is dedicated to the survivors of Wake Island and their families.

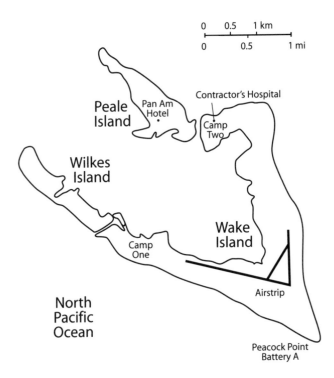

0   0.5   1 km

0   0.5   1 mi

Contractor's Hospital

Peale
Island

Pan Am
Hotel

Camp
Two

Wilkes
Island

Wake
Island

Camp
One

North
Pacific
Ocean

Airstrip

Peacock Point
Battery A

Chapter 1

Boise, 1941

"Come on, Maggie," Colin said, his gaze fixed on Maggie's bedroom window. He tried to believe he could will her to appear, that somehow he could make her feel his presence. His sister, Gwen, would have believed he could, but Colin had never been as romantic. Still, when the lace curtains fluttered up on the spring breeze, he expected to see Maggie's face; he even raised a hand to wave her down. But the curtains settled back in the window frame, and Colin settled back on his heels. He stared at the yellow Victorian Maggie shared with her mother and grudgingly pulled himself back to reality.

A Studebaker rolled by on West State Street, and Colin acknowledged the driver's two-fingered greeting with a nod. With his hand in the right pocket of his trousers, he rubbed the smooth surface of his father's gold watch. He'd been hoping to avoid calling at Maggie's door, being in no mood for Mrs. Braun's small talk or the way her eyes would narrow as she surveyed him, her gaze traveling up from his leather shoes to his forced smile.

Colin had just resigned himself to this fate when he heard someone call his name. He turned to see Maggie's uncle, Eddie, leaning against the screen door of the house across the street, arms folded across his thin chest. Colin groaned and promised himself he wouldn't let Eddie keep him long. He went to stand before Maggie's uncle, his foot on the lowest porch step, his fist tapping impatiently the iron railing.

"Beautiful evening," Eddie said.

The sun was setting far off over the horizon, lending a dreamy sharpness to the tree-lined town of Boise, Idaho. Shadows swelled across foothills the color of coffee with cream. And above the mountains, ribbons of pink and orange wove through the sky to wrap a faint crescent moon.

"Come in for a drink?" Eddie opened the door wider.

"Can't. I need to talk to Maggie."

"Something wrong?"

"No." Colin weighed how much he wanted to reveal. He knew how seriously Eddie took his responsibilities to his dead brother's daughter. He sometimes resented Eddie's protectiveness, but today he found it comforting. It would make it easier to leave Maggie.

"Maggie's here," Eddie said. "She's out back."

Colin nodded, relieved to dodge Maggie's mother, and set off around the house, feeling Eddie's eyes upon him. At the corner of Eddie's small backyard he hesitated, his hand once again finding his father's watch in his pocket.

Maggie was kneeling on a sheet, carefully painting the rungs of an old chair. Even in well-worn, blue slacks, her uncle's plaid shirt, and a faded pink scarf covering her auburn hair, she was striking. How clearly he remembered her kneeling, just this way, over the picnic basket she'd packed for their first date nearly four years before. She had been a nervous eighteen-year-old then who'd pouted when she discovered she forgot to bring the dessert.

He'd laughed and reached across the blanket they'd spread out under a tree beside the Boise River and reassured her he couldn't have eaten another bite. Even now he could remember how strong his fingers felt holding her small hand, how he kept clearing his throat before he spoke, afraid to say the wrong thing.

He shrank back, realizing he hadn't decided how to break the news to Maggie. He took his hands from his pockets and straightened his sweater. It would have helped to know he could count on Eddie to back him up, but he suspected Eddie would have doubts about his decision. This time he would have to win her over on his own.

As he stepped forward, Maggie looked up. She wiped her hands on her apron and smiled. "Were you watching me?" she asked as he approached.

"I could watch you all day."

She put her arms around his neck, fanning paint-streaked fingers away from his clothes. He lowered his head to kiss her, but she turned quickly in his arms, lifting her hair off her neck with the backs of her hands so he could untie the apron. Instead, he kissed her neck, his lips warm against her skin. She shivered and closed her eyes, arching toward him. When she stepped reluctantly out of his embrace, his hand trailed down her arm, catching her wrist. She glanced toward the back of Eddie's house.

"It's okay," Colin said, drawing her back. "He's on the front porch."

With a nod toward the neighbor's house, she asked, "And

what about Mrs. Coleman?"

"Ah, Mrs. Coleman," Colin conceded with a sigh.

She smiled and indicated the chair she'd been painting. "What do you think?"

Colin circled it slowly while Maggie watched. The chair's finish was ruined, and the wood had warped so badly the back leaned away from the base, but she hoped he could see that gave it character.

"It looks good," Colin said, but not like he meant it.

"It'll look better when I'm finished," Maggie assured him. "Uncle Eddie said I could have it. I thought we could use it in our kitchen, or maybe a den."

"I have good news, Maggie," Colin said, grabbing her hands. "I figured out a way to get some money together so we can get married."

In her mind, a picture formed of Colin in his father's best suit, her uncle standing beside her mother and a room full of family and friends. It was a picture that lately seemed so real it was more like a memory than a vision of something to come. But the picture faded as Colin began to speak, and she noticed his hand go to the back of his neck as it always did when he was unsure about something.

"There's this place called Wake Island," Colin blurted out. "It's out in the middle of the Pacific. The government is building a military base there, and they've contracted with Morrison Knudsen. I went down to M-K today to check into jobs on Wake."

She watched his face change from worry to excitement as she struggled to absorb his words. "Maggie, the pay is out of this world. In just nine months on Wake, I could get together enough money for a down payment on a house."

"Nine months?" She pulled away. "I thought you said we

could get married this summer."

"I know, but this changes things, don't you think? We could start off on our own feet. No help from anyone."

Maggie shook her head. "Military base? Colin, that sounds dangerous. The whole world is at war except us."

"It's not dangerous, sweetheart," he said. "I wouldn't go if it was. This is the opportunity we've been waiting for."

She was shaking off her shock, and the anger was coming through. He could tell by the flash in her pale blue eyes. "The opportunity *you've* been waiting for, Colin," she said.

"What does that mean?"

"For nearly three years now you've been saying you're going to marry me when the time was right. I've always known what you meant by that. That you needed to know you could provide for me first. Fine. That's how you feel. But this is how I feel." She began to pace. "I've never thought we needed a house right off. We could live with your family or even my mother. All *I* want is to be your wife." She stopped abruptly and yanked the sheet from under the chair. It toppled onto its side as she rolled the sheet into a twisted bundle. When Colin reached to help, she shoved his hands away, dropping the paintbrush into the can and carrying it toward the house. He rushed to open the door.

"Can we talk about this?" he asked.

"Sounds like you already made up your mind."

Colin tried to chuckle, but it came out a wasted gush of air. He followed her into the kitchen. "Actually, Patrick and I signed up today. We're leaving in two weeks."

"You and Patrick," she said. "I should have known he was a part of this."

"I'm sorry," Colin said, placing his hands on her shoulders. "I should have talked to you about this before I signed on, but there didn't seem to be time. I was afraid they'd fill the positions if I didn't act fast. I thought you'd understand."

"Did you? Then why did you look so nervous when you told me?"

They stood in the kitchen, staring at the black and white tiled floor, gathering their thoughts. The clock ticked loudly. In a moment, Colin took the wadded-up sheet from under her arm and the paint can from her hand and placed them on the counter. He pulled her toward him. "Maggie—"

She braced her palms against his chest and held him at a distance. "You know, Colin, I have a box in my room I was going to show you soon," she said. "I've been filling it for months with fabric samples for a wedding gown and magazine pictures of flowers I might like in my bouquet. I wrote to a hotel in McCall, thinking we might honeymoon by the lake." She pushed away from him. "I'm twenty-two years old, Colin. You're twenty-three. Most of our friends are married already. My God, even Patrick's married."

"Don't you think I want to be married?"

"You want things to be perfect, but they'll *never* be perfect. Why can't you see that?" She turned away from him and found she could no longer hold her shoulders back. Her mother would be disappointed in her behavior. Not very composed. Not very ladylike. She sighed heavily and raised her head, but she did not look at Colin. "Did you tell Uncle Eddie?"

"Not yet."

"I can imagine what he'll think. That I should have gone to college like he told me to. He never wanted me to be too dependent on any man, and that's exactly what I've become," she said. "I should have listened to him. I could have lived my whole life without knowing there was such a place as Wake Island."

"Everything will be all right, Maggie."

Maggie turned to face him, hating the quiver in her voice, the tears in her eyes. She couldn't stand for him to misinterpret her anger for something as childish as hurt feelings or fear. "You've always said you want our children to have the things we didn't have," she began. "Well, the most important thing missing from my childhood was my father, and I've seen what that's done to my mother. I promised myself I'd marry a man who would always be there for me and my children. I want it to be you, Colin, but I won't wait forever. I'll go on with my life. I swear I will."

She turned and walked through Eddie's cluttered house and out his front door.

"Maggie," Colin called feebly as he followed her onto Eddie's front porch. But she crossed the street without a backward glance and disappeared into her house, slamming her front door. Colin bit his bottom lip, wondering how he could have been so mistaken. He had expected her to be disappointed by another postponement of their marriage, but had never expected an ultimatum. It was not like Maggie to react so strongly.

Eddie Braun rose from his favorite rocking chair, the one that sometimes moved from one side of the screened-in porch to the other but always faced east—toward Maggie's house. "Have that drink now?" Eddie asked.

Colin slapped his worn fedora against his thigh and fought the urge to throw something. "A drink would be good," he said.

Eddie stepped into the house and returned quickly with two tumblers, each containing a finger-width of whiskey. Colin downed the whiskey then crossed to a low wooden bench against the wall, gathered up a scattered copy of the *Idaho Daily Statesman* and glanced at the date—April 3. He tossed the two-day-old paper on the floor and sat down, dropping his hat onto the bench then rolling the tumbler between open palms.

Eddie slid a cigarette from his shirt pocket and lit it with a Zippo lighter. "How's work?" he asked. It wasn't Eddie's style to ask straight out what was wrong. Colin had to laugh.

"Still busting my back," Colin said. "And for what? I'm never going to get rich delivering furniture for twenty dollars a week. So I quit today."

Eddie stopped rocking, and Colin felt his confidence slip. He set the tumbler on the bench. "You know a lot about the world, Eddie. What have you read about Wake Island?"

Eddie stroked his graying black mustache. "I believe Pan American uses it as a stopover for passenger flights to the Orient. I read once they have a nice hotel on Wake, but I don't recall much else there." He cocked his head. "I take it you saw the ad in the paper about the naval base being built there."

Colin nodded. "I went down to Morrison Knudsen to check it out."

"And?"

"I signed up. I leave in two weeks."

Eddie leaned forward, resting his arms on his knees. He dropped ashes between his feet and brushed them aside with one shoe. "How long will you be gone?"

"Nine months."

"Nine months is a long time to a young girl."

"You going to lecture me now too Eddie?"

Eddie took a sip from his drink then began fumbling through a stack of books on an end table. "What'd they tell you about the work?"

"Morrison Knudsen's already started building the base," Colin said. "I'll be loading and driving supply trucks. They asked if I could handle long hours and hard work, and I told them I could handle anything for that kind of money." Colin scooted over on the bench. "A hundred and fifty dollars a month to start, and that's with no income tax deducted. Then there are bonuses."

Eddie whistled, but said nothing. He was studying a page in an atlas. After a moment, he tossed the atlas at Colin's feet. "Page twenty-eight. Lower left-hand corner, two inches up. That's where you'll be going."

Colin held the page close to his eyes and stared at the tiny dot that marked Wake Island. "I know. It's in the middle of nowhere."

"Looks like maybe twenty-three hundred miles from Hawaii, maybe fifteen hundred from Guam, twelve hundred from Midway," Eddie said. "That should tell you how big that ocean is—and how far away you'll be."

Colin lowered the atlas to his lap. The two men were silent for a moment, but the old floorboards creaked loudly under Eddie's swaying rocker, and somewhere down the road a mother shouted for her sons to come in for dinner. In that moment, breathing deeply the familiar, Colin realized he couldn't imagine a world outside Idaho, and he suddenly felt very tired.

"My father used to say leaving Ireland closed his throat so that he couldn't talk for days, but America brought his voice back stronger than ever," Colin said. "Wish I'd paid more attention to his stories before he died."

"Colin, if you're doing this to be like your father—"

"Come on, Eddie. You know me better than that."

"Well, I can't help wondering if you gave any thought to those lumber camps in Oregon we talked about? You could get off on your own for a while, see some of the country. And they pay good wages."

Colin struggled to keep his voice even. As much as he respected Eddie, he hated how he always talked like he knew what was best for everyone. "I'll make more money on Wake than most jobs I could find stateside, Eddie. You know that. Just like you know I need to get some dough together if I'm going to marry Maggie." Colin set the atlas on the bench and folded his arms. "I'd hoped you'd back me up. So tell me, what's really eating you?"

As usual, Eddie was eager to share what he knew. "If you'd been reading the papers lately, Colin, you'd know what the Japanese are doing to that part of the world. For almost ten years they've been bulldozing over Asia like a runaway train. China, Korea, Manchuria . . ." He jabbed a finger toward Colin. "We don't pay as much attention to the Japanese as we do the Nazis, but that's a mistake. They're just as dangerous, especially now that they've signed a pact with Germany and Italy—"

Colin was sorry he'd asked. Eddie could go on like this for hours, and Colin had never been too interested in war talk. He had too many other things on his mind. For one thing, he should try to reason with Maggie again. "Can we talk more about this later?" he asked, rising from the bench.

Eddie followed his gaze and understood immediately. "I'd let her simmer a bit, son," he said. "She's got just a bit of my brother's temper in her."

"But she'll come around," Colin insisted.

"Hope so."

Colin glared at Eddie. "You saying she won't wait for me?"

"Not saying anything." Eddie blew smoke toward the ceiling. "If it's meant to be, it's meant to be."

Colin slumped against the screen and tapped his hat against his palm, his gaze once again finding Maggie's window. "Oh it's meant to be, Eddie," he said. "I know it is."

Chapter 2

Boise, 1941

Colin paced beside one of two buses waiting to transport the men on the first leg of their journey to Wake Island. He couldn't believe Maggie would not come to see him off. She'd refused to speak to him at first, but when he finally heard from her a few days ago, she sounded resigned to his decision, if not supportive.

He glanced over his shoulder at his mother. Laura Finnely had just finished reassuring Colin that Maggie would be here. There was nothing left for her to do now but nod and smile gently at her son. Colin looked over at his friend Patrick Gulley, who was standing at the edge of the small crowd stroking his wife's blond hair. He watched them for a moment, irritated to be missing a similar moment with Maggie.

A car horn sounded. Eddie's black Packard pulled into the parking lot and eased to a stop. Maggie jumped out of the car, catching her handbag strap on the door handle. She struggled to free it.

"Leave it," Colin shouted, rushing toward her. She let go of the handbag as he arrived at her side. He lifted her off the ground and held her close.

Despite an earlier promise to herself to remain aloof, to register her disapproval of this entire affair, arriving late had unnerved her, and Maggie found herself surrendering to the warmth of Colin's body, laying her cheek against his brown sweater, breathing its damp, musty scent, its zipper cool against her skin. All around, men were preparing to leave their families. Maggie heard the voice of a child begging her father not to go, a baby cooing, a woman crying. She held Colin tighter, her heart beating so hard she was sure he could feel it.

"I was getting worried," he said.

"I'm sorry." She lifted a shaky hand and touched the sandy brown hair at his temple.

"I've got something for you," he said, digging in his pants pocket. The bus driver honked just as Colin held out a tiny gift-wrapped box.

Maggie stared at it, and though she heard the bus driver calling for the men to board, she found she could not move. She looked helplessly into Colin's green eyes. He tore off the gift-wrap, letting it fall to the ground, and opened the box to reveal a small diamond solitaire. "I hope this proves I'm the marrying kind," he said with that cocky, slightly crooked smile that had once stolen her heart.

So many times Maggie had imagined this moment, but in her dreams it had taken place in a romantic setting—the park where they'd gone on their first date, or her mother's rose garden. This was not a dream, though, and the moment for which she'd waited was taking place in a rain-soaked parking lot, the air heavy with the smells of worms and exhaust, the bus engines rattling loudly.

And more than she wanted the ring, she wanted to hear Colin say he had decided he could not leave her.

"I picked this out months ago," he was saying as he took the ring from its box. "The jeweler was a friend of my father's. I've been making payments, and he agreed to let me pay off the rest with what I earn on Wake." He took Maggie's left hand. "May I?" he asked.

She nodded, catching her breath as he slipped the ring onto her finger. She stretched her hand out to study it and wondered if it would have looked bigger had the sun been shining. She instantly regretted her selfishness and told herself Colin had been wise to choose this modest ring, that it looked good on her small hand. "It's beautiful," she said, as the impatient bus driver shouted at the men.

Colin slung his duffel bag over his shoulder. Turning, he traced his fingertip down Maggie's cheek.

"Don't forget our agreement." Maggie said, catching his hand and holding it tightly against her cheek. "You'll come straight home when your contract is up. We'll get married then."

"I'll be home in nine months. I promise."

Eddie stepped forward and extended his hand, his eyes earnest. "Watch your back, son."

"I will, sir." He gave Eddie's hand a firm squeeze.

Patrick Gulley hurried over on legs so long and spindly he'd often reminded Maggie of a clothespin doll. He touched the bill of his wool tweed cap and leaned in close to Maggie. "Hey, Mags, be a doll and keep Ellen company for me while I'm gone. She's gonna stay on with my folks to take care of Ma, but I'm guessin' she might get lonely. Her family lives in Nampa, and she don't see 'em but once a month."

Maggie glanced at Patrick's wife, who stood with her head down, her handbag clasped tightly in her fingers. "I'll call on her soon," Maggie said with little enthusiasm.

"Knew I could count on you. Always thought Colin knew how to pick 'em." Patrick kissed her cheek. He nudged Colin and nodded toward the bus. "Let's get movin', buddy. Never waste time or good whiskey, that's what I always say."

Maggie walked with them to the bus, gripping Colin's hand in both of hers.

Colin turned to kiss her. "I'll be back soon, Maggie."

She smiled through the tears rolling down her cheeks. "I love you."

"Yeah, yeah, we all love ya." Patrick pushed Colin up the steps.

Maggie scrambled backward to get a better view as Colin maneuvered for a window seat in the half-filled bus. He pressed his fingers against the glass as Maggie walked beside the bus until it began to outpace her. It soon turned out of the parking lot and disappeared from view. Though the crowd was already dispersing, Maggie remained, watching the road, refusing to believe even now that Colin could leave her.

She felt a plump hand on her arm and turned. Colin's mother hugged her. "Come by tomorrow for dinner," she said.

Maggie nodded, trying to hold onto the moment when she could still see Colin's face in the bus window.

Something rustled at her feet, and it took a second to recognize the pieces of pink-and-white-striped paper that had wrapped the ring box Colin had presented her. Maggie watched them skid across the pavement. She squatted, the hem of her overcoat trailing along the wet cement as, one by one, she gathered the pieces.

"Here, let me hold those for you," Eddie offered, uncurling her fingers to remove the scraps of paper. He tucked them safely into the deep pockets of his coat.

"I feel like I'll never see him again," Maggie said, beginning to cry.

Eddie kissed her forehead and helped her to her feet. He put his arm around her shoulder and led her toward the car as the soft spring rain began to fall again.

Patrick combed his thick, brown hair and listed the things he might buy with the money he made on Wake: a new rifle, a suit, maybe a car. Colin was only half listening, his chin tucked into his palm as he watched the farmland and still-brown sagebrush rush past the bus. Not the prettiest scenery in Idaho, he thought, remembering the trips to the pine-scented mountains he'd taken with his father.

Only once before had he come close to traveling outside the state. His family and Patrick's had camped just this side of the Oregon border when Colin was eleven—before the Depression and before his father died. His favorite memory of his dad came from that trip. Beside the campfire, Fergus Finnely had passed a flask to Patrick's father, and they had laughed for hours while retelling stories about their families back in Ireland. Fergus had called Colin to his side often to use him as a prop in his stories or simply to drape his arm around his son. Even tipsy, Fergus knew just how to grip Colin's shoulders, look him square in the eye and make him feel like the most important person on earth.

At moments like this, Colin could remember so clearly his father's face and the sound of his laughter. His mother often said he'd inherited Fergus's square jaw and solid build—but also his stubborn streak. Colin preferred to think of it as a determined nature, a strong spirit. That's the way he'd always thought of his father, and that's what had made the news of his death so hard to accept. If only he hadn't been pouting over some stupid thing his father had said, Colin thought again, if only he had accompanied him on the hunting trip as he'd been asked to, perhaps he could have saved Fergus when his heart failed.

As the bus put more distance between him and Boise, Colin forced himself to consider what lay ahead. But the more he thought about Wake, the more his excitement and apprehension built, the more mixed-up he felt.

A man in the next row back kicked Colin's seat. "Sit still, will ya? You're botherin' me."

Colin turned to glare at the man, who was small but muscular. His cold gray eyes held a clear challenge.

Patrick cussed and rose to Colin's defense.

"Let it go," Colin said, his hand on Patrick's arm. "It's a long ride to California. No sense making enemies."

"Well, the jackass is right about one thing," Patrick whispered. "You're squirmin' like an ant on a hotplate."

"Sorry. Nerves, I guess."

Patrick scooted down in the seat, stretched long legs into the aisle, and yawned.

"You suppose this is how our fathers felt leaving Ireland?" Colin whispered.

Patrick shrugged and tipped his cap over his eyes.

But Colin felt like talking. "I've been thinking lately I might take some college courses when I get back. I'd like to start my own business someday. Maybe a lumberyard. I always liked the feel of wood in my hands, the smell of it when it's fresh cut. Boise's growing. People will be building more houses."

"Uh-huh." Patrick's head nodded forward onto his chest.

Colin frowned. He took his father's gold watch from his pocket and curled the chain into the palm of his hand. The watch had been a gift to Fergus from his parents on the eve of his departure from Ireland. His initials were inscribed inside the cover. The watch was still in good condition, except for a scratch on the face and a slight dent in the cover, and it was Colin's most prized possession.

Inside the bus it was fairly quiet, most of the men having drifted off. The excitement of the last few days finally caught up with Colin. He rested his head against the window, closed his eyes, and allowed the rocking of the bus to lull the tension from his body. He thought of Maggie as she looked when the bus pulled away, tears falling, dark hair framing her face, his ring on her finger, and again hoped he could prove to her he was doing the right thing.

Chapter 3
Wake Island, 1941

"You should get some ointment for that sunburn," shouted Red Warner as he slid the last two-by-four onto the flatbed. He tossed an end of rope over the back of the truck, and Colin caught it, grunting as he jerked it tight across the lumber stack and looped it around a slat in the sideboard.

"I'll stop at the infirmary when my shift's over."

Colin watched a flock of bosuns fly overhead. He'd become fascinated by these large birds that seemed to fly backward as they maneuvered to land in the strong northeasterly trade winds, their red feet and beaks bright against the pale blue sky.

"Some say they fly backward because they care more about where they've been than where they're going," Red said.

"Then they're not like me." Colin gazed at the green and turquoise waves striking the rocky shore. "I've got too much to look forward to. Can't see much sense in looking back."

"You will," Red said. "Someday."

With the load secured, Colin climbed into the truck's cab and dropped his broad-brimmed hat onto the seat.

"How about a lift to the office?" Red said, jumping into the truck.

Colin glanced back at the supply ship. He'd recently learned that just beyond the island's dangerous reef, the ocean floor plunged to depths of five hundred feet, making it nearly impossible for ships to drop anchor. Instead, they turned over their engines to hold position or drifted on the waves while cargo was lowered to the barge.

"As if this place didn't seem isolated enough," Colin said, gesturing toward the ship. "It's like the whole damn world drops away on the other side of those reefs."

Wake was nothing like Colin had imagined. Though he wasn't sure what he had hoped to find, he knew he had never expected a place so stark and barren, yet beautiful. Wake Island was a V-shaped coral atoll formed over an underwater volcano. The opening of the V faced northwest—toward Japan. What had once been the volcano's crater was now the lagoon, and Wake's three small islets had been part of the rim. Wake, the largest of the three islets, formed the base of the V. Of the other two islets, Peale was located at the northernmost point of the V, and Wilkes lay across the lagoon from Peale. Altogether they totaled less than three square miles.

Colin thought often about those men he'd traveled with aboard the USS *Burrows* who had taken one look at the tiny, sweltering island and gotten right back on the ship. They must be back in Hawaii by now, surfing, enjoying exotic fruits and the attention of tanned island girls. Colin envied them. He'd never seen a more spectacular place than Honolulu, where they'd been held over for nearly two weeks awaiting transport to Wake.

He sighed, and the truck bed swayed slightly as he pulled onto the crushed coral road, which ran the perimeter of the atoll. Before he'd been to Wake, Colin had never even seen coral. Now it was everywhere, some of it dead, the rest alive and growing, ensnaring beach magnolia and dwarf ironwood. It came in a variety of colors, pink and lavender, white and blackish gray, and could be porous or lacy, etched by the waves that beat relentlessly against Wake's shore.

Red hung his elbow out the window, his hat set back on his freckled scalp. The bright sunlight reflected off his fair skin, shadowing deep lines in his forehead and around his hazel eyes. He scrunched down in the seat, his knees braced against the dashboard.

Colin knew less about Red than any of the new guys he'd met on the *Burrows*. He knew only that Red came from Portland, Oregon, and lived with his parents when he wasn't working construction jobs. He had no wife or girlfriend. Colin guessed him to be about forty, which would make him nearly twice as old as most of the men on the island. Colin smiled, thinking back to his first conversation with Red while still on board the ship.

"I'm not here to socialize, just to get this job done and move onto the next one," Red had said. "Wake won't be like Hawaii, you know. No sandy beaches or pretty girls. No drinking till daybreak. Just a lot of hard work."

Now Colin batted Red's arm, raising his voice over the clamor of the engine. "I was just thinking about what you first told me about Wake—how it would be no picnic. Boy, you weren't kidding."

"I never kid," said Red, but with a half-smile.

The truck backfired as Colin downshifted in front of the superintendent's tent. "The *Clipper* came in this morning with the mail," Red said. "I can see if you got any letters and drop them on your bunk."

"Hold onto them for me, will you? Otherwise Patrick will read them before I get a chance."

Red nodded and jumped out of the truck.

Colin revved the engine and pulled back onto the road. The land was mostly flat, the highest spot on the atoll not more than twenty-one feet above sea level. The fifty-foot water tower seemed to soar into the sky. At some spots on the island, Colin could see far out ahead of him, but higher elevations were covered with thick brush and umbrella and hardwood trees. Dark green shrubs, some as high as ten feet, blanketed the interior, along with scrub trees.

On this tiny island, it took only a couple of minutes to get from one work site to the next. Along the way, he would pass diesel cranes, tractors, bulldozers, road scrapers and rollers, cement mixers, and trucks rumbling about. But on Peale another world existed, one sheltered beneath the blue and white flag of Pan American Airways, where tourists relaxed behind the French doors of The Inn, lounging in deep-seated wicker chairs, cooled by electric fans and waited on by white-clad Chamorro boys, natives of Guam.

Those travelers were on their way east, to the Orient, and for them Wake was only a one-night stopover, a quick trip around the lagoon in a glass-bottomed boat, a walk along the beach to collect seashells and coral, then a night's rest on comfortable mattresses behind painted, shuttered doors. Colin envied them almost as much as he envied the men who'd turned back toward home.

After only a week on Wake, he already knew the ruts and curves of the few roads better than he'd ever known the maze of streets back in Boise. He swerved to crush a rat as it darted in front of the truck. The rats had proven too smart to eat the poisoned grain laid out for them, and they were everywhere. Nearly as bothersome were the thousands of birds with strange names—fork-tailed tern, booby, man-o-war—who nested in the beach magnolia and shat on the equipment.

Colin stopped at one of the work sites and peered through the cracked windshield at men spidering over the frames of what would be the officers' quarters for the military detachment due to arrive in a few months. He knew Red had spent most of this first week on this project. From what Colin had heard, Red was a fine carpenter and a hard worker.

Colin lifted his canteen, wincing as the replenishing salt he'd added stung his cracked lips. The island's temperature averaged eighty degrees, but the humidity made it seem much hotter. With summer approaching, they'd been warned to expect upwards of one-hundred-degree temperatures.

Rusty Miller ambled over, stubby arms swinging at his sides. The men affectionately called him Chaplain because he led the Sunday night worship service on the beach and was always ready to lend an ear to any man with troubles. Chaplain's bunk was four down from Colin's in the barracks. He'd seen Chaplain reading his Bible every night and writing letters to his wife and three daughters.

On Colin's first uneasy night on Wake, Chaplain, who had arrived a couple of months earlier, stopped by to chat. He'd tried to help Colin make sense of the work on the island, taking a piece of paper and roughing out the plans for the base.

He started by drawing Pan American's Inn on Peale, and then marked Camp Two, the contractor's camp on the northern tip of Wake. Toward the base of the V on Wake, he sketched the airfield, and on her southern tip, Camp One, which would house the Marine detachment when they arrived. He explained how the crews would dredge a channel across a narrow part of

Wilkes to allow ships into the lagoon and that someday there would be a submarine base. He showed where they planned to enlarge the seaplane landing area in the lagoon near Peale. Then Chaplain had sat back, clearly impressed with it all, while Colin had simply shaken his head.

"It'll make sense soon," Chaplain had assured him.

"Do you miss home?" Colin asked.

"I miss my family, but the money I make here will give them a better life. My wife begged me not to come. But I told her I had a calling. I know God wants me on Wake for a reason."

Though Colin had never been an overly religious man, he was chilled by the look in Chaplain's earnest brown eyes. And Chaplain's confidence had given Colin the strength to make it through that first tough night, through a vivid nightmare in which Wake sank into the crater of the volcano and was washed over by the pounding surf.

Colin stepped out of the truck, hitching up his pants as he greeted Chaplain.

"Losing weight already, Finnely?"

"I think I sweated it off."

"Maybe God's giving us a little reminder. Must be *nearly* this hot in hell."

"Must be." Colin laughed and began unfastening ropes as more men gathered around to unload the truck.

———

Several hours later, Colin hurried toward the barracks before he was assigned something else to do. After delivering the lumber, he'd run canned goods and sacks of grain to the mess hall and erected a shelving unit at the camp hospital. He'd finished the day by changing a flat tire on the truck, and now all he wanted to do was rest.

He entered the eighty-man barracks, which was nicer than Red had led him to expect. It had two screened porches, running water, showers, electric lights, and indoor lavatories. As Colin worked his way down the aisle, he saw Kaminski, the man who'd kicked his seat on the bus, sitting on the edge of his bunk talking to a friend. He seemed not to notice Colin but then stuck his foot out to trip him.

"Watch where you're goin', mick," he growled, as Colin stumbled forward, hands out to break his fall. Kaminski stood.

Colin took his time getting back on his feet. He dusted off his palms and met Kaminski's glare. "Grow up, Kaminski," he said. He heard Kaminski growl something to his friend, but he was too tired to care. He collapsed on his narrow bunk just as Red approached.

"That fella giving you trouble?" Red asked.

"No, he's just a hothead. I can ignore him." Colin wiped the back of his hand across his sweaty forehead. "This heat really wears you out."

"You'll get used to it." Red dropped three letters onto Colin's chest.

Colin rose up on his elbow and tore open an envelope, pausing to breathe in Maggie's rose-scented perfume. A small picture fell onto the bunk. It showed Maggie wearing the dress and matching hat she knew to be Colin's favorite. He smiled and stared at the picture for several seconds before passing it over to Red.

"Very nice," was all Red said. He lit a cigarette and smoked quietly while Colin paraphrased the letter's contents.

"She's talking about wedding plans. She asked my sister to be her maid of honor and another friend to be a bridesmaid. She wants to know who's standing up for me besides Patrick."

"Patrick's an odd kid," Red said. "So moody."

"His father and mine came over from Ireland together. We've known each other all our lives." Colin felt guilty that it sounded like a justification. "Say, Red, how about coming to my wedding next February?"

Red scowled. "I'm not one for formal occasions."

"I guessed that." Colin laughed, then held out his hand to take back Maggie's picture. "Don't you think you'll ever find a girl and settle down?"

"Don't know. Guess I always figured any woman I'd want would find me."

"I've always felt like Maggie and I were just meant to be," Colin said. "Too bad her mother doesn't see it that way."

Red shook his head. "You don't just marry a woman, you marry her family. That's why you won't see me rushing for the altar."

"No girl would have ya, anyway," Patrick said, coming up behind Red and slapping him hard on the back.

"Yeah, no girl would have ya," echoed Frank D'Ambrosio, a wiry eighteen-year-old with dark, sleepy eyes who had taken to shadowing Patrick.

Red threw him an impatient glance and rose to leave.

"Hey, Red, why don't you come fishing with us Sunday night?" Colin said.

"We'll see."

"Don't do us any favors," Patrick muttered when Red was safely out of earshot. "I don't see why you like that fella, Colin. He's laced tighter than my grandma's corset."

"Red's all right," Colin said. "He's just serious."

Patrick made an unsuccessful grab for Colin's letters, then dropped down on Colin's bunk. "We're startin' up a poker game. Wanna sit in?"

"No thanks," Colin said, reaching under his bunk for the box where he kept his stationery. "I promised Maggie I'd try to write every day."

"And have ya?"

"Uh, I sent a postcard from Hawaii."

"That's what I figured."

Colin laughed. He rose, sidestepping Patrick's attempt to wrestle, and made for the door. "And stay out of my letters," he called over his shoulder as he walked out of the barracks into one of Wake's dazzling sunsets.

On the beach, the roaring surf drowned the noises of the men in camp. Green spider crabs scurried away from Colin's boots as he stooped to retrieve a glass ball from the edge of the waves. The colorful balls, used by the Japanese to buoy fishing nets, washed ashore daily. Colin had decided to collect a few and take them home, along with some of the prettier pieces of coral. He dropped his sweater on the rough sand and sat on it, leaning back against a slight bank. He closed his eyes, allowing the island breeze to penetrate his weary mind. Yawning, he positioned the pencil between stiff fingers and began to write:

Wake is quite a place, Maggie. Not what I expected at all. I'm driving and unloading truckloads of lumber, steel, and heavy machinery.

He paused, deciding against trying to explain the complicated work on the island. He tapped the pencil against the sheet and started again:

Patrick is bored stiff and wanting the one thing he can't get here—a drink. He never was good at taking orders and never imagined he'd get stuck cooking. I think he'd be on the next ship home if it weren't for me.

He scratched his neck and stared at the darkening sky, wondering why this was so difficult. Why did it suddenly seem he had nothing to say, as if Boise was worlds away? He looked back at the paper:

I met a new friend who reminds me of Eddie. He's older and spends a lot of time reading and thinking. Most of the other fellows are decent sorts, hard workers.

He reread what he wrote in the fading light, then slashed bold strokes across the sentences. He skipped a few lines and wrote in quick, illegible letters what he really wanted to say:

Do I miss you, Maggie? Sure. There are moments I can hardly stand it. But everything is so new here. The smells, the heat, this feeling of living on the edge of the earth. Not since I was sixteen, since my father died, have I felt so free. And, yet, I think I finally understand why Eddie says you have to be part of something bigger than yourself. I'm doing something important here. I can feel it. And these men are like brothers to me. Do I miss you, Maggie? You're the first thing I think of when I wake. But being here is something I want to do—I need to do—alone. I hope you can forgive that.

He jabbed the pencil point first into the sand, crumpled the letter and threw it as far toward the sea as he could. How was he supposed to explain to Maggie what was happening to him when he didn't fully understand it himself?

He kicked his boot at a rat and wondered what would be the use of trying to explain about the rats or the men who'd already been seriously injured on the job or the sunstroke or the hours of backbreaking work? How could a letter make her understand the excitement of swimming in a pool blasted out of a lagoon and enclosed with wire netting to keep out the sharks and moray eels?

Resting his head on his knees, Colin tried to imagine Maggie sitting on their favorite bench by the Capitol Boulevard Bridge back home. But the roaring surf, which had kept him awake his first night here, had lately become a lullaby. His tired mind formed only an outline of Maggie's figure, her slender legs crossed, shoulder-length hair stirring in the breeze. He rose, picked up his things, and headed back for the barracks, vowing that when he got home, he'd tell her everything.

Chapter 4

Boise, 1941

Maggie kicked off her pumps and raised her skirt to unfasten silk stockings and roll them carefully down each leg. She draped the stockings over the footboard of her bed and crossed to her vanity, reaching up to repin her hair. She watched her movements in the mirror, sucking in her breath to fill out her chest beneath the bodice of the dress she'd worn to church. She closed her eyes and imagined how she had looked when she first caught Colin admiring her at the Walgreen's soda fountain one summer day in 1937.

Maggie had been sitting with her friend Alice. An oscillating fan teased the stray hairs at the back of her neck. Nearby, two children stretched up on tiptoe while the soda jerk leaned both elbows on the counter to hear their orders. Alice was whipping her chocolate sundae with her spoon, worrying over the fate of a lost aviatrix named Amelia Earhart. Maggie understood her concern. She too had sat beside the radio with her mother and uncle listening for news, hoping the adventurous woman with the close-lipped smile had managed to land somewhere safely. It had seemed the most important thing in the world until Colin and his friends entered the soda fountain.

She watched him stroll to the counter and plunk down several coins to order three Coca-Colas. It was then that he'd noticed her, and she'd looked quickly at her milkshake, unable to decide which way to cross her legs. She could feel him watching her and glanced up a few minutes later to see him set down his empty bottle and saunter toward her. Her hand came up to lightly pat her upswept hair.

"Didn't we go to school together?" he asked, his mouth easing into a cocky smile.

Maggie nodded and lowered her eyes.

"You're Colin Finnely, right?" Alice said, kicking Maggie's shoe. "We were a grade behind you in high school. You still going around with Faye Delana?"

Maggie stirred her strawberry malt, feigning disinterest.

"No, Faye moved to St. Louis after graduation to live with an aunt." He dragged an empty chair to the table, straddling it backwards. "So what are we talking about, ladies?" he asked, dropping his hand casually on the table so it lay near Maggie's. She felt the heat from his skin and her fingers curled protectively around her glass, but she did not move her hand away.

Now, sitting at her vanity, she could almost smell the strawberries and chocolate and hear the clink of Alice's spoon as she scraped the bottom of her sundae dish and started up again about Earhart.

"A real shame," Colin had agreed, nodding at Alice, though his eyes were on Maggie.

Maggie sighed, letting her chest fall. Four years had passed, and she could look back on the naive, pampered girl at the soda fountain and feel confident she'd matured. She felt grown up and finally ready to be a wife and a mother, to run her own household and care for a husband. And she realized she had still not forgiven Colin for leaving, for not marrying her this summer as they'd planned.

She reached for the top drawer of the vanity, where she kept the only word she'd received from Colin since he left Boise more than a month ago. On a postcard, he'd written about the bus trip to California and the journey to Hawaii aboard a transport ship, but nowhere did he mention being happy she'd accepted his ring, or tell her how much he missed her. She told herself that exploring Honolulu must have kept him very busy, and he would surely write more often when he settled into his work on Wake.

A soft knock interrupted her thoughts, and she stuffed the postcard back in the drawer. She opened the door and greeted Ellen Gulley, Patrick's wife. Ellen wore no make-up or jewelry, though Maggie thought she should. At least powder to mask the freckles and a little rouge to bring some color to her face.

"Where's Gwen?" Ellen asked.

"Late as usual. Come on in."

Ellen commented on the warm weather and went to the window seat. The sun lit up her best feature, her long blond hair gathered into a braid trailing down her back. Ellen took cloth and an embroidery hoop from a bag. Maggie had seldom seen Ellen without her needlework. "Idle hands are the devil's workshop," Ellen would say.

Since the men had left, Maggie had become fascinated by this soft-spoken woman. Though she was what Maggie's mother called "plain," her air of delicacy and gentleness made her attractive in a distinctly feminine way. In Ellen's presence, Maggie stood up straighter and took shorter steps. Ellen had seemed shy at first, but Maggie soon realized she shared her confidences in subtle ways. Maggie was learning to listen carefully.

"How are you feeling?" Maggie asked.

"I'm recovered."

Maggie paused. "Then it wasn't morning sickness?"

"No."

"Are you sure?"

Ellen stopped her needle at the start of a stitch. "Quite sure."

Maggie reached over and touched Ellen's shoulder. "I'm so sorry."

"It's for the best, I guess. My hands are full with caring for Patrick's parents." Ellen resumed her stitching, and Maggie watched her for a moment.

"Have you heard any more from Colin?"

"No. I can't understand it. How about you?"

"Oh, Patrick's not much of a writer. I don't expect to hear much from him, but his mother is distraught. I wish, for her sake, he'd write more often."

"Take no offense, Ellen, but I have to ask. What on earth made you marry Patrick? The two of you are so different."

Ellen blushed. "Well, we met at a barn dance in Nampa, you know. He came with a friend from Boise whose family lives near mine." Ellen lowered her needlework. "I was usually with my mother and my aunt, and the boys paid little attention to me. But that night, Patrick was very persistent. He brought me lemonade, and asked me several times to dance. I turned him down, but after my mother and my aunt went looking for my father, he sat beside me. I barely spoke to him or looked at him, but he stayed until my mother returned. Then he asked to call on me. He came every other weekend for the next few months.

I guess you could say he wore me down, but it was more than that. No other man had ever taken such an interest in me." She looked at Maggie. "I know Patrick can be childish and crude, but he has a good heart and he loves me. That was something I thought I'd never have."

Maggie nodded. She still couldn't see Ellen and Patrick together, but if her acceptance of Colin's latest postponement of their wedding had taught her anything, it was that you couldn't help who you loved.

Strong footsteps beat on the stairs, and Maggie took a deep breath, steadying herself for the arrival of Colin's seventeen-year-old sister, Gwen, who burst into the room, her round face flushed, her sharp blue eyes alight beneath penciled brows. "Sorry I'm late," she said, bending to give Maggie a swift hug. "I'm such a mess. Can I borrow your brush, sis?" she asked, snatching it off the vanity before Maggie could answer. "I'm going to call you sis now that you and Colin are truly engaged."

Gwen began swiping at the red curls that encircled her face. She straightened her snug cotton sweater and smoothed her wide skirt across her full hips, then dropped the hairbrush into Maggie's lap and plopped down on the bed. "I saw your mother coming home."

"So soon? Did you say anything to her?"

"Nope. Just waved."

"Good." Maggie sat down again at the vanity.

"Do you know what I've been thinkin' 'bout today?" Gwen asked. "'Bout when Colin left." She fell back on the bed, grabbing the teddy bear Colin had won for Maggie at the State Fair. "Was that just the most romantic moment when he gave you the ring? Wish I could have been there, but Ma wouldn't let me out of school." She hugged the stuffed bear. "Someday I'm gonna meet someone who'll love me more than anything in the world."

Maggie exchanged a smile with Ellen. Gwen sighed dramatically and sat up.

"I see you're still not wearing Colin's ring," said Ellen.

"I haven't told Mother about our engagement yet."

"God, Maggie, why not?" Gwen asked.

"I've tried, but I can't find the right words. You know how she feels about Colin and me."

"I think it's that snooty English thing. Ma says the Brits are always puttin' on airs around the Irish."

"Do you think that's it, Ellen?" Maggie asked, concerned. "Mother will never tell me why she doesn't like Colin."

"I only know that the longer you wait to tell her, the harder it's going to be."

"I know . . . That's why I've asked Uncle Eddie to help me tell her tonight." Maggie took the ring box from the drawer in which she kept the postcard. She opened it and slipped the ring on her finger. Gwen kneeled beside her to admire the ring. "After tonight, I'll be able to wear this," Maggie said. "Think how Colin would feel if he knew it had been sitting in a drawer all this time."

"Oh I think he'd understand." Gwen giggled. "Let's face it. Even Colin's afraid of your mother."

Maggie watched Agnes move deliberately around the kitchen as she dished up supper. Eddie poked his head in, offering to help, but she turned him out of the room, smoothing her chestnut hair at the back of her head, where it was pulled into a loose bun. She took off the starched apron she wore over a brown housedress and hung it on a peg Eddie had made. She paused for a moment to rub lotion into her blue-veined hands, then handed Maggie two plates to carry into the dining room.

Eddie stood and took a plate from Maggie. He told Agnes the table looked nice, as he always did, though this was just an informal supper. They sat down and Eddie said grace. As they ate, he talked about the war in Europe—the recent falls of Greece and Yugoslavia, and the German siege of Tobruk, Lybia.

Agnes feigned interest, but Maggie knew she never kept up on the European war. "After all, America isn't involved," Agnes would say, but Maggie suspected her mother was choosing to close her ears for other reasons. Perhaps it had something to do with her youth in London, overshadowed by the first Great War, or maybe it had something to do with the death of Maggie's father, a veteran of that war that had promised to end all wars.

Eddie shifted to the latest developments in the East, explaining the significance of a recent pact between Russia and Japan. "It's intriguing," he said. "You know they are sworn enemies. I think Japan must be trying to seal things up peaceably so they'll run into less trouble expanding south into the Pacific."

This caught Maggie's attention and, worried, she glanced at her mother, who politely suggested to Eddie that war talk was not a suitable dinner conversation.

Eddie took her meaning. "I'm sorry, Maggie. I shouldn't talk about these things while Colin's over there."

There was a long silence, and then Eddie brought up the weather and Agnes asked about the vegetable garden he'd planted.

Maggie picked at her food and twisted her napkin in her lap. Finally, she found the courage to speak. "Uncle Eddie, why don't you tell Mother what you and Colin talked about before he left?"

Eddie stopped the fork on its way to his mouth. He stared at his niece as she shot up from her chair, piled her silverware and the empty breadbasket on her plate, and headed for the kitchen. "Tell her what you thought of Colin's plans for us when he gets back." She pushed open the swinging door.

"Where are you going?" Eddie asked.

"I'll be right back." She let the door close behind her and stood on the other side, peeking through the crack. She saw Agnes fold her hands on the table and stare at Eddie.

Eddie pushed his plate away and resettled himself in the high-back chair. "Looks like I'm on my own. Agnes, Colin asked Maggie to marry him, and she said yes."

Agnes said nothing.

"I think the kids would like your blessing. I gave them mine, of course."

Maggie squeezed her eyes shut, knowing Eddie's declaration had been a mistake.

"How kind of you, Edward, to give your blessing to *my* daughter," Agnes said. "How long have you known about this?"

"Colin proposed when Maggie went to see him off."

"That was a month ago." Agnes sounded hurt.

"He gave her a nice ring."

"I don't care about jewelry. I care about my daughter's future."

Eddie glanced at the swinging door and moved over to Maggie's chair to be closer to Agnes. "Whatever you've got against Colin, I don't see it. He seems to be a fine young man, and I think he'd make a good husband for Maggie."

Behind the door, Maggie held her breath, but Agnes remained rigid. "I have nothing personal against Mr. Finnely. I simply believe Margaret could do better for herself. After all, that boy has nothing substantial to offer in the way of financial security, he has only a basic education, and he certainly holds no influence in this town."

She lowered her voice, and Maggie could barely hear her. "You know, they say his father drank heavily. Perhaps he does as well."

"Nonsense," Eddie said. "He drinks no more than I do. Colin hasn't had many advantages in life, but he's worked hard. He's been supporting his family all these years and he wants to provide well for Maggie." Eddie rapped a finger on the table. "Sounds an awful lot like my brother when he married you."

Agnes frowned. "We are not speaking of Kurt. His actions and behavior were always those of a man who knew his own mind and had the potential to make something of himself, whereas Mr. Finnely has shown a certain recklessness in shipping off to some distant island without even consulting my daughter."

"That's not entirely fair, Ellie."

Maggie straightened. Eddie was the only one she'd ever heard call her mother Ellie. The nickname slipped out very seldom, and had always piqued Maggie's curiosity. Someday she'd ask Eddie.

Agnes rose, folded her napkin, and laid it on the table. "I'm not going to debate that boy's faults or merits with you, Edward. I am entitled to my opinion." She raised her voice and looked toward the swinging door. "Anyway, if I know my daughter, my blessing is inconsequential. She will do as she pleases. I'm going for a walk. Margaret can clear the table."

When she was gone, Maggie opened the swinging door.

Eddie shook a finger at her and tried to look angry, but Maggie only stepped up to him and kissed his cheek. Through the front window she could see Agnes walk briskly past the house, chin up, eyes forward, mouth set firmly, and Maggie dreaded the next few days of silence from her mother.

"Oh well," she thought, "at least it's done."

Chapter 5

Wake Island, 1941

"You're up, Colin," Patrick said. "Didn't you hear me the first time?"

"Sorry. Got a lot on my mind, I guess."

Patrick scowled. "That's always been your problem—thinkin' too much."

"Not something *you'll* ever have to worry about," Colin said, but his joke wasn't met with a smile. Patrick was in one of his difficult moods. To make matters worse, Kaminski had been glaring at Colin all night and now jeered at him from left field as Colin stepped up to the plate.

Colin hit a line drive and made it to first base. There was yet another delay as they waited for the next batter to rush back from the brush, where he'd been relieving himself beside one of the many bird nests scattered along the ground. While Patrick cursed from the sidelines, Colin scanned the crowd. Red sat off by himself reading a book, while Frank entertained Chaplain and several others with his imitation of Jimmy Cagney. A couple hundred men had shown up to the ballgame tonight. The others were probably swimming or watching the picture again at the outdoor theater.

Dan Teters, their charismatic superintendent, sat with his men, most of whom he could call by name, though they numbered close to one thousand now. Colin was beginning to learn that money wasn't the only thing that had brought these men to Wake. Some were looking for adventure, others running from problems. Some were killing time, like Red. The young ones, like Frank, wanted to put some distance between themselves and their parents. For a few, like Chaplain, the reasons were more complex.

The fifth inning ended with Colin's team behind by two runs. As the men jogged off the field, Kaminski ran up behind Colin, shoving him hard.

"Almost had you out that time, mick."

"Yeah, too bad you can't throw straight." Colin turned to leave, but Kaminski grabbed him by the arm and spun him around.

"You're always turnin' your back on me. You been 'fraid to fight me since we got on the bus."

"I'm not afraid of you, Kaminski. I'd just rather put my energy toward the game."

By now, other players had crowded around. "Come on, fellas," the third baseman said, stepping between them. "Let's play ball."

Patrick moved to Colin's side, glaring at Kaminski.

"We're not through with this, Finnely," Kaminski said. He stalked off toward the sidelines.

"That guy's a pain in the ass," the third baseman said to

Colin.

"Sure seems to have something against me."

"Nah. He's like that with everyone."

Colin was aware of Kaminski watching him as he made his way to a bench where a cup and a jug of water had been placed for the ballplayers. He snatched up the cup and poured himself a drink.

Red joined him. "There's one like him on every job," he said.

"I'm not much of a fighter, but that guy really burns me," Colin said. He looked up to see Red, with a furrowed brow, watching Dan Teters.

"What's the matter?"

"Something's going on, and Teters and the brass aren't telling us."

"What makes you say that?"

"He looks worried."

"Looks all right to me," Colin said. "Seems to be enjoying the game."

Red shook his head impatiently. "Superintendents are always pushing to beat deadlines, but this time something feels different. Somebody's puttin' extra pressure on him. For some reason, the higher-ups are wanting this job done sooner."

"I hear Teters talking a lot about how we're building faster than the crew on Midway," Colin said. "Maybe there's some sort of competition between the two."

"It's more than that."

Colin squinted into the sunlight, trying to read Teters' face, but Teters rose and excused himself. He headed for his small cottage and his wife Florence. The most approachable of the three women on the island, Florence was a pretty blond with an outgoing manner and quick smile. She was more than just a hostess for the journalists and visitors who stopped over on Wake; she was a reassuring presence for the work crews battling homesickness and fatigue.

Colin noticed several men watching the superintendent as he ambled toward home. "Maybe Teters is under some pressure, but I doubt there's a man on the island who wouldn't trade places with him tonight," Colin said.

Red turned to leave.

"Aren't you going to finish watching the game?" Colin asked.

Red shook his head and raised a book in his left hand. "Think I'll just read a few chapters and call it a night."

"I should knock off too. My mind's not in the game tonight. Been thinking about Maggie. We had talked about getting married this summer, you know. Strange to think I could be married right now."

Red looked at the ground, as if considering whether to go on. "Guys like you think you've got life all sewn up. You lay out your plans and expect them to come off without a hitch. Then one day you start to wonder if you're doing the right thing, or if you can handle it. Maybe you panic a little, and the next thing you know, you wind up in a place like this. Happens all the time. Funny thing is, there's usually a woman at the bottom of it."

Colin swirled the water in his cup. "I guess I know it's Maggie I want. I'm just not sure about the rest of it."

"You'll work it out." Red said, tapping Colin on the chest with his book.

"On the field, Finnely," someone shouted.

"Coming." Colin flipped his remaining water onto the ground and dropped the cup back on the bench. He trotted over to second base and glanced at Red's departing figure, considering his words. Then he pushed thoughts of Red and Maggie from his mind and fixed his gaze on the batter.

———————

Several months later, Colin sat with his back against the metal railing at the head of his bunk, his crossed legs growing stiff as he tried to focus on the cards in his hand. He and his friends had been playing poker for over an hour. Only Red, sitting straight-backed on the bunk beside Colin's, seemed able to concentrate on this late November night. Patrick sat at the foot of the bunk simmering in a foul mood. Frank rested on the floor opposite Red, fighting to keep his eyes open.

"God, I could use a beer," Patrick said again. "I tell ya I can almost taste it. When was the last time we got good and hoary-eyed, Colin?"

Colin didn't answer. He was thinking of a night nearly two years before when he'd taken Maggie dancing on her birthday, and she'd let him kiss her as they danced to *The Way You Look Tonight*. He could remember so clearly how beautiful she had looked in the golden light of the dance hall and how he couldn't pull her close enough to fill the ache in his body.

"Wake up, Colin, will ya?" Patrick snapped. "Red folded. Jesus you're all playing like crap tonight. And how come nobody's talkin'?"

"What do you want to talk about?" Red asked.

"Anything."

"Okay. With the Germans defeating the Soviets in the Crimea—"

"Christ, not war talk," Patrick groaned. "I'm sick of it."

But Frank awakened now. "Do you still think America's gonna get involved in the war, Red?"

"It's only a matter of time. We've made a point to show the

Nazis we're not as neutral as we claim to be. There's a better chance than ever you'll get your draft cards when you get home."

"Shit." Colin exchanged a frown with Frank. After all this work, he had no intention of returning home just to be forced into the Army.

The men finished up the hand in silence.

Frank hugged his knees and tapped bare feet nervously on the floor while Patrick dealt. "I was talking to one of the Pan American guys over at the hotel," Frank said. "He said we should be more worried about the Japs than the Krauts. He thinks the Japs are patrolling the ocean getting ready to attack the U.S. He said the radio blackout in the Pacific is making it hard to land planes on Wake."

"He said—he said. What're you, a parrot?" Patrick said.

Frank lowered his head.

"Ever since the Marines got here, things have seemed different," Colin said. "I heard U.S. subs were blinking secret messages to our officers the other night. Maybe it had something to do with those big ships we've seen circling. I heard they didn't respond to recognition signals. And then there was that squadron of planes that passed overhead a few days ago—"

"Major Devereux said they was *American* planes," Frank insisted.

"Then why didn't they stop here to refuel?"

"There do seem to be a lot of strange things going on lately," Red agreed.

"Well, nothin's goin' on in this game, that's for damn sure."

Frank glanced at Patrick nervously. "What're we gonna do if the Japs do attack, Pat?"

"Oh for cryin' out loud. When you gonna stop being such a baby, Frank? Hey, you fellas shoulda seen him shivering in his bunk the night the typhoon hit. Whoosh!" Patrick threw up his arms to imitate the fifteen-foot waves that had crashed against the reef, sending spray across the camp. "I thought the poor kid was gonna piss his pants."

Frank blushed, and Colin fixed Patrick with a disapproving glare.

"Don't worry, Frank," Red said. "We'll be off this island before any trouble starts."

Colin patted the boy's shoulder and tried to sound confident. "Frank, you know if the Japs attacked the U.S., our Navy would whip their asses back to Japan before they knew what hit them."

Frank nodded and rested his chin on his knees.

"It's raining," Red said.

"Guess I'll knock off for the night. My luck stinks tonight, anyway," Patrick growled, yanking off his shirt. Frank did the same, and they joined several other men spilling out of the barracks into the cleansing rain.

Red scooped up the cards as Colin unbuttoned his shirt and reached under his bunk. He retrieved a bar of soap from his toilet kit and joined the others outside. From around the camp, men wandered out of the ice cream parlor, the commissary, the barbershop. They ambled out of barracks units, some holding bars of soap, hoping, like Colin, for a good downpour to rinse away sweat, dust, and the itchy saltwater film left on their skin after bathing in the lagoon.

Colin surveyed the young men with whom he'd spent the past six and a half months. The dangerous construction work had left most with scars and burns, which they now compared, swapping stories and probing each other's fresh wounds, admiring the most gruesome trophies. Colin showed his index finger to one group, revealing a jagged cut he'd gotten from a nail that protruded from a piece of scrap lumber. After a moment, he slipped away toward the beach. Once this job ended, he guessed he'd never see most of these men again, yet he knew he'd always feel a connection to them and this place.

But what if Red was right? Would he be returning to Boise only to be drafted into a war? He stripped to his undershorts and tipped his head toward the sky. Closing his eyes, he imagined the soft raindrops were Maggie's fingertips brushing his face.

Details that had faded in the seven long months since Colin left Boise were lately becoming vivid again as his time on Wake was winding down. He could smell his mother's stew and hear his sister giggling at the supper table. He could picture Eddie sitting on his porch, feel the weight of Maggie's hand on his knee. He remembered how the snow-covered foothills seemed to loom over Boise and recalled the sting of the icy, mountain water as he waded with his father in their favorite fishing lake.

As the rain washed over his body, as he felt the heaviness of the air and his own concerns, he thought he could now write Maggie the letters he should have been writing all along. He could tell her how much he missed her and how much he needed her, tell her he never wanted to leave her again. He just hoped it wasn't too late.

Chapter 6

Wake Island, 1941

Tools, supplies, and a crew of six men jostled around in the flatbed of Colin's truck. The crew joked as they sped along the road just after eight o'clock on a Monday morning in December. A jovial mood had taken hold the past weekend, when the overworked civilians and Marines had been granted a much-needed day off. Even the commanding officers seemed to relax and enjoy the recreational activities on the island. Dan Teters visited with the men, though it was evident he missed his wife, who, along with dependents on other outlying bases, had been evacuated more than a month ago on orders from the Navy.

Colin had allowed himself to be swept up by the heightened morale, if only to take his mind off the fact he hadn't received any letters from Maggie this week. If she were mad at him, she had a right to be. But this last letter he'd written, the one he'd dropped in the mail a few days ago, would make up for his past stale words.

"Hang in there, Maggie," he muttered.

"What?" asked the skinny kid riding in the cab with Colin.

"Nothing. Just talking to myself."

The boy nodded. "I do that sometimes. Seems like I do it more since I got to Wake. Wonder why that is?"

Colin shrugged. The boy pointed to a man walking briskly along the side of the road toward the airfield. "Captain's in some kind of hurry," he said. Colin pulled over to offer Captain Henry Elrod a ride, and the kid slid to the middle of the seat as the pilot jumped in.

Marine Fighter Squadron 211, under the command of soft-spoken Major Paul Putnam, had arrived less than a week ago with a dozen Grumman F4F-3 Wildcat fighter planes. The pilots had become instant heroes. Now that they were flying regular patrols, the island seemed less vulnerable. Colin ignored rumors that the planes, though rugged, were outdated and that their repair manuals and spare parts had failed to arrive. Like everyone else on Wake, Colin needed to believe the pilots were invincible, even if they hadn't had much experience with this model of plane.

"What do you think of Wake, sir?" the kid stammered, unable to conceal his awe. Colin wondered if he himself had looked that way the first time he spoke to the indomitable Captain Elrod a few days before.

Captain Elrod frowned. "Well, we were expecting things to be further along."

Since the pilots had arrived, readying the airfield had taken high priority. The runways were long but not wide enough for more than one plane at a time, and that would pose a problem should the pilots need to take off in a hurry. The squadron's ordinance officer had been busy trying to rig the planes for the hundred-pound bombs that were the wrong size for the Wildcats. And the protective revetments, which would shield the planes from enemy view, had not yet been completed, so the planes were in clear sight.

Colin stretched his aching neck to one side. The day off had passed too quickly. He couldn't remember a time when he hadn't felt rushed. As soon as one project was finished, another more important one took its place. No matter how hard they worked, sometimes it seemed the island would never be ready for defense.

The men leaped off the flatbed even before Colin brought the truck to a complete stop at the airfield. As he got out to help unload, an aide raced toward them. He was wild-eyed and sweating profusely, but he looked relieved when he spotted Captain Elrod.

"Sir." He saluted sharply. "Major Putnam has ordered you to report at once."

"What's going on?" Colin asked.

The aide still addressed Captain Elrod. "The Japs are attacking Pearl Harbor. Really attacking it, sir. This is no drill. Major Putnam thinks they could be heading here next."

The men dropped their tools and converged on the aide, all asking questions at once. "That's all I know," the aide insisted, pushing them back.   Without a word, Captain Elrod took off at a dead run for Major Putnam's headquarters. The aide made a move to follow, but Colin caught his arm.

"What can we do?" he asked.

"I don't know. Go about your business, I guess. I've got to get back to headquarters."

Colin released the aide's arm and turned to find all the men in the work crew looking directly at him.

"Did he say, 'go about your business?'" one man asked. "What the hell does that mean?"

"Jesus," one worker muttered. "We're at war."

"Dirty bastards," said another, clenching his fist.

"My folks are gonna be worried sick," the kid whimpered.

They all turned to look at the boy, and one man put a hand on his shoulder. Colin didn't know the names of all of these men, but he knew he'd never forget the fear in their eyes and the way their blistered hands rubbed hard at their faces.

He took a deep breath and knew exactly what he had to do. "If they're coming, we've got to be ready. Everybody get to your work details."

The men mumbled in agreement and stooped to gather their tools. Colin jumped back in the truck and sped toward the airfield's storage buildings to drop off the camouflage netting and other supplies. When he was finished, he asked for an assignment.

A sergeant got him started digging foxholes around the airfield. "Keep 'em shallow, son. There's saltwater six feet down."

Colin put his back into the work. But then his movements slowed as he thought of home. Across the International Date Line it would be Sunday, December 7. His mother and Maggie would be at church. Until today he had never imagined he might not see them again.

He drove the shovel into the ground with a renewed energy.

At eleven forty-five Colin considered skipping lunch to keep working, but he'd overslept this morning and missed breakfast. He knew he needed to keep up his strength, so he decided to take the truck to Camp Two, where he could round up more shovels, picks, and men and bring them back, along with food for the civilians and GIs at the airfield. As he approached the truck, he caught sight of Red jogging toward him with Private Marty Johansen, a stocky, tow-headed Swede. Marty's detachment had arrived in October, and Colin had been shocked to recognize him marching into Camp One beside his fellow Marines. Colin and Marty had been high school classmates back in Boise, and they'd shared a couple of evenings lately catching up on news from home and drinking the coveted beer Marty was able to sneak out of the Marine camp, much to Patrick's raucous delight.

Colin approached Red and Marty.

"If you're going to camp, we could use a lift," Red puffed.

"Why aren't you with your detachment?" Colin asked Marty.

"I had to bring bandage rolls to Major Putnam. They want me to be a medical aide if the Japs attack. Guess I never should have told them my dad is a doctor." Marty laughed nervously. "I'm supposed to report to the Navy doc. He's taking over your civilian hospital since it's bigger and better equipped than our aid station."

"Are the Marines ready if the Japanese . . . you know?"

Marty looked about as if he wanted to be sure no one would hear him. He spoke quickly. "There aren't enough rifles and pistols to go around, and the few helmets we have are World War I issues. Thank God the gun batteries are in place and camouflaged. Those antiaircraft guns are the only things standing between us and an invasion. If they could just get the airfield ready. We need those planes."

"Don't count on it." Colin frowned.

"Shit. We should have had more time to train," Marty said. "But we've been too busy digging our goddamn gun emplacements with picks and shovels while you Civvies putzed around on your Cats. Maybe if you'd have given us a hand, we could have gotten the defenses ready sooner and gotten back to training."

Colin jabbed a finger at Marty's face. "Teters offered to lend you crews and equipment, but Major Devereux said he didn't have permission to use us. Meantime we've had a contract to fill, and our work was just as important as yours."

"Shh." Red raised his hand, cocking his head. "Anybody hear that rumbling?"

"What rumbling?"

"Sounds like planes."

Colin looked up. Over the southern end of the atoll, a formation of twin-engine bombers approached. "Are those the B-17s we've been expecting?"

The color drained from Red's face. "They're Japs! Get down!" He forced Colin to his knees and dragged him under the truck. Marty wriggled under beside them as the air began to whistle. The ground vibrated, shrubs tearing out at the roots. Small rocks bounced like popcorn in a hot skillet. Colin shielded his face with his arms.

Black smoke snaked under the truck, and they all began to cough. "They must have hit the gas tank," Red sputtered. He shook Colin's shoulder and pointed out toward the airfield. Colin raised his head cautiously, peering through the smoke. The pilots of squadron VMF-211 were running toward the Wildcats.

Bullets tore up the ground around the planes. Colin cried out as square-faced Lieutenant Conderman fell, struck by machine gun fire. Nearby, Lieutenant Graves was scrambling into his cockpit when a bomb scored a direct hit. The plane burst into flames. Colin buried his face in Red's shoulder, unable to watch. Twenty feet away, the ground ripped apart. Bits of coral pummeled Colin's head and arms, leaving bleeding scratches on his dust-covered skin. He tried to still his shaking muscles and struggled to breathe.

"God almighty," Marty swore. "They're trying to kill us. What'd we ever to do them?"

Overhead, plane engines buzzed again. "We're sitting ducks," Colin screamed, glancing up at the truck's underbelly, imagining it dropping down to crush him. He scooted forward, intent on getting out from under the vehicle, but a Japanese fighter swooped down, the orange ball of the Rising Sun blazing on its wings. It flew so low Colin could see the pilot sitting forward in his seat, firing off shots. Red pulled him back and pushed his head down. Colin dug his fingers into the ground, driving bits of sharp coral under his fingernails. Metal rang above him as the Japanese fighter strafed the truck, and Marty cried out. A bullet drilled into the ground an inch from Colin's left arm.

With the bombs and bullets pulverizing the airfield, Colin turned to his mother's oldest advice and whispered the Hail Mary, focusing on the rhythm of the prayer as he repeated the lines over and over. So intent was he, his body drawn up in a ball, the back of his head wedged against the truck's tire, that when Red finally shook him, he shoved Red's hands away and curled tighter.

"It's over," Red shouted, his face near Colin's.

Colin stopped praying and raised his head, listening. He could hear the surf, the shouts of men, and somewhere the spit and crackle of a fire, but he could no longer hear the bombs or the hum of plane engines. Red crawled out from under the truck, crouching as he looked up at the sky.

Colin could now see Marty, whose face was streaked with blood from a cut on his forehead. Colin stared at him for a moment, panting for breath, swallowing the fear that had closed his throat. "You okay?"

Marty took a moment to nod.

Colin inched forward, watching the sky, and slowly pulled himself from under the truck. He gripped the wooden railing of the flatbed with both hands and lay his head against the wood, now splintered by machine-gun fire. Dust and smoke enveloped him, clinging to his moist skin.

Colin raised his head and watched as Red helped Marty out from under the truck. Marty put a hand on Red's shoulder to steady himself and lifted his right foot. The blood-soaked toe of his leather boot hung loose. "Damn near shot my toes off," he said with a shaky laugh, but the tears in his eyes gave away his pain. "Thought I was never gonna see Becky again."

"Who's Becky?"

"His girl," Colin answered.

"I was gonna ask her to marry me as soon as I got leave."

Red lowered Marty to the truck's running board and carefully removed the boot. Marty had lost the tip of his big toe, but the others were intact. Colin dropped down onto the running board beside him and helped Red wrap Marty's foot with Red's blue handkerchief.

"How long you figure we were under that truck, Red?"

"I don't know. Ten, twelve minutes."

"Must have been longer than that," Marty insisted. "Seemed like a lifetime." He tried to stand, but fell back. "Can't get my knees to stop shaking," he explained, embarrassed.

Red pointed toward the southern sky. "They must have come in behind that rain squall. Our lookouts probably never saw them."

"Think they'll be back?" Colin asked.

"Yeah . . . they'll be back."

"Hey, you men," someone shouted. "Get that truck over here and give us a hand with the wounded." Red and Colin exchanged a worried look, then Red snatched his hat from the ground where he'd dropped it and rushed off to help.

Colin stood up from the running board and held out a hand to Marty, pulling the big man to his feet. They held hands a few seconds longer than necessary, each staring into the other's dirty face. Then Colin bent to pick up a chunk of coral to break off the fragmented pieces of the windshield. He wrapped his own handkerchief around his hand and swept the glass off the seat, helping Marty into the truck.

"Hope this thing starts," he said, tapping the bullet-riddled hood. He opened the driver's side door and paused. He dropped to his knees and reached under the truck to retrieve the bullet, still a little warm, that had so narrowly missed killing him. He tossed it into the cab and jumped in.

Smoke pulled away from the truck as it moved forward, and Colin glanced around the ruined airfield, wondering in which direction to head. But everywhere he turned, he saw men rushing toward crumpled heaps on the ground. "My God. That could have been me," he said to himself, tightening his grip on the steering wheel.

The carnage that surrounded him seemed to press Colin back against the seat of the truck. He felt heavy and tired. He thought about Patrick, who would have been preparing lunch at the mess hall before the attack, and hoped he was all right. And where would Frank have been?

Before him, on the ground, a corporal knelt beside Lieutenant Conderman, the pilot shot down while running for his plane. The corporal looked up and motioned the truck over. Nearby another Marine lay dead, his blood bright red against the starched white coral. Colin smelled burnt flesh and tasted bile in his throat. He swallowed hard and jumped out of the truck to help the corporal, shrinking back at the sight of Lieutenant Conderman's mangled body.

The corporal ordered him forward, and Colin forced himself to comply. Together they lifted the barely alive pilot onto the flatbed of the truck. Conderman opened his eyes and glanced at Colin, and something told Colin the pilot wouldn't survive. He looked away.

"Get him to the hospital, quick," the corporal ordered.

"No... Get the other wounded first," Conderman sputtered.

"But, sir."

"That's an order."

The corporal nodded reluctantly and turned to leave. Colin stepped in front of him. "Where's Captain Elrod?"

The corporal pointed at the sky. "Up there. He was on patrol."

Colin scoured the dark clouds, hoping to see the Captain bringing his plane safely toward the runway. But there was nothing in the air except flocks of screeching birds, unnerved by the attack. Colin helped Marty climb onto the back of the truck and told him to hold a handkerchief over a bullet wound in Conderman's neck.

There was a picture Colin couldn't get out of his mind—the Japanese pilot grinning as he fired on the men, on these good men Colin had come to think of as friends. He slammed his fist against the side of the truck and fought back the hatred that stiffened his muscles again, making it hard to move. He had a job to do. There was no time to feel. He stuck out his jaw and climbed into the cab, easing the truck forward for Conderman's sake, refusing to look as he passed the dead Marine, determined to gather as many wounded men as he could fit on the flatbed and get them to the hospital at camp.

The bullet rolled between his feet on the floorboard.

Chapter 7

Wake Island, 1941

Colin's foot slipped off the accelerator. He stared ahead at a body lying in the road and slowly got out of the truck.

"Looks like he's dead," Marty said, climbing down from the flatbed, where he'd been monitoring a dozen wounded men.

"Well I can't drive over him," Colin said. "Help me move him."

Colin covered his mouth as he approached the body lying face-down, one arm torn off above the elbow. He took a deep breath and grabbed the dead man's shoulders, rolling him over. Kaminski's bulging eyes gaped above a hole where his nose should have been. Colin dropped him and doubled over to vomit.

He wiped his mouth on his sleeve and remained still for a moment, hands on his knees, thinking of all the times Kaminski had baited him, insulted him, and he wondered why this man's death had moved him to lose control. Better men had died today as far as Colin was concerned, but maybe that was it. Death was so indiscriminate.

"Are you all right?" Marty asked.

Colin nodded and turned to help Marty move the body to the side of the road.

"What about that?" Marty pointed toward Kaminski's disconnected arm.

"Leave it there. I'll drive around it."

Colin pulled slowly into Camp Two. Gasoline fires blazed where tanks had been hit, black smoke wafting toward the sky. Many of the tents and outer buildings were destroyed, but Colin's barracks unit appeared undamaged. Dazed men drifted across the compound. Like the glass fishing balls caught in the current off shore, they moved in circles, waiting for some force to propel them forward.

Wounded soldiers and civilians lay on the ground in front of the contractors' hospital or sat propped against friends. Colin pulled an unconscious soldier from the truck's cab and called for help unloading the men from the flatbed.

"Wounded inside—dead over there," said a medic, indicating a row of sheet-covered bodies.

"Those are all dead?" Colin gasped.

"Yeah. We're putting them in the cold storage until we figure how to get them home."

Colin's empty stomach churned. He imagined his own body arriving home in a coffin, his mother and Maggie weeping at his graveside. But what if his body never made it back? What if there was nothing left for them to bury? He could be blown to bits or the Japanese could decide to leave his body to the rats. He felt the urge to run, to leave the shrieks and moans of the wounded behind him, but his feet were weighted to the ground.

He heard someone call his name and turned to see Patrick

hobbling across the courtyard holding up Frank, who clutched his head with one hand, blood seeping between his fingers, while his other hand barely covered a wet spot at his crotch.

"Thank God you're okay," Colin said, throwing an arm around Patrick's shoulder. He grinned at Patrick for a moment, then glanced at Frank. "What happened?"

"Ah, stupid kid," Patrick said. "Soon as the raid started, he ran right out in the open. A bomb exploded, and he caught some shrapnel in the head. Lucky for him it's just a little piece. It's still in there, though, see?"

Frank whimpered as Patrick pried his hand away to show Colin a short, twisted piece of metal protruding from Frank's skull. With a glance at Frank's terrified eyes, Colin managed a tight smile. "Heck, that's not so bad."

He and Patrick guided Frank to a medic, who examined the wound quickly and motioned Frank inside the hospital. He stopped Colin and Patrick at the door. "Too crowded in there as it is, fellas," he said. Frank glanced over his shoulder at Patrick, blood and tears mixing on his cheeks as the medic led him inside.

"Damn them Japs," Patrick fumed. "They'll pay for this." He turned to Colin. "You okay?"

"I'm fine. Where were you when it happened, Patrick?"

"Standin' in the doorway of the mess hall lookin' for one of our servers that hadn't shown up yet. Then the bombs started fallin'. I ran outside. Saw a couple fellas get hit right in front of me. See this blood?" Patrick showed him a stain on his pant leg. "That's from Brooklyn Hayes, you know that big New York kid who hit all the home runs? Bomb landed practically square on top of 'im; blew 'im into the air like a rag doll."

"How many of us do you think they got?" Colin asked.

"Maybe fifty—dead or wounded. Hard to tell, the way men

were scatterin' all over the place. They'll probably still be finding 'em into tonight."

Doctor Khan shouted to the men waiting outside the hospital, "If anyone here's got the stomach for it, we could use some help." His eyes met Colin's, and he paused. But Colin shoved his hands in his pockets and looked at the ground.

"Guess maybe I could be of some help," another civilian said warily, and Colin watched the doctor tug him inside.

"Hey, Patrick," someone called. They turned to see a dredge operator named Smitty running toward them. "I'm heading for the brush," he said. "You fellas should do the same. Get enough food and water to last at least a week or two."

"You mean hide out?" Colin asked.

"Hell, yes. There ain't enough guns for us, so how we supposed to protect ourselves? I heard even Teters is tellin' men to head for cover. Me and Rickles know of a good spot over by Peale. Get your gear, Patrick, and I'll show you where it is."

Patrick glanced at Colin, wavering. "I think I should make sure Frank's okay first."

"Suit yourself," Smitty said. "But you're makin' a big mistake."

"What do you think, Colin?" Patrick asked when Smitty had gone. "Should we hide out?"

"I don't know. Seems like there's still a lot of work to do."

They stood for a moment considering Smitty's offer, listening to the cries of the wounded inside the hospital and the sound of a hammer beating hard and fast against wood. Patrick scuffed the dust with the toe of his boot, picked up a splintered piece of wood and threw it against the side of a barracks unit. "Guess you're right. I reckon I'd rather be busy than hunkered down in a foxhole waiting for some bomb to bust me open."

Colin pointed at Dan Teters, who was hurrying past,

surrounded by men asking questions. Colin and Patrick ran to catch up to them. Teters was directing some of the men to Peale to help extinguish a fire at The Inn, adding that several of the hotel workers had died.

"I've got a truck," Colin offered. "Do you want me at the fire or the airfield?"

Teters turned toward Colin, but kept walking. "Round up some men and get to the airfield. Bring the truck back here tonight in case we need it elsewhere."

Colin motioned to Patrick, but Patrick shook his head. "You go. I'm gonna help out around here so's I can keep an eye on Frank."

Colin stared at the man he'd once known as a lanky, reckless boy, the friend whose pranks and caustic sense of humor had gotten them both into trouble and had often been a source of frustration for Colin. Yet it had always been Patrick he'd turned to when he needed a hand, and he'd counted him as his one constant friend. Now he was surprised to realize he thought of Patrick as a brother.

"Watch out for yourself," he said, giving Patrick a quick hug.

"Don't worry 'bout me. Dyin's for those too old to lift a beer, that's what I always say."

Patrick winked and turned back toward the hospital. Colin watched him for a moment, then headed for the mess hall. There he was able to get Chaplain and five other men to agree to accompany him to the airfield. They gathered food and fresh water and scavenged extra tools. Colin loaded canned fruit, bread and cheese onto the truck without the slightest desire to eat. In the end, he wrapped a piece of bread in a handkerchief and put it in his pocket, hoping his queasiness would pass.

Chaplain rode up front with Colin, but neither spoke as the

truck maneuvered around loose shrubs and deep potholes in the road. When the shredded airfield finally emerged through a lingering haze, Chaplain leaned forward, his breath stopping short. "I didn't expect so much damage," he said.

Colin saw him rub the corners of his mouth vigorously, and he knew Chaplain was trying to collect himself, to be the calm presence the men expected him to be. Finally, the gentle man cleared his throat and nodded toward the airfield. "Looks like they left the landing strip intact, but demolished everything around it. They must be planning to use our own strip when they land to take the island. Do you know how many planes they got?"

"I heard seven of the planes on the ground were destroyed. The others are in bad shape. They knocked out the air-to-ground radio and blew up the maintenance equipment too." Colin stopped the truck, staring at the charred remains of Lieutenant Graves' Wildcat. "VMF-211 lost half their squadron. They'd counted thirty men dead or wounded when I left. I took some of them to the hospital myself."

"What about the four pilots on patrol?"

"I wish I knew. Captain Elrod was up there."

"You friends with him?"

"Nah. Just talked to him a couple of times." Colin looked at Chaplain. "I guess you could say I admire him."

Chaplain hung his head. "So we have only three planes in working condition. We're not much of a match for the next raid, are we?"

Colin's silence answered for him.

They got out to unload the truck, and Colin swung a shovel over his shoulder. He caught sight of the aide who'd spoken to Captain Elrod before the attack and ran to catch up to him.

"Is the patrol back?"

The aide looked disheveled and annoyed by the interruption. "Yeah. With the cloud cover, they never even saw the Japs. They must have flown in right below our boys. Captain Elrod hit some debris on his landing and wrecked his plane."

"But he's all right?"

"Hell yeah. It's gonna take more than a few Japs to ground Hammerin' Hank. They're clearing debris and patching the runways. I'm sure they could use your crew and truck."

"We'll head right over," Colin assured him.

A plane roared low overhead, and Colin ducked. But it was only the Pan Am Clipper *Philippine*. The *Philippine* struggled into the air, bullet holes lined up like rivets in her hull. "Looks like the attack didn't ground the Clipper. Must be on its way to Midway," someone said.

"The passengers will tell them what happened here. They'll send reinforcements soon," Chaplain said.

As the Clipper climbed sluggishly, Colin's heart beat hard. It occurred to him the Pan Am passengers might be the last people to leave the island alive and, for a moment, he envied them. But the feeling quickly passed. Somehow he felt his place was here, among the soldiers and civilians who had worked so hard. Though Wake's defenses were not yet as strong as he would have liked, Colin felt sure they could compensate for the island's shortcomings with energy and ingenuity. And though he suspected most of the men had secretly prayed this day would never arrive, or at least that they'd be long gone when it did, he believed with all his heart they would defend Wake now as their home.

Looking up at the sky, he only hoped the Clipper pilot knew he carried with him the hopes of sixteen hundred men. As the crippled Clipper finally nudged the low gray clouds, the men erupted into a cheer. Colin fingered the bullet that had nearly killed him. He was keeping it in his pocket now as a kind of good luck charm, along with his father's watch.

"Okay, everybody," Chaplain shouted as the Clipper disappeared and a silence settled over the men. "Let's get to work."

Chapter 8

Wake Island, 1941

They had gathered around Eddie's kitchen table ten minutes before noon on Monday morning, December 8th. A plate of sandwiches grew stale in front of them while the coffeepot percolated loudly. A small radio warbled a song about bluebirds over white cliffs, but they had not gathered to hear music. They'd come together to hear the President declare war.

Maggie concentrated on the wood grain in Eddie's dark pine table, tracing the lines with her finger as they swirled and stretched across the surface—anything to keep from meeting her mother's gaze. It was infuriating to see the way Agnes looked at her with pity and concern, as if she already knew Colin was dead. She'd been hovering over Maggie since they heard the news yesterday about Pearl Harbor, denying Maggie the time to herself she so desperately needed, forcing her to take walks and help with housework, thinking, as usual, she knew what

Maggie needed—to keep busy, to keep her mind off what had happened.

Maggie thought of Colin's mother. She had wanted to be with Laura today, but Agnes had insisted she stay home with her own family. And she thought of Ellen and wondered if her hands were still, just this once.

But mostly she thought about Colin, of the letters she'd found in her uncle's car, the ones she'd asked him to mail a few weeks ago and he'd apparently forgotten. What must Colin have thought when he received no mail from her?

No one knew yet whether Wake was in danger. The news on the radio had dealt mostly with the devastation at Pearl, the fires and sunken ships, the dead sailors and terrified civilians, the blow to America's pride and the almost instantaneous lines forming at recruiting stations across the country. The end of peace.

Maggie had called the Morrison Knudsen offices this morning, but they couldn't say if their workers were safe. And she'd called the governor's office and the air base on the outskirts of Boise. No one could tell her anything. It was as if Wake Island didn't exist.

"Is it cold by the window? Do you want my sweater?" Agnes offered.

Maggie shook her head without looking up. Eddie reached over to pat her hands. She moved them into her lap.

The music stopped. And through the crackling airwaves President Roosevelt's voice filled the kitchen:

Yesterday, December 7, 1941—a date which will live in infamy—the United States of America was suddenly and deliberately attacked by naval and air forces of the Empire of Japan . . .

Maggie rose, clutching the kitchen counter with both hands. She stared at the radio on the counter, the President's voice pounding in her ears:

. . .Last night, Japanese forces attacked Hong Kong. Last night, Japanese forces attacked Guam. Last night, Japanese forces attacked the Philippine Islands. Last night, the Japanese attacked Wake Island . . .

She felt herself sliding to the floor, almost as if she were sliding into a bathtub, feeling weightless, as if there really were water to buoy her. Eddie dropped down beside her, wrapped her tightly in his arms. Her mother crouched in front of her, clasping her hands. The tile floor was cool beneath her dress, and her gaze fixed on a dark scuff rising from the base of the white kitchen cabinet like a column of black smoke swirling into a cloudy sky.

Though his mouth was near her ear, Eddie's voice sounded low and hollow, as if traveling through water. "Don't worry, honey. Everything's going to be all right."

She closed her eyes, feeling she deserved their pity and protectiveness. She wasn't strong, as she'd promised herself to be. She was numb—and Eddie's arms were warm and soothing. She accepted the glass of water her mother held out to her and sipped obediently.

She would let them care for her now because she needed them to, but when this numbness wore off, and she stood against the force of her fear, she vowed to face it alone in her room, surrounded by photographs of Colin and by the things he had given her. She would teach herself to be strong for his sake. She would teach herself to believe he could yet come home.

Chapter 9

Wake Island, 1941

"Something's out there all right. I can feel it," Colin said.

The faint light of a half moon was giving way to dawn on the morning of December 11, three days after the first attack. Like the other men at Battery A at Peacock Point on the tip of Wake, Colin watched for movements on the ocean that would confirm Japanese ships lurking out at sea. He wondered how the Marine lookouts had ever detected something on the dark waves two hours earlier, when they'd dared to wake Major Devereux. With a pair of powerful field glasses, Devereux had confirmed the approach of a Japanese task force. He'd informed his superior, Naval Commander Cunningham, and sent the news out to the gun batteries over field telephones. The Marines were now positioned behind the guns, adhering to strict orders to hold their fire.

Colin and Red had left their dugout near the airfield when

darkness fell. They'd helped move, sandbag, and camouflage the guns at Battery A. This tactic had been working well to mislead the Japanese reconnaissance pilots who accompanied the daily air raids. The dummy gun emplacements were hit with regularity while the camouflaged guns escaped serious damage.

Once the work was completed, Lieutenant Barninger, in charge of Battery A, dismissed the handful of civilians. Some returned to their foxholes, but Colin and Red volunteered to serve the Marines as ammunition=passers. Patrick had remained on duty at the mess hall, and Frank was no doubt with him.

Colin sat on a sandbag, hugging his knees. "Maybe this is it, huh, Red? We can't stand out against a whole fleet."

Red, his arms folded tightly across his chest, only shrugged. But his upper lip twitched, and Colin knew he too was nervous. A rat snapped at Colin's ankle, sinking sharp teeth into his boot. Colin killed it with a rock, cussing as he kicked its carcass aside. The air raids were affecting every creature on the island. The once-skittish rats had turned vicious, attacking men in their dugouts. Dead birds lay in heaps, knocked from the sky by concussions from bomb blasts. The flies feasted on them and on the human excrement no longer confined to the latrines. The flies then spread dysentery across the island.

Colin took his father's watch from his pocket. 5:15 a.m.

"There she is," Red said.

Colin dropped the watch into his lap and leaned forward on his hands. A Japanese cruiser turned to port side out past Peacock Point and led the task force westward on a course parallel to Wake's southern coast.

Colin jumped up to help the Marines remove camouflage from the two 5-inch guns. His muscles tensed as the soldiers swiveled the barrels of the guns to follow the ships. An earlier air raid had taken out the battery's range finder, so Lieutenant

Barninger would have to guess at distances.

"Where's the order to fire?" Colin asked Red.

"The commander must be trying to bluff them. Make them think we're disabled. Draw them in."

Colin's fingers tightened around the cold steel of the ammo belts.

The Marines cussed under their breaths as long minutes passed. Suddenly, orange light streaked across the water and shells thundered toward the island. The ground shook, and Colin stumbled backward. The air swelled with smoke and dust—and still Wake's guns were silent. Colin's finger twitched. He longed to wrap it around the trigger of the gun, to do something besides sit here and wait to be killed.

"Dammit, Red, I can see those ships plain as day. What's Cunningham waiting for?"

"Just a little closer," Red urged, an eerie glint in his hazel eyes.

From his vulnerable perch on the roof of the command post, Lieutenant Barninger shouted the long-awaited order. The Marines cried out with voices to match the roaring surf as their guns opened fire. The first volley missed the flagship, a cruiser, but hit the destroyer the cruiser had been screening. Like a frightened jackrabbit, the cruiser turned sharply and sped away from Wake on a zigzag course, still firing. Colin ducked as coral and vegetation sailed overhead. One of the soldiers swore and fell back, grabbing his ankle.

The Marines hammered the cruiser, shells striking her just above the waterline, and she began to lose speed. Hit again, she turned starboard. Colin shouted encouragements to the Marines as they turned their guns on a destroyer, which had come between the cruiser and the atoll to lay down a smoke screen. The destroyer quickly retreated, leaving the cruiser to limp away.

Colin passed another ammo belt to the gunners just as the Wildcats roared in formation over the island. Red shook his head. "Four planes against a task force? Let's hope the Japs don't have an aircraft carrier out there."

But Colin would not be discouraged. "Blow them to hell, fellas!" he screamed as the Wildcats angled toward the Japanese ships. Soon one Wildcat began falling toward the ocean. The pilot forced the sputtering plane back toward the airfield. Eventually it dropped out of view over the island. Colin lowered his head and said a quick prayer for the pilot's safety.

The battle raged on as the under-equipped Marines fought fiercely to hold the island. Miraculously, the Japanese Task Force began to retreat at 7:00, with the remaining Wildcats in pursuit. Colin and the others gathered around the field telephone. Earliest reports suggested several direct hits and a few sunken enemy ships. Wake's commanders were estimating a high loss of life on the Japanese side, but so far, no new deaths had been reported on the island. Colin sighed his relief.

The Marine wounded during the attack, a private named Thorpe, had caught some shrapnel in his leg. Colin passed him a canteen while the Marines congratulated each other and bragged about the victory. An explosion rocked the horizon, far out at sea.

"Must be that destroyer going down. The one on fire," Red said.

Colin swallowed hard, thinking for the first time about the Japanese soldiers dying out there in the ocean. Their bodies would likely wash to shore, and he hoped he wouldn't pull duty retrieving them. He'd seen enough death in the last three days to last a lifetime.

Colin and Red offered to help Private Thorpe to the new

hospital facilities in the ammunition magazines east of the airfield. Constructed of reinforced concrete and steel, and built partially underground, they were the safest places on the island. The hospital at Camp Two had suffered direct hits on the second day of raids, despite the large red cross painted on the roof. Now when Colin closed his eyes at night, it wasn't Maggie he saw, but the image of the bombed-out hospital, sick and wounded men murdered where they lay. If this was the type of enemy they were facing, he doubted they could hope for mercy should the Japanese take the island.

He pushed those thoughts from his mind as he supported Thorpe, who hopped on his good leg. After a few minutes, they passed near the dugout, and Colin called to Chaplain, who'd reluctantly chosen to sleep off a headache the night before and hadn't accompanied them to Battery A. Chaplain ran toward them now and relieved Colin, taking Private Thorpe's arm and drawing it over his shoulder.

"How's your headache?" Colin asked.

"Better, till that shelling started," Chaplain said with a grin. "I ran to Major Putnam's headquarters to see if I could help, but there was nothing for me to do but watch. I saw Captain Elrod crash land his plane on the beach . . ."

Colin froze, realizing Elrod had been in the Wildcat he'd seen falling toward the island.

"Don't worry." Chaplain said. "He came out of it without a scratch. I'm convinced there's nothing can touch Elrod." He went on to tell about Captain Freuler's perfect landing though his shot-up engine cut out just short of the airfield.

There was a moment of silence among them as they considered the recent events. "That leaves us with only two working planes," Colin said. As he walked he felt heat rising in his face. He pressed his hands against his stomach as if to hold in the swell of victory he could feel dissipating.

"Where the hell are our reinforcements?" he asked, but no one answered. Their silence irritated him. "It's a friggin' miracle we've held the island this long, wouldn't you say?" Still no answer. "You *realize* the Japs could have landed today."

"They didn't," Red said.

"But they'll be back. You know that, Red."

"Take it easy," Chaplain said softly.

Colin held his hands up to stop them. "Don't you know what kind of trouble we're in?" Despite his efforts to retain control, his voice was rising. "Aren't you sick of acting so fucking brave all the time, keeping your hopes up, trying to believe we'll actually make it out of here alive?" He thrust his hand toward the ocean. "Don't you realize we could have died today, and still nobody can tell us where the hell our reinforcements are?"

Private Thorpe raised his head slowly. "You oughta listen to your buddy and take it easy, pal."

Met with the soldier's condescending glare, Colin snapped. "Go to hell," he hissed. He shook his head in disgust and waved his hand to take in his friends. "In fact, to hell with all of you." Chaplain called out to him, but he was sprinting toward the beach, his pulse hammering in his temples. He snatched up pieces of coral, someone's discarded food can, a piece of metal, and hurled them into the ocean toward the Japanese ships he could see now only in his mind.

Exhausted, his head aching, the muscles in his arm strained, he dropped to the ground. He covered his head with his arms, blocking out the bright morning light, and began to rock. For several minutes he rocked back and forth. Then he sobbed for Maggie and his family, for the mountain trails he'd hiked, for Eddie's confident guidance, for everything he'd been fool enough to leave behind. Everything he may never see again.

———————

That night, Colin came to stand beside his friends at the edge of a long trench. Patrick breathed the slaughterhouse stench through a handkerchief, and Frank covered his nose with his sleeve. In the trench lay more than seventy sheet-wrapped men, civilian and military lying side by side, their shapes rolling together like foam on the waves.

Colin refused to cover his nose. He felt it only right the smell should sicken him. Everything about their deaths should sicken him. He nodded to Patrick and Frank, but he couldn't look at Red, not after the way he'd lost it this afternoon. Red put a hand on his shoulder, though, and Colin buckled with shame.

Chaplain, looking somber, stood beside John O'Neal, a Mormon lay preacher whose deep voice flowed gently across the trench as he prayed for the souls of the men who had died since the first raid on December 8th. Finally there was time to put them to rest in a common grave, all hopes of transporting them home now dashed since the power to the cold storage units had been knocked out. Four Marines fired rifles into the air, and a bulldozer quickly covered the trench. Colin helped camouflage the area, and Commander Cunningham issued a new order.

From now on, the dead would be buried where they fell.

Chapter 10

Wake Island, 1941

Colin emerged from the two-foot-deep dugout and stumbled into the underbrush to relieve his aching bowels. Like most of the men on the island, the relentless strain of work, missed meals, and unsanitary conditions were taking a terrible toll. He eased up his filthy dungarees and shuffled out of the brush, a gust whipping open his short-sleeved shirt. The night was moonless and charged with the energy of an approaching storm. Colin took short breaths of wet, heavy air and turned his face to the wind. He closed his eyes, believing he could fall asleep where he stood.

For sixteen days, they had held the Japanese forces at bay. Though the daily air raids were smashing away at what was left of the island's meager defenses, the men, sick and exhausted, still hadn't considered giving up. But on this black, turbulent night, two days before Christmas, Colin knew they could not hold out much longer.

He felt a tap on his shoulder and spun, bringing his fists up. Red stepped out of his reach, his shoulders drooping, his eyes barely open.

Colin lowered his fists. "Jesus, Red. Don't sneak up on me like that."

"Sorry."

"You look like hell."

"I just need some rest," Red assured him. "I'll be back on my feet by morning."

Colin had no doubt of that. Come morning he would see several men who looked as bad as Red, as bad as he himself must look, drifting around the island searching for ways to stave off the inevitable. "Where's Chap?"

"Finishing up some work detail."

Colin shook his head in disbelief. "He must be the only man on the island who isn't sick, wounded, or just dog-ass tired."

Red rubbed his forehead with an oil-blackened hand. "I told him to wake us if the food truck comes around."

"You know it's funny," Colin said, shaking his head. "Patrick used to be so pissed about his job as a cook. Now he's all puffed up driving that food truck like he's the most important man on the island."

"Damn near is," Red said. "Just wish he came by more often."

Colin buttoned his shirt. "I can't believe it's never going to be that way again."

"What way?"

"Like before the attack," Colin said. "When we were just working and playing cards. Not a care in the world."

Red sighed heavily. "Let's get some sleep, huh?"

Colin turned to follow him into the dugout when he caught

sight of movement in the brush. He pivoted to his right, unsure whether to fight or run. Chaplain's face emerged from the darkness. Colin opened his arms as Chaplain collapsed against him, breathing hard. "They're here. They're on the island," Chap sputtered.

Colin's bowels churned, and sweat dampened his unshaven lip. "It's probably the reinforcements we were promised," he said, helping Chaplain stand again. "They're overdue."

"Dammit Colin, it's the Japs."

"Where are they?" Red asked.

"South Beach and Peacock Point. Major Putnam says other landing boats are heading for all points of the island."

The three men stood with their feet fixed to the ground, listening to the wind scrape bits of coral across the plywood cover of the dugout. Red mumbled something to himself, and Chaplain stared into the darkness, his hand rising and falling atop his heaving chest.

"So this is it," Colin whispered.

"We should report to Major Putnam. See what we can do," Chaplain said. But none of them moved. They waited with their lips parted as if to speak, but there was nothing left to say. With only a glance at the dugout that had provided them cover for two long weeks, they started off limping in a single, silent line, heads down, feeling the defeat they had fought so long. But as they neared the airfield and saw other dark figures moving steadily ahead, heard strong footsteps crushing coral, they came together side by side, bumping each other until their feet fell into brisk, even strides.

They gathered with other civilians and what was left of squadron VMF-211, four able-bodied officers and thirteen enlisted men. Over the last several days of bombing raids, all the Wildcats had been disabled. VMF-211 had been grounded at last.

Major Putnam and his executive officer, Captain Elrod, addressed their squadron. "Major Devereux has ordered us to back up the Marines on the South Beach," Putnam said. He turned to the civilians. "We have no guns to spare, so you men stay here. You'll be safer."

There was only a second's pause before the steel crew's superintendent, Pete Sorenson, moved to tower over Putnam. "Do you really think you're big enough to make us stay behind?" he asked.

Colin and the other civilians closed in around Putnam. The major glanced at each of them and smiled wearily. "Okay. We'll be glad to have your help." He turned and led the Marines toward the South Beach. Colin and the other civilians followed.

The Japanese sailors bore down on 211's position near the three-inch antiboat gun manned by Lieutenant Hanna and his crew. Captain Elrod commanded a flank of Marines situated nearby in dense undergrowth. Though dawn was approaching, it was difficult to see beyond twenty feet. Beside his foot lay a steel pipe Colin had picked up to use as a weapon. He passed the last ammunition belt to a Marine with a Thompson machine gun and instantly missed the comforting weight of the belt and the illusion of security it had provided.

His ears rang with the thundering of the surf, the blasts of gunfire, and Captain Elrod's shouts to his men. Colin kept the Captain in his view, feeling safer with Elrod standing firmly between him and the enemy, providing cover for his men while they reloaded. The small troop had so far repelled several Japanese assaults, but a Marine sergeant had died, shot through the chest only a few feet from where Colin and Chaplain crouched. The sergeant's .45-caliber pistol had flown from his limp hand and landed beside Chaplain, who had wiped his hands on his tattered black overalls and picked it up.

"Do you know how to use it?" Colin asked, hoping Chaplain would turn over the gun to Colin.

Chaplain didn't answer immediately. He nodded slowly, then placed both hands on Colin's shoulders. "Take care of yourself, my friend."

Colin snatched at Chaplain's clothes and tried to call him back as he disappeared into the underbrush. He stared after Chaplain a moment, remembering the time they'd sat in the empty mess hall while Colin told Chaplain about his father's death. He'd never confided in another man the way he had to Chaplain that night. Not even Patrick. "Goddammit, I should have stopped him."

Someone screamed nearby, and Colin jerked his head around looking for the sound. He felt unbearably alone. He bolted, running doubled over in the direction he had last noticed Red, stumbling over something and losing his grip on the steel pipe. He dropped onto all fours and felt around until he found it again, and only then did he notice what he'd tripped over. He backed away crab-like from Pete Sorenson's corpse and got to his feet again as quickly as he could. In a flash of light from an exploding shell, he saw Red brandish a pick handle, ready to smash Colin's skull. Colin cried out, and Red redirected his blow just in time. He seized Colin behind his neck and pulled his head toward his chest, mumbling apologies.

They sank to the ground together, and Red shouted over the whir of bullets into Colin's ear. "Major Putnam was wounded. Shot through the jaw by a sniper."

They ducked as a shell burst nearby. "How much longer do

you think we can hold this position?" Colin shouted.

"Not long."

Slivers of light streaked the sky, reminding Colin of a long-ago fishing trip with his father when they'd risen early to catch trout. "It's almost dawn," he muttered, dreading the horrors the daylight would reveal.

From this position, Colin could glimpse Captain Elrod firing toward a mass of Japanese troops crawling over each other up the beach toward Lieutenant Hanna's three-inch gun. "Kill the sons of bitches!" Captain Elrod cried, his gun cracking. Suddenly the young, handsome captain spun, struck by a bullet, his body lifting and turning in a strange, rhythmic dance.

"Oh God, no!" Colin screamed, jumping to his feet. Red forced him back to the ground, pinning him down, his strong hands digging into Colin's forearms.

"Get ahold of yourself, Colin," Red shouted, shaking him once.

"He's dead."

Red gripped his shoulder. "Listen, we're isolated over here. We need to get to Captain Tharin's troops." He hauled Colin to his feet, and together they broke through the brush toward the left flank of 211's line. Colin hesitated, shocked by the sight of an enlisted man, James Hesson, standing in blood-soaked dungarees as he mowed a hole in a line of Japanese troops with a machine gun.

He turned back at the sound of a strange thud and saw Red fall backwards, his left hand covering his shoulder. Colin dropped the steel pipe and cradled Red in his arms.

"Did the bullet go through?" Red asked calmly.

Colin bent him forward and ripped at Red's shirt, baring his shoulder. He shook his head. "I can't tell. I need to get you help." Taking his dirty handkerchief from his pocket, he pressed it into Red's hand and instructed him to hold it tightly against the wound.

He put his hands beneath Red's armpits and lifted, but the earth rocked, propelling Colin forward onto his friend. He heard Red cry out and felt a tingling in his own elbow.

Then he was in a tunnel, and the walls were closing in.

———————

Red's pinched face hovered above him. "That's right, Colin, wake up."

As Colin drifted back to consciousness, he tasted blood in his mouth, touched his finger to his tongue and pulled it away bloody. Red helped him sit up. Only a few yards away, a shallow crater marked the spot where the grenade had landed. Colin stared at a piece of shrapnel embedded in his left arm just above the elbow. "God, that's gotta hurt," he stammered.

"Give it a minute. It will," said Red.

Colin's teeth chattered as a sharp pain streaked through his body. He could still hear gunfire, but it sounded far away now.

"What's happening?"

Red helped him to his knees and pointed across to the beach. The Marine commander, Major Devereux, was talking to Captain Tharin, who stood with his head high, his hands fisted at his sides. A sergeant held a white rag tied to a mop handle, and Colin was stunned to see Japanese soldiers standing beside him, their guns trained on the defeated Marines.

Colin shuddered. "What do we do now?"

"We surrender." Red started to rise.

"Wait. Don't you hear that? They're still fighting somewhere on the island. We should try to join them."

Red looked down at Colin, his eyes moist. "It's over, Colin.

What we need to do now is stay alive."

"Red . . . Captain Elrod said the Japanese don't take prisoners."

Red's eyes rolled upward as he fought to maintain consciousness. Colin knew his friend was losing too much blood and needed medical attention. His own arm throbbed. He reached for his canteen before he remembered he'd left it at the dugout. "All right," he conceded. "Let's go." He helped Red to his feet.

"Hold up a minute," Colin said, emptying the contents of his pocket. "I can't let those bastards have this." He looped his father's watch chain around the lowest branches of a beach magnolia. The watch swung gently, the morning light flickering off its gold surface.

Colin showed Red the bullet that had nearly killed him the day of the first raid, rolling it back and forth across his palm. "Guess I won't be needing this anymore." He threw it with as much strength as remained in him, watching it land somewhere off in the brush. He glanced back at the surrender scene. "I don't want to do this," he confessed.

Red only nodded, lowering his head to Colin's shoulder.

Colin took a deep breath and wrapped his good arm around Red's waist, hauling him to his feet. He scanned the area for enemy soldiers and became keenly aware of the place between his shoulder blades, waiting for the bullet he half-expected to hit him in the back. As they moved toward Devereux, Colin noticed a man clad in black overalls reclining on a slight rise, one knee propped up, an arm draped despairingly over his eyes.

"Chaplain?" he called. "It's over." He let go of Red and took a few steps toward Chaplain. "Chap? You all right?"

He hesitated before dropping to his knees and moving Chaplain's arm. Above vacant brown eyes a small, neat hole was fixed in the middle of Chaplain's forehead. The blood puddling below his head reached Colin, staining the knee of his pants. He sat back on his heels, clutching Chaplain's hand, his tears wetting his shirt.

"Colin, I need you," he heard Red say. With stiff fingers, Colin retrieved from Chaplain's breast pocket a picture of his three daughters. Their sweet faces beamed up at him, and Colin choked back a sob.

He heard Red's warning but not before a Japanese soldier burst through the brush, his bayonet stopping to quiver inches from Colin's throat. The soldier breathed heavily, but his arms were steady. Colin's throat closed, the air forcing from his mouth in a frightened moan. Unable to move, he focused on the wild black eyes of the soldier.

The soldier took a step backward, motioning for Colin to rise. Colin struggled to his feet, raising his good hand and the photograph slowly into the air. Somehow he hadn't expected the enemy to look so real. The pilot he'd seen in the cockpit that first day of the raids had seemed more like something from a cartoon. Younger than Colin and, surprisingly, taller, this soldier's dark eyes darted from side to side beneath his webbed helmet, and sweat clung to his sunken cheeks. His roughspun khaki uniform fit loosely over his slight frame, a wide belt fixed on the last notch across his waist.

The soldier motioned with his rifle for Colin to join Red. He kicked Chaplain's body with his black, split-toed boot, grunted and stepped over him. Then he shouted an order in Japanese and directed Colin and Red to move toward the open. Colin hesitated, wanting to take Chaplain's body with him, but the bayonet pricked his lower back.

He took his first step into captivity.

Chapter 11
Wake Island, 1941

Sharp coral fragments dug into Colin's knees. He'd been stripped to his undershorts and could feel the sun slowly burning his back and the soles of his feet. Before the Japanese had taken his clothing, he'd painfully removed the largest piece of shrapnel from his arm and tied a sock around the wound and the few tiny shrapnel pieces still embedded inside. A guard had confiscated the photograph of Chaplain's daughters and torn it in half, scattering the pieces at Colin's feet. He'd glared at Colin, challenging. Colin tried to look defiant, but his right eye began to twitch, and he was forced to look away. The guard grunted his disgust and bumped Colin hard as he passed.

A medic had bandaged Red's shoulder but left Colin's wound untreated as he rushed to help a seriously injured civilian. Though his elbow ached terribly, Colin's more urgent concern was the wire with which he had been bound. The Japanese had tied his hands behind his back—ignoring his cries of pain—then strung the wire around his neck. If he relaxed his shoulders or let his arms drop, the wire would strangle him. Though the guards had tied Red's hands, at least they hadn't run the wire to his neck. His wounded shoulder could never have supported the weight.

The prisoners had been instructed to keep silent, but when the guards occasionally circled to share cigarettes, Colin whispered to Red. "If they know we're civilians, maybe they'll treat us better."

"Don't count on it," Red said weakly. "Even though we aren't military, we still fought against them. That should only give them more reason to hate us."

"Do you think they'll shoot us?"

"Maybe. Unless they want to save ammunition. Then they could just march us into the sea with our hands tied and let us drown."

"I'm not going to die that way," Colin said. "I'll run first. *Make* them shoot me."

Somewhere the battle continued. Communications had been cut, and Major Devereux must still be working his way around the island ordering pockets of resistance to surrender. Colin nursed the vain hope that somehow the Japanese could still be defeated.

The guards finally waved their arms for the men to rise. Colin did so slowly, the joints in his knees popping loudly. The prisoners were arranged into two rows, and the guards kicked at their ankles to get them moving. Overhead, a Japanese plane exploded, shot down by the remaining free Americans, its parts raining over the island. The men jostled one another excitedly and grinned, until the guards cursed and kicked them harder.

They were marched to the airfield, where they were finally untied. Holding his elbow close to him, Colin rolled the tension from his shoulders and rubbed at painful indentations on his wrist. To his surprise, the men were directed toward a pile of confiscated clothing. Colin snatched a pair of shorts and one of the last shirts, which he draped over Red's shoulders. They sat down on the runway, and the guards aimed machine guns at their chests.

As the hours passed, Colin searched the faces of each new arrival for his friends. Frank came first, dragged from a hospital truck and dropped to the ground. He crawled to the front row and sat cross-legged, his head in his hands. Colin knew he'd been admitted to the hospital the night before with dysentery but was still dismayed to see the boy looking so pale and shaken.

Patrick arrived shortly after Frank, winking nervously at Colin as the guards shoved him toward the back. His face was covered with dried blood, and his left calf was wrapped in a bloody bandage. When Marty arrived with a handful of Marines, Colin finally relaxed a little, though he couldn't stop feeling someone was missing, couldn't fully accept that Chaplain was not the man sitting to his left.

"I still can't figure out what's keeping our reinforcements," Colin whispered.

"They're not coming," said the man who should have been Chaplain. "Commander Cunningham got a message from Pearl during the battle. Our task force was recalled."

"You're lying."

"Like hell. I heard it straight from Cunningham's aide."

"Then that's it," Red whispered.

Colin hung his head and closed his eyes. In Boise, his mother would be hanging the Christmas wreath, his sister, Gwen, would be wrapping presents. Maggie would be baking sweet rolls for the neighbors, and Eddie would be shoveling the walk. Colin imagined himself among them, feeling the crisp winter air on his face.

A sharp kick brought him back to reality. A Japanese soldier was gesturing for him to straighten the line. Colin repositioned himself, his eyes on the soldier's back. His right eye twitched again, but this time with hatred, not fear. He promised himself that if he did not die today, he would fight with every ounce of strength left in him to survive this war. No matter what it took, he would see Maggie and his family again.

For the next fifty-four hours, the men were left in the open. The first cold night, Colin dug into the warm earth with his hands to escape the chilling wind and rain. Then during the day, the sun scorched his bare back and neck, and he could think of nothing but water.

On Christmas Day, the men were finally issued tainted water brought in gasoline barrels. A Japanese admiral strode across the airfield dressed in a stark white uniform, wearing ribbons and a sword. The men began to jeer until the guards fired a volley over their heads. An interpreter came forward to read a proclamation. Colin raised his head to listen, his eyes on the stony features of the man who'd been introduced as Admiral Kajioka, the man in whose hands rested the fate of the hundreds of men huddled together on the runway. In broken English, the interpreter began:

"*Here it is proclaimed that the entire island of Wake are now the state-property of the Great Empire of Japan,*" the interpreter read. "*—Japan who loves peace and respects justice has been obliged to take arms against the challenge of President Roosevelt. Therefore, in accordance with the peace-loving spirit of the Great Empire of Japan, Japanese Imperial Navy will not inflict any harms on those people—though they have been* *our enemy—who do not hold hostility against us in any respect. So, they be in peace!"*

"Does that mean they're not going to kill us, Red?" Colin asked.

"At least not now."

The interpreter paused, staring into the faces of the Americans. His voice rose and became threatening. *"But whoever violates our spirit or whoever are not obedient shall be severely punished by our martial law."*

Kajioka turned, and Colin followed his gaze to the top of the flag mast, where a battered American flag barely stirred in the trade winds. Colin realized what must happen next. He cursed under his breath as two soldiers stepped forward. With each squeak of the pulley, as the American flag was lowered, Colin folded in upon himself, feeling it as a blow to his stomach. Red leaned against him, shaking his head.

When Colin raised his eyes at last to see the banner of the Rising Sun snapping at the top of the flagpole, tears streaked his sunburned face. But he did not look away.

He vowed never to look away again.

Chapter 12

Boise, 1942

"Please come in," Mr. Phillips said. "Sorry to keep you waiting."

Ellen nodded politely and allowed him to lead her into the office with one hand at her elbow. Maggie hung back, measuring him with her eyes. He was middle-aged and balding, with a thick mustache and a paunch hanging over his belt. He guided Ellen to a chair across from his wide desk and offered a second chair to Maggie.

She and Ellen had agreed Maggie would do the talking, but now that they were here, surrounded by aerial photographs of Morrison Knudsen's jobs around the world, Maggie found herself letting Mr. Phillips lead the conversation.

"It's a pleasure to meet you, Mrs. Gulley," he said to Ellen. "I believe we've spoken on the phone."

"Yes. It was kind of you to return my calls."

"It was the least I could do," he said. "Mrs. Braun, I'm sorry I don't find your husband's name on my list."

"Colin and I are engaged."

"Oh, I see." He picked up a file from the corner of his desk and took from it a typed list. "Colin who?"

"Finnely."

He shuffled pages. "Ah yes, truck driver. I believe I've spoken to his mother." He replaced the file and folded his hands on the desk, looking gravely from Ellen to Maggie. "Ladies, you have the sympathy of myself and Mr. Morrison. The safety of our workers has always been of utmost concern to our company. We are grieved, indeed, by this unfortunate turn of events. You have my assurances that Mr. Morrison is, as we speak, working with the government to do everything we can for our men on Wake and for their families."

His words were reassuring, but his tone lacked conviction. Maggie had felt more sincerity from Harry Morrison. But their brief phone conversation had taken place two weeks ago, and much had changed since then. Her cheeks grew hot when she remembered the radio announcer who had called the men on Wake "expendable" and the *New York Times* article that had concluded, "they may yet be annihilated." Even the president had warned the public to prepare for Wake's defeat. If the whole country had given up hope for Wake, could Mr. Phillips have done any less? She decided to get right to the point, before she lost her nerve.

"Can you tell us if Colin and Patrick are alive?"

"I cannot. Our information does not extend to the names of individual workers."

"Can you tell us if the government is sending reinforcements?"

"It is my understanding they are, but I have no way of knowing for sure."

"Can we speak to Mr. Morrison?"

"I'm afraid not. He's asked me to handle all matters concerning the families."

Maggie struggled to keep her voice steady. "I can't believe *no one* can tell us what's happening. We've tried everyone we can think of. I even called the White House. Are we supposed to just sit back and wait while no one does anything to help them?"

"I appreciate your distress, Miss Braun. I can only begin to imagine—"

"Is it true you'll be stopping the men's paychecks?" Ellen asked meekly.

For the first time, Mr. Phillips looked shaken. "Surely you can understand our position. Our portion of the Wake job was funded by a consortium called Contractors Pacific Naval Air Bases, or CPNAB. They were funded by a contract with the Navy. Since all work has ceased, all contracts are terminated. Therefore, payments to the workers must naturally stop."

"What about their families?" Maggie demanded. "They are dependent on those paychecks."

"We are very sorry for any inconvenience. It is our hope the government will provide assistance."

"They won't," Ellen explained. "Since our men are civilians, not military, the government is bearing no obligation to support their families."

Mr. Phillips opened his desk drawer and took out a blank check. "I can offer you a small amount from my personal funds. I'm sure Mr. Morrison will reimburse me. He is very sincerely sorry he cannot do more."

"We can't accept your money," Ellen said. "We'll find other ways to get by." She rose and held out her hand, thanking Mr. Phillips for his time. Maggie was not so generous, turning away from him and heading toward the outer office.

He followed them to the door. "If there's anything more I can do for you, please let my secretary know."

They stepped into the outer office as Mr. Phillips's secretary was hanging up her phone. She turned in her seat and glanced nervously at Maggie and Ellen, but her eyes settled on Mr. Phillips. "That was Mr. Morrison," she said. "He's had communication that the Japanese have captured Wake."

Maggie stepped back, dropping her handbag. So the moment had come. She had wondered how she would react and was relieved to be in this office among strangers, where she was forced to remain composed. She bent quickly and retrieved her handbag and, though her heart beat painfully, she was able to walk steadily to the coatrack and collect their coats, handing one to Ellen as Mr. Phillips and the secretary spoke words of encouragement. But Maggie was no longer listening. She wanted to be far from Mr. Phillips' stale voice and this tidy office where Colin had signed the contract that should have fulfilled his dreams.

She hurried out of the room, annoyed with Ellen for pausing to again express weary gratitude to Mr. Phillips. Maggie leaned against the wall in the hallway, pressing her hand against her ribs, feeling each hard breath.

Nearby an office door opened and two finely dressed gentlemen stepped into the hall. One was tall and handsome, with black hair combed back and alert brown eyes that looked at Maggie with concern. Maggie resented his attention at such a terrible moment and quickly turned her back on him. She grabbed Ellen's arm and rushed her out of the building. She grasped at her open collar as they were met outside by a blast of sharp, winter air.

Next to where she'd parked Eddie's car was a pickup truck with a homemade sign in the back window. It showed a hand in the thumbs-up victory salute with the words "Wake Up!," which had lately become a national slogan. Wake's defenders had provided America with her first victory and a little revenge for Pearl Harbor when they repelled a Japanese landing on December 11. The nation had puffed up with pride when a supposed communiqué was received from Wake's Marines declaring, "Send us more Japs." Maggie had heard newscasters urging people to take up the battle cry "Remember Wake." But all of that would soon be forgotten, she thought, like the men themselves. She climbed into the car and slammed the door. She pounded her open palms against the steering wheel. "Why is this happening?" she shouted. Then she looked at Ellen, whose tears ran freely, and, for a moment, Maggie was baffled by her own reaction. Shouldn't she be crying too? Instead she felt rage, more than she'd ever known.

"We should go home and listen to the newscasts," Ellen suggested, shivering in her oversized coat.

"No, I want to go to the Red Cross and ask how long before they'll get information about prisoners."

"Maggie . . . there might not be any prisoners."

Maggie's eyes narrowed. "I'm not giving up, Ellen," she snapped. "If you are, I can let you off at home."

Ellen looked at her hands. "No. I'll go with you."

"Not another word about them not being alive."

Ellen nodded.

"Good. Talk about something else for God's sake," Maggie said.

"Please, Maggie. We must never take the Lord's name in vain."

Maggie laughed. How could Ellen worry about such a ridiculous thing at a time like this?

Ellen blew her nose gently into her handkerchief. "I thought

Mr. Phillips was helpful," she said quietly.

"Oh piffle, Ellen. The man was a dolt." Maggie turned the keys hard in the ignition.

"Why are you raising your voice to me?"

Maggie looked at her friend's sullen face. She sighed heavily. "I'm sorry, Ellen. It's just . . ."

"Never mind." Ellen lay a hand on her shoulder.

Neither spoke for a moment while the car idled loudly. Maggie felt some of her anger subside and immediately missed it, for in its place came pain. "I wonder if Colin's mother has heard yet?" she said.

"This will break my mother-in-law's heart," Ellen said. "Patrick was her favorite son. She's so ill, and Mr. Gulley is helpless without her. We so depended on Patrick's paychecks."

"Couldn't his brothers help?"

"His younger brother joined the service."

"Already?"

"The day after Pearl Harbor. And his older brother lives in Philadelphia and must care for his own family. He sends money when he can." Ellen lifted her chin. "I suppose I'm going to have to take a job."

"Doing what?"

"I don't know, Maggie."

Maggie stared across the parking lot where she'd last seen Colin boarding the bus. She wondered what she would have said to him had she known she might never see him again. She couldn't have stopped him from going—she knew that now—but at least she could have told him how much he meant to her, how much she loved him. She pressed her fingertips to her eyes to hold back the tears.

"Ellen?"

"Hmm?"

"Did you ever consider going to college?"

"No." Ellen blew her nose into a lace handkerchief. "What a funny thing to ask."

"Why is it funny?"

"Oh Maggie, my family could never have afforded college."

"I could have gone, you know? My uncle wanted me to, but I wasn't interested. I was going to marry Colin," Maggie said. "Now I wish I'd gone. At least I'd be trained in something."

"What would you have been?"

"Maybe a teacher."

"You'd have been a good teacher," Ellen said.

Maggie smiled faintly. She reached for her friend's hand and took a deep breath. "Okay, so you'll take a job. And I will as well. And I'll help you with the housework and tending to Mrs. Gulley until the boys come home." She squeezed Ellen's hand. "We'll get through this, Ellen—together."

Chapter 13

Wake Island, 1942

In his dream, Colin was back on the runway, guards shrilling orders somewhere in the black night. Someone hummed "Away in a Manger" while the head of a decapitated man cried for help as it lay along the side of the road.

Colin awoke with a start, drenched in sweat, and rolled off his bunk. Leaping over men sleeping on the barracks floor, he dashed for the latrine. Shortly after the surrender, when his case of dysentery was still in its early stages, Red had managed to scavenge some charcoal from the hospital for Colin to eat. Since then, his condition had greatly improved, though he no longer trusted his bowels. Many of the other men had not been so lucky. A few had died from the disease.

In the barracks washroom, Colin stared at himself in the long, cracked mirror. Gone was the wide-eyed boy who'd arrived on Wake over seven months ago. His once vivid-green eyes had turned listless and sunken, ringed with dark circles. His sandy-blond hair hung shaggy and dirty to his collar. On his usually clean-shaven chin, a beard was coming in with a red tint that reminded him of his father. The scratches he'd acquired on his arms, face and legs during the invasion had scabbed over and were peeling now. The wound above his elbow had closed with the small pieces of shrapnel still inside, but not before it had festered for several days. Colin still couldn't straighten his arm completely.

Thank God Ma can't see me this way, he thought, remembering the way his mother had always cried whenever he hurt himself as a child, insisting on tending to even tiny wounds.

They had been moved back to Camp Two on Christmas Day. The sick and seriously wounded, Red and Frank among them, were taken to the hospital, but their treatment had been superficial as most of the medical supplies had been confiscated by the Japanese to treat their own wounded. The healthier prisoners were crowded into a few barracks, two hundred men to each unit designed for eighty. Colin and Patrick had maneuvered through the lines to ensure they'd be placed in their previous unit. But when they reached their bunks, they found them occupied. A fevered man lay writhing on Colin's bunk, watched over by his friends. He wore one of Colin's work shirts, though it fit him snuggly.

Colin was able to get past the fevered man's friends long enough to look through his belongings. The Japanese had picked through the barracks, removing anything of value, including Colin's leather toilet kit and his Saint Christopher medal. They'd left their boot tread marks on Colin's photographs and had scattered the fishing balls and bits of coral he'd collected. But he was able to find one long-sleeved shirt, a dirty pair of dungarees, and the beat-up work boots he'd kept under his bunk. He held them up to show Patrick the holes in the soles. "Even the Japs didn't want these boots," he said, pointing to a pair dangling by their laces from Patrick's hand. "They left yours too, huh?"

"Finally came in handy having such big feet."

Colin and Patrick slept on the floor that first night, but the next morning the fevered man was removed to the hospital, and Colin and Patrick reclaimed Colin's bunk. Colin shared it with Patrick, and later Red when he was released from the hospital, though his gunshot wound had not yet healed.

Colin had soon been assigned to drive a jeep for a Japanese officer, Captain Kurokawa. The Japanese had organized work details, and many of the Marines and contractors had spent the past two weeks clearing debris, setting up barbed wire, building new gun emplacements. In a sense, they were doing what they had always done on Wake, readying the island for defense. Only now they were working for the enemy, and engaging in sabotage whenever they could find the chance: pouring saltwater down rifle barrels, dumping sand into the recoiling mechanisms of the antiaircraft guns, burying inner pieces of machine guns.

Colin left the latrine and headed back to his bunk, hoping for another hour of sleep before he'd have to drive the Captain on his rounds. But someone gripped his bandaged left arm and yanked. Colin clamped his jaw shut to keep from screaming in pain. A burly guard propelled him through the door into the early morning sunshine. He lost his balance and fell to his knees. The guard dragged him up and shoved him toward the road, where Captain Kurokawa waited beside a jeep. The small Japanese officer snapped an order to the guard, who saluted and lumbered back to his position outside the barracks door.

Captain Kurokawa stared up at Colin. The officer's black eyebrows knit together. His tone was harsh, for the benefit of the guard, but his eyes betrayed concern.

"Are you able to work?" he demanded.

Colin shrugged. The captain ordered him into the jeep, then climbed into the passenger seat, the guard watching suspiciously as they drove away. They passed the barbed wire the Japanese had erected, the unused barracks units, and the demolished aggregate plant and storehouses. Then the buildings of Camp Two slipped behind them, and Captain Kurokawa relaxed in his seat.

"Where are we going?" Colin asked, leaving off the "sir" he knew was required.

Kurokawa ignored the slight. "I need to check all the work details today," he said in perfect English. "Let's start near the South Beach."

Initially he hadn't spoken much except to direct Colin's driving, but in the past several days, the officer, who couldn't be much older than Colin, had initiated conversations of a personal nature, asking about Colin's home and family. Colin had told him little at first, preferring to nurse his hatred. But when the Captain brought him an extra piece of bread one day and asked him again to tell him about his home, he reluctantly agreed.

In turn, he'd learned that Kurokawa had been raised in San Francisco from the age of three until his parents took him back to Japan when he was fifteen. He'd been planning to return to America to attend college in California when he was drafted into the Imperial Navy. He said more than once how much he regretted that missed opportunity.

"You look better today," Kurokawa said.

"It comes and goes."

"Your friend Patrick was disciplined in the mess hall this morning. Don't worry. It was only a slap, and the stew kettle was overturned. I'm afraid your men will miss noon meal today."

"It won't be the first time."

Kurokawa frowned and was silent for a moment. He took

three crackers from his pocket and handed them to Colin. "I brought you these."

Colin hesitated, then took the crackers.

The captain looked grim. "Do you understand the Code of Bushido?"

Colin shook his head.

"It's the Way of the Warrior," Kurokawa said. "For a Japanese, the greatest honor is to die for the Emperor. To be taken prisoner disgraces not only the soldier, but also his entire family. Better to kill yourself. It is only because your men fought so well and so bravely that our soldiers are able to look at you with anything but contempt. You are lucky your treatment has not been worse."

A truck rumbled toward them, and Colin pulled off the road to let it pass. The South Beach lay off to the side, gutted and torn from the invasion. Colin was still unable to pass this point without hearing the loud pops of gunfire, without a lump rising in his throat at the memory of Chaplain's lifeless body.

Kurokawa laughed, the sound turning Colin's stomach. "When we came ashore, my men were afraid of you civilians," the captain said. "They thought you must be convicts banished to hard labor on this island. And as hard as you fought us, they feared you must be very brutal men."

Colin turned the wheel to pull back onto the road, but Kurokawa stopped him. "I should not be telling you this," he said seriously. "Tomorrow a boat will come. Most of you will be taken to a prison camp. A few hundred of your most skilled workers will be kept on the island to continue the work of rebuilding. I have seen the list for transport . . . Your name is on it."

Colin stared at the captain, trying to make sense of his words.

"I can arrange for you to stay on the island if you like."

"What good would that do? I'd still be a prisoner."

"Yes, but at least things are familiar here, and the barracks are in good condition. There's still plenty of food and . . . there's the chance your American troops will retake the island."

Colin put both hands on the steering wheel and looked out across the ocean, the water reflecting the brilliant colors of the coral reef, the cloudless blue sky washing into the sea at the horizon. One of the American officers had fixed a broken radio and for a few days, until it was discovered, the men had heard news from the United States. They knew of President Roosevelt's ambitious plans to turn the focus of American industry toward winning the war, to build thousands of planes and resurrect the United States Navy from the carnage at Pearl Harbor. But Colin had heard nothing to lead him to believe the military planned to retake Wake. They had been abandoned during the battle, and it seemed now they were forgotten.

"Leave my name on the list."

Kurokawa looked surprised. "Why?"

"I don't know . . . I guess I was raised to believe in fate. My mother would call it God's will. It seems to me if my name's on that list—then I'm meant to go. Besides, I can't let Patrick go alone."

"Things could be much worse for you."

"Maybe, but there's too many memories here and too many broken dreams. This place was supposed to be my motherlode, my chance to build a good life for me and my girl."

Kurokawa sat in silence for a moment. "I would like to see America again someday."

"So would I." Colin's eyes met Kurokawa's briefly, then he looked away. "I need to ask a favor, though. I left something in the brush over there, and I need to take it with me."

Kurokawa glanced at the expanse of dense vegetation along

the beach and frowned.

"Please, sir. It's very important."

"I will grant this, but hurry. If anyone sees, I will tell them we noticed a movement, and I sent you to search the brush. I've been told there are still a few of your men in hiding."

Colin jumped from the truck. Several minutes passed as he searched frantically for his father's watch, scratching his hands as he parted the scrub brush. Kurokawa became impatient and ordered him back to the jeep just as a flicker of light caught Colin's eye, and he bent to untangle his father's watch from the branches of the dwarf magnolia.

"What is it?" Kurokawa demanded, his pistol drawn.

"It's okay. It's not a gun." Colin raised his hand slowly.

The captain took a step forward and lifted the watch from Colin's palm.

He looked it over and handed it back.

"It belonged to my father."

"Then I can see why you would want it back, but they will take it from you on the ship tomorrow."

"I'll find a way to hide it."

"Come, we must get to work now."

Colin pushed the watch deep into his pocket as he walked back. He started up the jeep and edged onto the road, comforted by the weight of his father's watch against his thigh.

Chapter 14

The Nitta Maru, *1942*

The *Nitta Maru* hovered on the waves, sleek and menacing. Her engines churned, turning over to keep her from being carried onto the treacherous reef. Rumor had it the ship had once been a luxury liner and had set a transpacific speed record, but to Colin it looked more like a coffin.

He waited in line with Patrick. Frank, pale and barely recovered from dysentery, wavered between them. Ahead, Marty Johansen stood with his Marine friends. From time to time he'd turn, keeping his eye on Colin. The men had been given an hour's notice to prepare for transport, and most carried white linen sacks packed with a change of clothes and the few personal items that had not been confiscated. Patrick stood on one foot with his sack tucked beneath his arm, mouthing curses in the direction of the flat-faced guard who had just kicked his ankle. Colin gripped the edge of the sack slung over his shoulder and looked around hopefully.

"I haven't seen Red all morning."

"Last time I seen him he was looking for his boot. Somebody probably stole it," Patrick said.

"I think the guards grabbed him for a work detail," Frank said. "Wish I was a carpenter like Red. Then I'd get to stay on Wake too."

"Not me," Patrick growled. "I'd be damned before I'd help the Japs rebuild this shithole."

The men were called to attention and shown a list of rules from the captain of the ship. Colin read the rules, his forehead creasing. It was forbidden to: *show resistance or antagonism; attempt to run away or carry unnecessary baggage on board; demonstrate individualism or selfishness; take more than one meal or use more than two blankets; talk without permission; walk without order; or touch the ship's wires, electric lights, switches, materials, etc.*

"In other words, they can kill us for twitchin' a finger if they want," Patrick whispered.

The orders also stated that because the ship was *narrow and ill-equipped* they should expect the food to be *scarce and poor*.

"What's that supposed to mean?"

"It means take what you get and be glad for it," Colin said.

"The punishment for disobedience will be death," shouted a Japanese officer. Colin exchanged a look with Patrick. Frank began to tremble and mutter fearfully. Patrick clamped a hand over Frank's mouth.

Captain Kurokawa passed by without glancing at Colin and headed toward the front of the line. He stood to the side supervising as several guards shook down the men, removing any valuables they may have missed in the barracks searches.

Colin limped forward, walking on the side of his boot, the toes of his left foot curled to raise his arch and protect his father's watch. He'd removed the chain last night and secured the watch to the bottom of his foot with a used, bloodied bandage. His sock covered the bandage. He hadn't told even Patrick about the watch and now, as he watched the soldiers beat a man for trying to sneak a wedding ring on board, he wondered if it was worth risking his life for.

He tensed as his turn came up. One soldier ordered him to open his shirt, remove his boots and drop his pants. Captain Kurokawa lunged forward, shoving Colin out of the way. He slapped the soldier hard across the face, berating him in Japanese, his hand indicating the long line of men and gesturing for the guard to move faster, faster. Kurokawa grabbed the next man in line and thrust him at the soldier to be searched. Colin quickly stepped forward in line. For several seconds, he stared straight ahead, his heart racing, but the soldiers had forgotten him. Finally, he ventured a glance at the man who had saved his father's watch, but Captain Kurokawa was marching away, his hands behind his back, his body ramrod straight.

Moments later, the barge sliced through the rough, turquoise waters, ferrying the men toward the *Nitta Maru*. Colin's gaze remained fixed on the island the Japanese had renamed *Otori Shima*, Bird Island. He was leaving behind Chaplain, buried in a shallow grave marked only by a two-foot mound of sand and gravel. And leaving Red to labor in the relentless heat.

He remembered his first view of Wake's three tiny islets from the deck of the *Burrows* so many months ago. Wake had lured him with the promise of high wages and adventure—or was it the chance to find himself, as Red had suggested? As the barge neared the icy gray hull of the prison ship, he began to tremble. He knew a part of him would never leave the shimmering coral atoll, her pounding surf and the stench of gunpowder and decomposing bodies. How often in his nightmares would he revisit Wake's rocky shore and peer across an endless ocean for the reinforcements that would never arrive?

He scanned the vanishing beaches for a glimpse of Red's floppy hat, aching for the older man's wisdom and dry sense of humor. More than once, Red's levelheaded actions had saved his life. Last night they'd spoken in the crowded barracks, their heads close together as Colin repeated Captain Kurokawa's warning about the transport. Colin's skin crawled as something told him Red would not be boarding the ship.

Judging from the look in his eye, Red must have known it too. He seized Colin's wrist. "Listen to me," he said. "They can control your body, but they must never be allowed to control your mind. Do you understand?"

"Yes."

Red let go and sighed heavily.

"If you get home before me, would you telephone Maggie? Tell her to wait for me."

"I'll do you one better, my friend," Red said. "I'll go to Idaho myself."

Since the first raid, Red had held Colin together, and now he wasn't sure how he was going to learn to survive on his own.

The waves burst between the barge and the ship, nearly smashing the smaller boat against the *Nitta Maru*. Colin warned Frank to stop crying as they were stuffed into cargo nets and hoisted to the deck. On board, the Japanese sailors rifled through the prisoners' sacks, tossing them aside and beating the men for having no valuables.

The prisoners formed a single-file line to be sprayed with a decontaminant that settled mostly on their clothes. The Japanese sailors formed two rows, laughing and yelling as the first bewildered prisoner was forced between them. The sailors pummeled him with rifle butts, swords, bamboo clubs, and bare fists. Then the next man was pushed through the gauntlet.

Patrick ran through doubled over, his arms covering his head. Frank followed, tripping on his way through. Several sailors fell upon him as he tried to stand. Coming up behind, Colin grabbed Frank's shirt at the shoulders and hauled him to his feet. But Colin was slow, still hobbling on the side of his boot to protect his watch. A sailor rammed his rifle butt into Colin's kidney, and Colin arched backward, crying out.

On the other side of the gauntlet, Patrick seized his arm and pulled him away from the sailors. Other guards shoved them toward a ladder leading into one of the ship's empty forward cargo holds. Colin descended the ladder, fighting to control his fear as steel walls echoed the heavy breathing of the men who had preceded him into the dark hold. Marty waited at the base of the ladder to lead Colin and the others to a spot by the starboard wall, where he had been sitting with another Marine. All the men, roughly twelve hundred, were eventually crowded into holds on three decks. They sat shoulder to shoulder.

Sweat poured from Colin's brow, stinging a gash below his right eye, a painful reminder of the gauntlet.

It's hotter than hell in here, he thought, laboring to breathe the stifling, rank air. The men maneuvered into positions that allowed the most comfort, some standing while others sat or lay down. Colin sank to the hard floor, his shoulder against the ship's warm iron hull, his hand covering his bruised lower back. He felt the ache in his bowels again and wondered how he would relieve himself.

A murmur went up among the men as the hatch screeched closed, the sound reverberating through the hold. Colin winced as it slammed into place, leaving them in blackness. In the absolute silence, he closed his eyes and felt the others pressing against him. Then he started to hear things. First it was only hundreds of men breathing, then the soft moans of the sick, the muffled sobs of the younger boys—the sounds of fear and hopelessness. Colin put his hands over his ears, pressing hard until he could hear only the blood rushing in his veins.

"They can control your body," he heard Red say, "but you must never let them control your mind."

Colin took a deep breath and forced his mind to a place far from the cargo hold, to the wide-open spaces of Idaho and a picnic by a meandering creek where Maggie sat on a checkered blanket.

"Why didn't I stay on the island with Red?" he asked himself. But he could feel Patrick's breath on his face, Marty's shoulder against his, and Frank trembling at his feet. He knew he belonged here with his friends. He could never have stayed on the island without them. They had only each other now, and on each other they must depend.

Chapter 15

The Nitta Maru, *1942*

As much as Colin hated the dead men for making the air even more foul, he envied them being free of this hellhole. From time to time, the Japanese sailors pointed their guns into the hatch, and Colin would think it was all over, hope it was all over. Then they'd withdraw their guns, and he'd remember again how much he wanted to live.

He shuddered, recalling the prisoners tying the dead to ropes to be hoisted from the hold. Colin had looked up once as the bloated body of a civilian twisted on the rope. He'd looked away quickly, but not before the image had singed his mind.

"When are they going to dump the dead guys again?" he asked Patrick. In the darkness he could see only the outline of Patrick's face, but he could feel, with irritation, his friend's body against his, as it had been for the past ten days. "It's not just the smell. We could use the room."

Colin and Patrick sat with their knees drawn up so Frank could lie down at their feet. He'd been sick for the last four days, his dysentery returned. Sometimes he made it to the overflowing five-gallon can in the corner to relieve himself; more often he did not. But he smelled no worse than anyone else. The stench of feces, urine, vomit, stale sweat, infected wounds, and decomposing bodies had permeated the skin of every man in the hold.

Colin tapped Frank with his foot, listening for a groan that would indicate he was still alive. He pulled his thin, ratty blanket tighter around his shoulders and flexed the stiff muscles in his thighs. He stretched out his legs, determined to lay them across Frank's bony chest, actually holding them suspended over the moaning boy before slowly drawing them back.

He leaned forward to keep his back off the cold hull. Many times since they left Wake, he'd wished he'd never followed Marty to the starboard wall of the hold. In the first few days of the voyage, the steel hull simmered as the temperature soared above a hundred degrees. But as the ship crossed into northern waters on its way to Asia, the temperature plummeted, and the steel turned cold. Still, it helped to have something to lean against, something solid, not another man.

Marty stirred at Colin's right, waking from a sleep in which he'd mumbled again about his girlfriend, Becky. Colin asked him how he was doing by nudging him. Marty nudged back. Since the *Nitta Maru* left Wake, the Japanese had proven they were intent on enforcing the absurd rules they'd issued. The men kept as still and quiet as they could, fearing the brutal beatings doled out by the guards.

Marty was particularly careful not to draw attention to himself. Twice the sailors had taken him and several of the other large men on deck to use for practicing their judo throws. His height and bulk provided a special challenge to the sailors, most of whom were much smaller. Of course, the prisoners were not allowed to fight back, and when they passed out or went limp, they were dropped back into the hold.

Colin was beginning to wonder if the Japanese also harbored a prejudice toward redheads. It seemed they were often the targets of random beatings and, on the second day out, two Marines from VMF-211 and three Navy seamen, two of whom had red hair, had been taken on deck to empty the waste cans. They had never returned. Although no one knew for sure what had happened, it was rumored they'd been beheaded. Colin was glad now that Red had been left on Wake.

On Marty's other side, Private Arthur Gaines licked condensation off the hull of the ship. In the early days of the trip, Colin had sucked sweat from his own arms until dehydration dried up the perspiration. Patrick had tried drinking urine, only to vomit it back up. One man had lost his mind and bitten another to drink his blood. He'd been beaten unconscious by the wounded man and his friends and had not yet awakened. Colin hoped he never would.

Arthur whispered something to Marty, and Colin strained to hear. In the last ten days, he'd learned just enough about Arthur to become interested in the man. He knew Arthur had been raised in California by his mother's mother—a Japanese woman brought over to marry his grandfather, an American. He could speak some Japanese, something he'd never mentioned on Wake. Not even Marty had known of his friend's Japanese blood until after the island had been taken.

"I've found most folks have a low opinion of the Japanese, so I generally keep it to myself. Course, it'll be worse now," Arthur had whispered to Marty, who'd passed it on to Colin. They agreed to keep his secret.

Arthur had taken a serious risk a few days back, hanging close to Marty so the Japanese would also grab him for judo practice. On deck, he'd eavesdropped on the casual chattering of the sailors, hoping for news of the war. He came back with fresh bruises and a twisted ankle but very little information. He confirmed, however, that the pings they'd heard were the sounds of American sonar bouncing off the hull of the *Nitta Maru*. He thought he'd overheard that the *Nitta Maru*'s guide ship had been sunk. Colin now worried this unmarked prison ship might be next. To be killed by Americans seemed too ridiculous to imagine, yet Colin would never have imagined any of the things that had happened to him in the past few weeks.

He hung his head, exhausted. The first few days had been too hot to sleep, and then too cold. The steel deck and cramped conditions afforded no comfort. Besides, he feared what might happen while he slept. He couldn't risk a beating again for breaking the stillness rule by shivering. And he certainly didn't want to be murdered while he slept by some sadistic guard or by a fellow prisoner desperate for his worn work boots or his place by the hull.

Moment to moment, Colin struggled to control his nerves. His right eye twitched more often now, and he'd taken to rubbing his left palm when the tension got to him. One thought hovered constantly at the front of his mind: How long can I survive this? He'd tell himself he was still young and only moderately weakened by the lack of food, that his family needed him, that he should survive to honor his father's memory, that he couldn't give the Japanese the satisfaction of destroying him. But in the end, it was Maggie who kept him alive. To be with her again was worth whatever suffering he would have to endure.

The top hatch creaked open. Frank raised his head slightly. A large food bucket swayed on a rope as it was lowered into the hold. Twice a day, the men received a cup of food and, once a day, a cup of water. Colin wished it were the other way around. Though his stomach ached constantly, he could stand the hunger better than the debilitating thirst.

Two prisoners were ordered to ration out dippers of watery rice gruel flavored with rotting fish heads, guts, and eyes. Colin ate from his mess kit, glad for the dim light that hid the food. He ate slowly, despite his ravaging hunger, making the sparse meal last. Many times he thought of the piece of bread he'd stuck in his pocket the first day of raids on Wake and tried to believe there had ever been a time he couldn't eat.

"Wonder what the officers got today." Patrick sounded annoyed. The officers were being held in a cramped mailroom on the upper deck and were rumored to be getting better treatment and food than the enlisted men and civilians in the holds. Colin rarely thought about them, but they seemed to be always on Patrick's mind.

Colin wiped his empty cup with the tail of his filthy shirt. His beard itched, and his shaggy, matted hair curled into his ears, tickling. He fumbled with the broken zipper on his dungarees. Most of the time, he left it unfastened to make it easier to urinate, but if he really worked at it, he could get the zipper back up. Now that it was so cold, it seemed wise to keep it fastened. Besides, he was losing weight and could almost pull the pants down without undoing them.

"I think my birthday came and went," Patrick whispered. "January 17. Can't keep track of the days down here. I'm twenty-five . . ." His teeth chattered loudly. "Oh boy. I'm thinkin' I'm not gonna make it."

"You damn well better." Colin put an arm around his shoulder and drew him close, whispering in his ear. "Remember that blizzard in Boise a few years back? I was digging out my mother's walkway and thinking how much I hated to be cold. Imagine that. Me with a wool coat and my dad's old fur hat, griping about the cold."

Patrick wiped his nose with the back of his hand and stammered, "That first day on board, when we were fightin' just to breathe down here . . . I thought things couldn't be worse . . . Wouldn't mind a bit of that heat now. . . Better to be fryin' than dyin', that's what I always say."

Colin smiled, relieved to hear the folksy sense of humor returning to Patrick's voice. He glanced over at Arthur, wondering how he could stand it in only the shorts and thin shirt that were part of the uniform issued Marines on tropical islands. Frank groaned, struggled to his feet, and lurched over bodies toward the overflowing can in the corner. Colin shook his head. "Poor Frank."

"Least he can go. I haven't crapped since we left Wake."

Colin stared at the ladder that led out of the hold and imagined climbing it to stand in the fresh air on deck. But what would he see there? Only icy waters leading to a hostile country farther from home than he'd ever imagined venturing. "We're going to walk out of here, Patrick. If I have to carry you every step of the way."

Patrick lowered his head to Colin's shoulder, and the heat from his body warmed Colin. When the boredom or fear got to him, Colin would list the items in his mother's home room by room, starting with the kitchen, which he imagined to be filled with the rich scents of baking bread and stew simmering on the stove. Each time the list differed. He'd forget an item or add one. But trying to get it right gave him purpose, kept his mind off his suffering, kept him connected to home.

He closed his eyes and began: *back door that sticks, chair, window with blue striped curtains, sink . . .*

Chapter 16

China, 1942

Hands trembling, Colin dragged himself from the hold and struggled to his feet, his legs barely supporting his weight. The wet air that chafed his sore throat hinted of snow, and Colin was mildly surprised to find none on the deck of the ship. After twelve days in the hold, his muscles were stiff, making it difficult to move. He followed the prisoner in front of him, keeping his head low as he passed the guards, squinting at the deck until his eyes adjusted to the light. A guard slammed Colin's shoulder with a rifle butt, and Colin reeled forward. One by one, the prisoners staggered onto the deck and formed uneven lines. Colin's watch remained hidden under his left foot, and he imagined it wound, its steady ticking stirring his shaky pulse.

His eyes opened wide at the sight of Patrick, bent forward, matted brown hair stuck to the sides of his face, sour breath hissing through chapped lips. His once-tan face had turned chalky and heavy circles pulled at the lower lids of his cloudy eyes. He scratched the stubble on his chin, long fingernails leaving red scrapes in his dry skin.

Had he not known Patrick was behind him on the ladder coming out of the hold, Colin might have doubted this horrible creature could be the friend he'd known all his life. My God, he thought, touching his own face with icy fingers. How must I look? He got his answer in Patrick's eyes.

Arthur, Marty, and Frank emerged from the hold, each seeming more ghost-like than the one who preceded him. For the first time, Colin thought to look around. The ship appeared to be docked in a large, muddy river. "The Huangpu," Arthur whispered.

A few days back, they had stopped briefly in Yokohama, where they'd been allowed on deck. Arthur had overheard they were headed for China, to a camp near Shanghai. Looking out across the land, Colin hoped to see the city. He remembered Eddie saying once that he would like to visit Shanghai, that it was a cultured place with a large population of international businessmen and their families. But from the deck of the ship, he could see only small riverboats and a gathering of smiling peasants, bundled in layers of warm clothes, watching from the dock.

Using bamboo sticks, the Japanese sailors beat the men into single file lines. They herded them down the gangplank, past two or three sailors who acted as swatters. The men were then turned over to the Japanese army.

Colin struggled to hold his head up. Terrified, he decided to make himself invisible by keeping to the middle of the group, avoiding eye contact, and moving quickly when ordered to do so. Beside him, Frank whimpered. Colin gritted his teeth, hating the boy. He wanted to slap Frank hard across his face. "Quit sniveling. Act like a man," he whispered, though Frank seemed not to hear him.

They marched down a narrow, muddy road alongside a slow-moving canal. The landscape was barren and quiet, with only a scattering of villages and tiny houses that seemed made from the same clay soil he walked upon. Families worked their fields, tending to the winter rice crop with barely a glance at the passing prisoners.

Colin was remembering other things Eddie had told him in one of his rambling observances of human nature. He'd said the Japanese believed all Asian people to be superior to whites, and they had overrun China as part of their plan to unite the Asian peoples under their rule. So Colin figured this whole procession was about one thing: a chance for the Japanese army to show the conquered Chinese how they had defeated the powerful white man. But most of the sunken-cheeked Chinese farmers who bothered to glance up at the prisoners did so not with arrogance, contempt, or even pity, but with an odd blank stare that left Colin feeling hollow.

The prisoners jogged nearly five miles, their legs and groins cramping painfully, many of the sick and wounded falling to the side of the road, where they were kicked by the guards and then left behind. The rest arrived at Woosung Prison Camp as the sun set. Passing several nondescript buildings, they entered the camp through its only gate, which hung loose on its hinges.

As a young boy, Colin had visited a friend's ranch and watched as sheep were herded toward a chute leading into a pen. Invariably, at the entrance to the chute, a sheep would attempt to bolt in the opposite direction only to be met by a herder with a stick delivering quick, hard blows to the nose to turn the animal. It had seemed cruel to Colin, a city boy. It seemed more so now that he understood that urge to run. He knew if he looked too closely at the barbed wire, the electric fence, the guards aiming rifles from the watchtower, he would break from the line before he reached the gate and be shot down. So he stared straight ahead, losing himself in the blue, stained shirt worn by the prisoner in front of him. When all the prisoners were in the compound, the gate finally swung shut on shrieking hinges. Colin's knees buckled, and he dropped to the ground. Patrick reached to help, but Colin knocked his hands away. Standing again, he took several strained breaths, then raised his eyes at last to see where fate had brought him.

The camp consisted of seven grey, run-down barracks units. Rectangular—roughly a hundred feet by twenty feet—with pointed roofs. They reminded Colin of the horse stables on that ranch he'd visited. Behind the barracks were crude wash racks and overflowing latrines. This portion of the camp was enclosed by a dirt road. Beyond the road but within the wire, other ramshackle buildings dotted the fence line. From an old water tank that looked about thirty feet high, icicles hung nearly to the ground. Dried weeds tangled everything.

The prisoners waited nearly an hour before Colonel Yuse came to stand before them. Appearing to be in his sixties, the commandant was squat with no neck. He wore his short-brimmed cap low over his eyes and a cape over his brown uniform jacket, which hung open revealing a clean white shirt. His baggy pants were tucked into knee-high black boots. He climbed onto a chair to address the prisoners, waving a short bamboo stick and barking orders in Japanese.

His interpreter, introduced as Isamu Ishihara, stood beside him. He was tall and scowled at the prisoners while twisting a short riding crop in his hand. He explained in broken English the camp rules, which were strict yet open to the interpretation of the guards, just as they had been on the ship. Colin was issued two damp cotton blankets, a thin straw mat, a pillow, and a plate, bowl, and spoon. He was directed to Barracks Four, which was divided into sections of three-sided rooms, empty except for six-foot-wide sleeping platforms built out from the walls and raised two feet off the ground. There were windows but no insulation, and the wind pried its way in through the cracks in the walls. A single bulb dangled in the middle of the room, illuminating a rat as it ran along a ledge designed to hold the men's belongings, if they'd had any left. There were nails under the ledge for hanging the pouches that held their eating utensils.

Colin, Patrick, and Frank claimed a portion of a platform. Arthur and Marty had been taken to one of the military barracks, separated again from the civilians. The men devoured a watery soup, licking the sides of their bowls. Afterward, Colin just managed to get Frank to the door before the boy vomited it back up. Disgusted, Colin left Frank in Patrick's care and returned to the sleeping platform.

He lay down, dragging his blankets up over his shoulder. "I should keep clear of Frank," he told himself. "If I'm going to survive, I'll need to stay strong. Frank's just bringing me down."

He heard Frank and Patrick return, felt their warmth as they lay down beside him. After a few moments, Colin rolled over to look at Frank's boyish face, his closed, sunken eyes, his puffy lips forming silent words. Overcome with shame, Colin scooted closer, sharing one of his blankets with Frank.

They shivered through the night, huddled together, the nearly useless blankets wrapped tightly around their filthy bodies. A cold breeze snaked through the floorboards. The sparse barracks echoed the coughs and groans of the prisoners, the shuffling of their feet as they paced the hall to keep warm, the click of rats' claws on the wood floors. By morning, the others had drawn so close to Colin he could not shift his position.

Despite the uncertainty of what lay ahead, he greeted the morning light filtering through smudged, frosted windows with relief. He'd always hated mornings back home, drawing his curtains to keep out the light so he could sleep a little later. He'd shrugged off his mother's appreciation of Idaho sunrises and silvery morning frosts. Now, staring at the blistered boards of the barracks, he could only thank God for the dawn, for keeping him alive through one more night in captivity.

A Japanese bugler woke the men. They folded their blankets as ordered, stacking them on the platforms, and swept the floor with freezing hands. They stood at attention outside the barracks as a Japanese officer and his guards arrived for inspection and struggled to perform morning *tenko*, counting off in Japanese *ichi, ni, san, shi, go, roku, shichi, hachi* . . . Frank barely managed to stand through the inspection, collapsing as soon as the men were dismissed. Colin and Patrick helped him back into the barracks before wrapping themselves in blankets and venturing into the compound for a look around. They ran into Marty and Arthur, who told tales of their own sleepless nights.

Marty pointed at the buildings beyond the dirt road. "They said the galley and bathhouse are over there, so the rest of those shacks must be storage."

Colin indicated the buildings outside the fence. "Those must be quarters for the guards."

"I'd like to get my hands around that commandant's neck," Marty grumbled.

"Hell, you could as easily squash him under your boot," Patrick said. The men chuckled softly, eyeing the guards. Sticking together, the prisoners ambled past the other barracks units, keeping track of who resided in each. They exchanged casual greetings with the camp's other inhabitants—British embassy personnel from Shanghai and the crews of two sunken gunboats, the H.M.S. *Petrel* and the ironically named U.S.S. *Wake*. They met a young Marine whose troop had been captured while awaiting transport to Manila and a handful of civilian crew members from merchant ships overrun by the Japanese. They learned that Allied civilians from Shanghai, including women and children, were in a separate camp.

"Why aren't we there then?" Colin wondered. "We're civilians."

"Because we acted as guerrillas on Wake," Arthur said. "From what I've been able to gather, we're lucky they haven't shot us. The Japanese have a particular dislike for guerrillas."

They continued exploring the camp, stopping just short of the electric fence to gaze beyond the lock-jawed guards toward the hazy skies above Shanghai, less than fifteen miles away. "Maybe we can escape," Marty said.

"If we could get to the city, we could find us a boat," Patrick said.

"The Japanese control the harbor," Colin reminded him.

"Okay, we could bribe some Chinese peasant to hide us on his boat."

"With what money?"

"We could steal some."

Arthur shook his head. "Fact is, fellas, we wouldn't make it to the city. We'd stick out like sore thumbs among all those Chinese. Besides, what about our groups of ten? You heard what the guards said when they numbered us off. If one of our group escapes, the other nine will be shot."

"They wouldn't dare," Patrick said.

"Want to bet?"

"Okay, so we stay here and do what we're told," Colin said. "We can handle that. The war won't last long anyway."

"Well, I gotta find some way to keep busy, or I'm gonna go nuts in this place," Patrick said.

"If it stays this cold and they keep holding out on food, you won't have to worry about keeping busy," said Arthur. "You'll be dead."

Patrick seized Arthur's shirt. "I've had enough of your smart mouth. You wanna roll over and give up? Be my guest."

"Lay off, Patrick." Colin nodded toward the guards. "It's not worth it."

Patrick shoved Arthur backward and stormed away.

"Guess you shouldn't have said that, Gaines." Marty chuckled.

Colin pulled the blankets tighter across his shoulders. "Patrick's got a temper," he said by way of apology. "But he's right, Art. We don't need you telling us what we already know."

With a last glance toward the city, Colin went to look for Patrick. When he didn't find him in the barracks, he decided to wait outside. He kicked at the frozen earth with the toe of his boot and got an idea. Inching along the outer wall of the barracks, he found a spot where the earth pulled slightly away from the foundation and felt his blood begin to warm.

He hurried into the barracks and sat on the platform. Nearby two men slept. With his back to them, he took off his boot and carefully unwound the bloody bandage. He removed the watch and, keeping it in the bandage, hid it in his pocket. Pulling his boot on, he wrapped his blanket around him and hurried out of the barracks.

At the spot he'd chosen, he sat with his back to the wall and hid his hands beneath the blanket he had stretched across his knees. He dropped the watch into the crack, sucking in his breath as a guard passed. He could feel the sweat rising on his forehead but didn't dare wipe it away. Behind the shield of the blanket, he scraped loose a layer of dirt with the spoon he'd grabbed from his mess kit and covered the watch, praying it would be safe until he found a better place to hide it.

He rose slowly and moved to the end of the barracks, untucking his shirttail to glance at a loose, crooked seam. Before he'd left Wake, he'd taken his favorite picture of Maggie, folded it in half, and sewn it into his shirt with a medic's needle and thread. As with the watch, he'd told no one about the picture.

At one time, he had planned to buy so many new things for himself and Maggie. So important had they once seemed that he'd left her to go in search of the money to acquire them. Now the only two things that mattered were a badly creased picture and an old, dented watch. The irony struck him, and he started to laugh. He laughed harder, his sides aching, until the other prisoners stopped to stare and the guards turned in his direction.

Chapter 17

Boise, 1942

The room was filled with the sound of a tapping typewriter and a very tall man gruffly issuing orders over a telephone. Maggie made sure no one was watching before she quickly straightened her silk stockings so the seam ran in a neat line down the back of her calf. They were the last pair she had left. She wore a tan, two-piece suit and wedge-heeled shoes, her dark hair swept up. She'd decided against a hat—the only one she owned that matched was out of fashion—but she didn't feel fully dressed without one. She brushed at her jacket sleeve and hoped she looked older than her twenty-three years and more confident than she felt.

Papers were piled neatly at the front of the high, wooden desk in front of her, and three sharpened pencils lay atop a ledger. The walls of the Mountain Bell office were empty except for a couple of pictures and a hanging calendar, which showed the date—Friday, February 21. Maggie felt overheated and lightheaded sitting beside the radiator and wished she'd eaten breakfast.

Miss Achurra, the chief switchboard operator, crossed the room, heels clicking on the wood floor. She thrust a skinny hand toward Maggie and apologized in a soft, nasal voice for keeping her waiting. Maggie shook her hand, lifting slightly from her chair as the tiny woman eyed her through gold-rimmed glasses attached to a chain. Miss Achurra sat across the desk from Maggie, her thick lips forming a stiff smile.

"You are here to apply for a switchboard position?"

Maggie could only nod, the words stuck in her throat.

"You were recommended by Mrs. Gulley. She's having a bit of trouble learning the numbers, but she'll be a fine worker." Miss Achurra cocked her head. "I can tell those things about people." She opened a small notebook and wrote as she interviewed Maggie. "What type of schooling have you had, Miss Braun?"

"I completed high school."

"Have you worked before?"

"No." Maggie spoke quickly now. "But I was secretary of the math club in school, and I've organized the church bazaar for the past three years. My mother takes in sewing, and I've helped with that. I learn quickly and have an excellent memory. I'm a hard worker, Miss Achurra, and very responsible."

"Are you punctual?"

"Yes, ma'm."

"Punctuality is crucial in this job."

"I understand."

Miss Achurra nodded, satisfied. She lay down her pencil and folded her hands on her desk. "Why do you wish to work for Mountain Bell, Miss Braun?"

Maggie hesitated. "My fiancé's been gone almost a year. He was working on Wake Island when it was attacked. No one can tell me if he's alive or . . ." She scooted to the edge of her chair.

"Please. I *need* this job."

Miss Achurra paused. "You'll work a split shift, 10:00 a.m. to 2:00 p.m. and 6:00 p.m. to 10:00 p.m., five days a week. Pay is twelve dollars a week, and the government deducts twelve cents for Social Security. Are these terms acceptable?"

Maggie nodded vigorously.

"Wait here while I speak to Mr. Satler."

Miss Achurra crossed to the tall man's desk and waited patiently until he hung up. She bent and showed him her notebook. Mr. Satler glanced at Maggie, nodded, and picked up the receiver again.

"You can start on Monday," Miss Achurra said, coming back to her desk. "I hope you will enjoy working for us."

"Thank you. I won't let you down."

Miss Achurra showed Maggie out, closing the office door behind her. Maggie stepped outside and stood under the thick, stone archway of the Mountain Bell building waiting for Ellen, who would arrive for work soon. Main Street bustled today with people rushing to complete shopping and errands before the snow started again, and Maggie recognized a couple of people who, thankfully, were too busy to stop and chat.

As they passed, she heard one mother and son arguing over whether or not he should enlist in the Army or wait to be drafted. Everywhere, there were signs of the war. Posters depicting the Axis leaders in fearsome caricatures had sprung up on walls from churches to doctors' offices, blue stars representing sons at war were proudly displayed in the front windows of homes, the neighbor girl had solicited a dime from Maggie to buy a war savings stamp at school. Even on the days when Maggie wanted to forget the war and her fears for Colin, she could not escape the headlines screaming of Allied losses or the dramatic newsreels of Pacific islands falling one by one to the Japanese or even the jabs at the enemy worked into the scripts of every popular radio program. The war was everywhere—in everything she saw, touched, even ate. Often, these days, it was even in her dreams.

Ellen appeared at last, beating mittened hands together. "I've only got a few minutes. Did you get the job?"

Maggie nodded, her breath swirling in the frigid air. "For a minute, I thought Mr. Satler might turn me away."

"Mr. Satler leaves all those decisions to Miss Achurra. He doesn't want to be bothered with us women." Ellen, recovering from yet another cold, coughed delicately into her mitten. She looked tired and frail.

"I need to go home and tell Mother." Maggie sighed. Agnes had been predictably upset when Maggie mentioned applying for work, maintaining she'd always felt it unbecoming for women to work outside the home. Maggie had reminded her that since the Depression, many women had gone to work to help support their families, and now that the men were leaving for the war, more women were entering the workforce, but Agnes had remained unconvinced. This morning, she had taken tea and toast to her bedroom, while Maggie drank tea alone at the kitchen table.

Maggie opened the door for Ellen, and she couldn't help smiling despite her concerns about her mother. "I think I'll go to Anderson's first and look at fabrics," she told Ellen. "I'll need some new skirts for work."

A truck sprayed melting snow onto the sidewalk. Maggie pulled her scarf over her head, wrapping it around her throat and tying it behind her neck. Across the street, a young man passed the storefronts, hunched into his bulky overcoat, a dark fedora pulled low on his head. Maggie watched as he paused to peer through the window of a shop. From this angle, he looked so much like Colin that Maggie nearly called out to him. She stopped herself, though. Her romantic daydreams of Colin's sudden return had shattered when Wake fell and now seemed foolish. She knew she had to accept this war and Colin's capture, but she had not yet learned how to stop hoping for a miracle. Her eyes filled with tears as the stranger walked away.

"Are you all right, miss?" someone asked.

Startled, Maggie turned. "Yes, thank you."

The gentleman's upturned collar brushed his long jaw. He raised a hand, revealing an expensive gold wristwatch. His thin mustache twitched, and then he smiled at her. His dark eyes shone and something about the way he looked at her caused her to catch her breath.

"Haven't I seen you before? At Morrison Knudsen?" he asked.

"I don't think so." She moved past him, her heart fluttering, but he followed.

"Then perhaps we've met somewhere else?"

"No," she lied.

"You seem upset. Can I walk you somewhere?"

"No, thank you. I'm fine." She ducked her head against the breeze and ran across the street, feeling his eyes on her. At the corner she glanced behind her and found that he'd moved on. She saw his well-dressed figure enter a cigar store farther down the street. How odd for her to run into this man again and how embarrassing that both times she had been visibly upset. She headed home, forgetting about the fabric. As the blocks passed, her pace slowed. She paused and rested her hand on the metal horse's head of an old hitching post. She felt foolish now. There had been no reason to be so aloof, but the man had taken her by surprise, and she hadn't liked the way her pulse stirred when he looked at her. "I hope he doesn't work downtown," she told herself, at the same time fixing his features in her memory. It wasn't everyday she met a man with such style and finesse in

Boise. It was natural to be curious about him, she told herself. She tapped the rings dangling from the horse's nose and walked away to the chiming echo of one ring striking the other.

Chapter 18

China, 1942

"Wake up," Patrick said, shaking Colin. "Teters escaped."

"What? How?"

"Stole a shovel and dug under the electric fence behind Barracks Three. Commander Cunningham and two Brit officers went with him. They say them officers know the area 'round Shanghai, and they took along a Chinaman to interpret. So maybe they got a chance, huh?"

Colin sat up. It was still dark. With any luck, the guards wouldn't discover the missing prisoners until morning *tenko*. "How'd you hear?"

"Had to go to the *benjo*, and I heard it there from a fella from Barracks Three. 'Less somebody rats 'em out, they should be long gone before midday."

Colin rested his head in his hands. "Do you know what this means? If Teters gets free, he'll tell our families we're alive. He'll get us help somehow." They sat in silence, listening to the snores and coughs of the other men.

"Should I wake up Frank?" Patrick asked.

"No. Let him sleep. He looks worse every day. We should try and sleep too."

Patrick nodded and lay back on the platform. Colin closed his eyes, but he knew the effort was fruitless.

By morning, a thick fog had rolled in to match Colonel Yuse's mood. Colin knew in order to save face, Yuse would have to recapture the escapees, and quickly. The men gathered by the hundreds near the fence to watch the bloodhounds pick up the trail. Colin noticed a small rock at his feet and picked it up, longing to hurl it at the dogs—anything to slow their progress.

"When Colonel Useless don't get 'em back, there's gonna be hell to pay 'round here. He'll cut back rations and God knows what else," Patrick said.

"It'll be worth it."

Colin believed that completely and would have gone on believing it had the Japanese not led Teters and the others back through the gate of Woosung two days later. Bound as he had been on Wake, Dan Teters marched into camp, the Japanese prodding him forward with their swords. As he passed his men, Colin could read the apology in his eyes.

Arthur came to stand beside Colin. He'd been eavesdropping on the guards.

"What happens now?" Colin asked.

"They'll be taken to a prison in Shanghai."

"Will they kill them?"

"Probably not the officers. I can't say for sure about your boss."

Colin watched as Teters was marched up the steps to the commandant's office.

"So that's it. We've got no leader now. No one to speak for the civilians."

Arthur shook his head. "I told you escape was impossible."

Colin looked at the second electric fence already being added to enclose the camp. He noticed the smug looks on the faces of the guards as they whacked at prisoners with their sticks, forcing them to disperse. After nearly two months in camp, it was finally sinking in. Colin would be here for the duration, and the only hope he had left was that the war wouldn't last long.

"This one's for Becky," Marty said, throwing a curve ball that struck out the batter.

Hovered over second base, Colin raised a half-hearted cheer with what little strength he could spare. He tugged at the waist of his dungarees, held in place now by a belt of braided string. Patrick stepped up, managing one practice swing as he moved toward the collapsed cigarette box that marked home plate.

"Easy out," Colin jeered, picking a louse from his hair and popping it between his fingers.

Patrick pointed the bat at Colin and mimed the ball going straight over his head. Someone laughed. Colin glared at the skinny Japanese guard who stood far out in right field enjoying the banter. Colonel Yuse had approved the softball games, possibly because of the Japanese fascination with American baseball. The foreigners in Shanghai's International Settlement had donated the athletic gear through the Red Cross, as well as books and chessboards. Though several guards usually watched the softball games, this was the first time one had asked to play. Colin beamed as Patrick opted to bat unnaturally as a right-hander, rather than risk hitting the ball to the over-anxious guard in right field.

Except for the sick, the entire camp, nearly eighteen hundred men, had turned out to watch the game on this mild March evening. But Colin missed Dan Teters. His calm demeanor had always been reassuring and somehow Colin still expected to see him sitting on the sidelines, cheering them on.

Colonel Yuse perched on his box far off to the right, away from the stench of the prisoners. Beside him the interpreter, Ishihara, smoked a cigarette and tapped his riding crop against his thigh. Though he wore a military uniform and headed the guard detail, Ishihara, they'd discovered, was a civilian working for the Imperial Army, which had refused to take him as a soldier. This must have been a point of great dishonor for Ishihara, and the men enjoyed speculating about it. "I'm sure it's that he's not mentally fit," Colin had said. "Because when he's beating on you, there doesn't seem to be anything *physically* wrong with the bastard."

Rumor had it Ishihara had grown up in Hawaii, but unlike Captain Kurokawa back on Wake, his upbringing had turned him hostile toward Americans. The men had nicknamed him the Screaming Skull because of his extended jaw and small, round eyeglasses. But lately another nickname had fixed itself to the interpreter—the Beast of the East. Colin preferred this one. It fit the viciousness of the man who derived obvious pleasure from whipping prisoners with his riding crop and administering torture for minor infractions of the rules.

Colin touched his bruised cheek, his pride still stinging from Ishihara's latest tirade at morning *tenko*. When one of the prisoners had failed to answer quickly enough, Ishihara had marched down the line of prisoners, slapping each across the left side of the face. Colin had managed to roll with the blow the first time, but when Ishihara traveled back down the line, beating them from the other side, Colin's timing was off, and he wore the proof on his swollen right cheek.

Frank had passed out with Ishihara's first blow and remained unconscious on the ground until the prisoners were dismissed. Colin glanced at the barracks, wondering how Frank was doing. He'd offered to help him to the compound to watch the game, but Frank had refused to move. When Arthur, who wasn't much of a baseball fan, volunteered to stay with Frank, Colin left quickly, before Arthur could change his mind.

Patrick fouled out, and Colin's team trudged to the sidelines, the skinny guard looking disappointed as he jogged past them from right field. A quartet stood behind home plate singing "Take Me Out to the Ball Game." Colin hummed a few bars, smiling at the memory of his parents and sister watching him play baseball in high school.

Marty was talking to a lieutenant from the North China Marines, who had arrived a week after Colin. In stark contrast to the Wake Islanders, these Marines entered camp in full winter dress, sporting fur caps with flaps and carrying duffel bags and footlockers filled with blankets, clothing, food, and personal items. They had been stationed up north at the embassies in Peiping and Tientsin and assumed they would be repatriated soon. After all, the Geneva Convention granted diplomatic immunity to embassy personnel. Even though the Japanese had never signed the Geneva Convention and had proven they had no intention of honoring it, the Marines were confident they'd be going home soon.

"Good game," said the lieutenant as Colin joined them, but Colin only nodded. He hadn't yet made up his mind how to feel about the North China Marines. They seemed pompous and arrogant, keeping to themselves and snubbing their bedraggled counterparts, especially the civilians. But Marty had met among them someone from basic training, who had given him a spare overcoat and a pair of wool underwear. He'd even given Arthur an extra set of khakis and donated a wool blanket to Frank. Some of the other North China Marines had shared extra clothing, but others guarded their possessions jealously.

The civilians had acquired bits of additional clothing of their own—ill-fitting, cast-off Japanese army uniforms, which they wore along with their clothes from Wake. Colin's lightweight soldier's jacket covered his blue work shirt, but he still wore his old boots, passing up a newer, but smaller, Japanese pair. He gave those boots to Frank.

"Looks like Useless has had enough of the game," Marty said as the Japanese colonel waddled away, a soldier following with his box. Ishihara remained.

"I think I'll bow out the last few innings," Colin said. "Just don't feel strong enough to make it through today."

"I'll get somebody to fill in for you." As Marty waved for a substitute, Colin noticed a fresh scab on the back of his hand.

"What happened?"

"Weasel got me. Said I got more than my share in the food line. Took my own spoon and jabbed straight for my eye. I got my hand up just in time. I'll be damned if that little runt doesn't have it in for me."

"They sure do seem to hate you big guys."

Marty snorted, then gestured Colin in closer. "Hey, listen. That lieutenant told me he got a letter from home today."

"How?"

"Red Cross came to the gates this morning with a bag of mail. Guess the Commandant was feeling generous, or maybe he was napping and they didn't want to wake the old goat. Anyway, the R.C. was able to distribute a few letters."

Colin could barely contain his excitement. "What did it say?"

"Not a hell of a lot. Once the American censors got to it and then the Japs, all the lieutenant could make out was that it was from his mother and his family's doing well."

"That's something, at least." Colin scowled at the lieutenant, realizing he was jealous.

"The R.C. is pretty persistent. Next time it'll be us."

Colin glanced at Ishihara. "I doubt it."

Someone gripped his arm. He turned to see Arthur, wheezing from his short run from the barracks. "You better come quick. Something's wrong with Frank. I sent for Dr. Shindo."

Colin's breath turned cold. He went to the sidelines and motioned to Patrick, who was playing shortstop. Patrick called for a replacement and joined Colin, who quickly explained. Silently, they walked side by side to the barracks, Marty and Arthur trailing behind. They paused in the doorway, looking into the dank, shadowy room to see Dr. Shindo bent over Frank, holding the boy's limp wrist between his fingers.

Patrick puffed out his chest and took long strides to the sleeping platform where Frank lay covered with the wool blanket, his dark, sunken eyes fixed on the ceiling. "What's the matter with him?" Patrick asked, his voice cracking.

The clean-cut young doctor shook his head and closed Frank's eyes with a slender hand. "Too late. Very sorry," said Dr. Shindo, the only sympathetic Japanese Colin had met since Captain Kurokawa. He lay a hand on Patrick's shoulder briefly, then strode past Colin, carrying his black medical bag, his eyes filled with pity.

Colin forced himself to look at Frank, and he was stunned by what he saw. He'd slept beside Frank for two months, brought him food, helped him to *tenko*, fetched the doctor to tend to his dysentery and pneumonia. Yet he'd long ago stopped noticing how the boy's soiled clothes billowed around his emaciated frame, how his cheekbones jutted out of his face like the rising granite walls of the canyons back home. He sank down on the platform next to Frank.

"Stupid kid," Patrick swore, swiping at tears streaming down his face. "I knew he'd never make it. He didn't have the balls."

"You were a good friend to him, Patrick."

"Bullshit. I only let him tag along 'cause he treated me like a god . . . He didn't know from nothin'. Just a baby. He needed me to tell him how to act, ya know?" Patrick was crying freely now. "He wouldn't go to the infirmary 'cause he wanted to stay with me . . . then I left him here to die alone."

"You couldn't have known he was going to die today," Marty said.

Patrick yanked the wool blanket from Frank's body and thrust it at him. "Here, take your goddamn blanket back 'fore somebody steals it." He pushed past him out of the barracks, slamming his fist against the doorjamb as he left.

Marty held the fetid blanket away from his body.

"Wish the Japs would let us write to his family," Arthur said. "Where was he from?"

"I can't remember," Colin realized with horror. "Somewhere in California."

"Come on, Marty," Arthur said. "Let's get permission to bury the body."

Their footsteps echoed in the hallway. Outside the cheers of the men at the softball game rose and fell. Colin knelt down. Frank was Italian, so he figured he must have been Catholic. He wished he could remember the rosary. He felt he owed Frank something in death, because he hadn't given him much in life. He took the boy's stone-cold hand and said, "I'm sorry, Frank. I'm so sorry." Then he started to cry.

Chapter 19

Boise, 1942

Now that the sun had set, it was finally cooling off in Reilly's Place. Maggie leaned against the long, ornate bar—a relic from the previous century—waiting for the drinks she'd ordered for her customers.

Verna slammed an empty glass on the bar and called for a refill. "It's so stuffy in here," she complained, blowing her bangs off her forehead. "This place could use a few more windows."

"It could use a lot of improvements." Maggie glanced around at the scratched round tables and black chairs with their worn fabric seats. Dark spots on the wallpaper marked where bawdy pictures had once hung. Now they'd been replaced by small, fuzzy depictions of wildlife and mountain vistas painted by the owner's wife. Tobacco smoke stains streaked the high ceiling, and the glass fixtures on the heavy chandeliers glowed dusty yellow. "Still, there's a bit of charm to this old place," Maggie admitted.

"I wonder what it was like when it was a real saloon?"

Verna rolled her eyes, uninterested, and left to deliver a drink to a stubby old man sitting alone in the corner. Maggie watched her lean in close to tell him something, then put her hands on her hips and join in as he erupted into laughter. Verna was the mother of two small boys. Her husband had abandoned them before the war, so she worked a day shift at the phone company and Friday and Saturday nights at Reilly's while her mother watched her children. She had trained Maggie at the phone company, patiently demonstrating how to run the switchboards and teaching her tricks for memorizing all the phone numbers in Boise. Now Verna was teaching her a very different set of skills.

Maggie kneaded her bare ring finger. The jeweler had arrived a few days before to reclaim her engagement ring unless she could pay for its balance. Twisting his hat in his hands, he'd explained he'd done Colin a favor because he'd known his father, but now he needed the money. She'd talked him into giving her the summer to raise the funds, and he'd agreed. So she'd taken this job Verna had told her about, waitressing on Saturday nights at Reilly's Place on Tenth Street.

Reilly's was a respectable bar, frequented mainly by couples enjoying a nightcap after a show at the Pinney Theater or a movie at the Ada. So when two soldiers burst into the bar like dust devils, blowing over chairs as they circled each other on their way to a table, everyone turned to look.

"Here comes trouble." Verna snapped her chewing gum. "Want me to take 'em?"

Maggie sighed. "Tempting. But I guess I need to learn how to handle these situations."

"Atta girl. Take the upper hand, sweetie. Show 'em who's boss."

Maggie took her time getting to the table, holding her tray in front of her as a shield. The soldiers had already been drinking, maybe at the rowdier, men's-only bar down the street. She lost her nerve and stopped abruptly at another table to settle the bill with a middle-aged man and his wife. She stood aside as the couple rose, sorry to see them leave. She took a deep breath and turned to the soldiers.

"What can I get for you, gentlemen?"

"How 'bout a kiss, doll?" snickered the pimple-faced one.

The other squinted at Maggie from beneath thick, black eyebrows. "Hey, I think I know you. You was in the grade after me at Boise High. Maggie Braun, right?"

Maggie nodded, surprised.

The soldier propped hairy arms on the table and spoke into his friend's face. "This gal turned down my kid brother Arnie when he asked her to a dance. Thought she was too good for him."

Maggie inched backward. "I remember now. It was nice of your brother to ask, but I already had a date to that dance. Now, can I get you something to drink?"

"Braun?" said the pimple-faced one. "Ain't that a German name? Oughta ship all you Krauts back where you come from. Don't you think so, Frease?"

"I dunno, Ingle." Frease eyed Maggie's chest. "Why should them stinkin' Nazis get to poke all the pretty girls?"

Ingle laughed, fingering Maggie's sleeve.

She pulled her arm away, her heart racing as she looked over her shoulder for help. But the proprietor's office door was closed, and Verna was busy with a table of soldiers and their dates. Maggie indicated the tobacco bulge in Frease's cheek. "There's no spitting in here," she said, her voice frail.

He pushed his chair back and circled the table, bringing with him the stench of sweat, tobacco, and beer. He hovered over

Maggie like a storm cloud over the mountains. "Come on, doll. You can break the rules for an old schoolmate, can't ya?"

She hugged the tray to her chest and shrank back, stepping on someone's foot. A hand took her arm and guided her gently to the side. She felt a tingle along her spine as she recognized the gentleman she'd seen at Morrison Knudsen and again on the street when she got the job at Mountain Bell.

"Seems like you boys have had some fun. Why not call it a night?" He stood with his feet apart, his jacket in the crook of his left arm with his hand resting casually in his trouser pocket. His starched white shirt fell in crisp lines from narrow shoulders and his right arm hung loosely at his side. He rubbed his thumb methodically across his fingertips, cocking his head slightly to the left, his dark eyes darting from one soldier's face to the other.

Ingle wobbled to his feet, bracing his hands on the table. He took in the gentleman's expensive suit, his mouth moving to a sneer. Frease scowled. Chairs scraped the floor as the bar's patrons turned to watch. Verna dropped her tray on a table and ran to the proprietor's door.

"So you like givin' orders, *civvie*? Why don't you get yourself an officer's uniform?" Frease brushed imaginary dust from the gentleman's shoulder. "What's the matter, pansy-waist? Ain't got the balls to fight for your country?"

The gentleman winced. He caught Frease's hand, bending it back. Ingle stepped forward.

Mr. Reilly's heavy footsteps shook the floorboards. He shoved Frease back, knocking him into the table. "No trouble in my place. You boys get on out. Come back when you're sober." He rounded up the soldiers the way Maggie imagined he'd once handled his cattle, herding them, bawling, toward the door. He stood in the doorway wiping chubby hands on his pants and shouting for them to keep moving or he'd call the cops. "Show's over, folks," Mr Reilly announced. "Come on girls, I'm not paying you to stand around." He plowed past Maggie.

Verna laughed, repositioning the scattered chairs as the patrons turned back to their conversations. Maggie lay her hand over her heart and took her first full breath in several minutes. "Are you all right?" the gentleman asked.

She nodded.

"William Preston," he said, his dark eyes smiling.

"I'm Maggie."

"I've been hoping we'd run into each other again."

Her stomach tightened. She took a damp cloth from her apron pocket and turned her attention to scrubbing the table. "Thank you for your help. No one's ever talked to me the way they did."

"Put a uniform on an ignorant man, and he suddenly thinks the world owes him something."

Maggie straightened up. "Are you against the war?"

"Not at all." He tapped his chest. "Bad heart. The military won't take me."

Maggie blushed, patting the snood that held her hair at the nape of her neck. "I'm sorry. It was rude of me to ask. Can I get you a drink, Mr. Preston?"

"Scotch—and call me William."

She returned his smile and walked slowly to the bar, uncomfortably aware of the movement of her hips.

Verna put her arm around Maggie's waist. "I see you've met Will. He comes in from time to time. You know who he is, right?"

Maggie shook her head.

"His father's Roger Preston, the retired banker from back east. They live in the white brick house on Warm Springs Avenue."

Maggie gasped. "Uncle Eddie says Roger Preston contributes

heavily to the college."

"Heck, Maggie, he could buy the college if he wanted to." Verna smiled at William. "He's a looker, don't ya think? And he sure seems to have noticed you."

"Don't be ridiculous, Verna. I'm engaged."

Verna shrugged and went to talk to William herself.

Maggie caught a glimpse of herself in the mirror behind the bar. The gold locket around her neck sparkled like starlight on a smooth lake. Colin had given it to her the Christmas before he left for Wake, and she'd worn it every day since the island had been taken. It had been six months since his capture, and still she had no word of his condition or whereabouts. Ellen had heard nothing either. There were rumors, though, about Japanese atrocities on Bataan and elsewhere. Maggie did her best not to listen and made her Uncle Eddie promise not to tell her the worst of the war news, at least not while the United States was still mostly losing ground in the Pacific. But the tide was turning, Eddie promised, using the Battle of Midway as his proof. He urged her to keep up hope. Some days, though, it almost seemed as if Colin never existed. As if everything she'd known before the war had been a fantasy.

She fingered the locket for a moment, watching the patrons' reflections in the mirror and wondering how her life had taken such an ugly turn. It all seemed so unfair. But Ellen would have told her to stop thinking about things she couldn't change and concentrate on those she could. So she took a deep breath and, leaving the tray on the bar, went to give William Preston his drink.

Chapter 20

Boise, 1942

Maggie loved summer nights in Boise. Though the temperature could get quite hot during the daytime, the nights were cool and dry. Even though her feet ached, she was looking forward to her walk home after a long evening in the stuffy bar. She was waiting for Verna to fix her shoe buckle so they could walk together.

"Well, look who's here," Verna said, rising.

Maggie turned to see William leaning against his black '39 Jaguar parked at the corner. Its chrome grating and oversized headlights gleamed beneath the street lamp.

"I was concerned those soldiers might return," William said, approaching. "Can I offer you ladies a ride home?"

Maggie shook her head. "That's kind of you, but—"

"We'll take it." Verna stared intently at Maggie as she steered her toward the car and said, "Maggie, you sit up front."

Maggie glared at her and reluctantly climbed in as William

walked around to the driver's side.

"This is sure a swell car," Verna said, settling herself in the back seat.

"Thank you. My father bought it in California."

"So," Verna said, leaning forward. "Tell us what it's like to be rich."

"Oh Verna." Maggie cringed.

But William only chuckled. "I guess I don't think of us as rich. My father worked very hard for the money he made."

"But you told me once you went to college back east. That must have cost a pretty penny."

"Verna, stop," Maggie pleaded.

"It's all right." William touched her arm gently. "I don't mind." He turned in his seat to look at Verna. "It was my father's dream for me to go to Harvard—so I chose Yale. But I did get the business degree he wanted for me. I can tell you, though, I never felt accepted there. I could have been the richest man in Idaho, and it wouldn't have mattered. A boy from out west is still a backwoodsman as far as they're concerned."

William started the car and they drove a few blocks to Verna's tiny, green-trimmed house. She thanked William, taking her time getting out of the car and smirking at Maggie from the sidewalk as William pulled away from the curb. Maggie pressed up against the door, biting her thumbnail and watching the houses roll by. They approached an intersection and stopped. She stiffened, wondering what to expect.

"Maggie?"

Her stomach tightened.

"Which way?"

"Oh," she felt her cheeks flush. "Straight."

He smiled but said nothing more until she directed him to park in front of her house. "I'll walk you to the door," he offered, but Maggie had already scrambled out of the car. He caught up to her on the walkway and pointed at the porch swing. "Can we sit down for a minute? I know it's late, but I'm leaving for Seattle tomorrow, and I'm not in the mood to go home yet."

"I don't know . . . my mother might not like it."

"I promise I won't stay long."

A cricket chirped from the high grass in the neighbor's yard, and the breeze rustled Maggie's hair. She could smell her mother's roses, distinguishing the scents of the different varieties. She glanced at the front window and back at William. "I guess a few minutes couldn't hurt." She led him around the house to the bench Eddie had built for Agnes and placed beside the rose garden.

Maggie sat down, but William stood at a polite distance, hands in his pockets. "Your garden is quite beautiful," he said, but he was looking at Maggie.

She pretended not to notice, but found she couldn't suppress a small, satisfied smile. She decided that, just for a moment, she should enjoy feeling pretty again—and desired. It had been so long since Colin left and it felt good to talk to someone who knew nothing about her, who didn't think of her only as Colin's fiancée and didn't expect her to always be brooding over his capture.

She looked up at the two-story Victorian, the steep roof piercing the night sky, the leaves of the red maple brushing her upstairs window. "What do you think of our house?"

William studied the house for a moment. "It's very nice."

"My parents put every cent they had into it. They paid cash. I think they must have been planning a large family, plenty of kids to fill all the rooms. Instead, there's only me."

William nodded and reached out to stroke the petals of the nearest yellow rose. "I'm an only child, too," he said. "But I think my parents wanted it that way. My father's a very busy man, and my mother, well, she's never taken much interest in me."

"Mine takes too much interest in me," Maggie said, keeping an eye on Agnes's bedroom window. She shivered.

"Are you cold?" He began to remove his jacket.

"No, please don't. I'm fine." She looked William in the eye for the first time since they'd left Reilly's. "Why are you going to Seattle?"

"My father's opening a new branch of his bank there. Since he's retired now, or so he says, he wants me to get things up and running."

She paused for a moment, then moved over on the bench, and William sat down. She kept her hands in her lap but turned to face him.

"What's Seattle like?"

He sat back and stretched out his legs. "Quite special, really. It's bigger than Boise, of course. Nearly every place is." There was no sarcasm in his pleasant laugh, and Maggie found herself responding with a warm smile.

He looked into her eyes for a moment, then raised a hand to paint a picture in the air. "In the distance, there are singular snow-capped mountains—dormant volcanoes really—soaring into the sky. The snow is so white it almost hurts your eyes, yet you can sense the darkness just below it. I find myself looking up often expecting to see those mountains come to life." He shook his head in wonder. "You know the city's built on steep hills that slope into the ocean—"

"I'd love to see the ocean," Maggie said. "Colin often wrote about it."

A shadow crossed William's face, and Maggie cursed herself. She was not yet ready for this moment to pass, yet she'd ended it with her own carelessness. How many times had her mother told her to keep quiet and let the man speak? She'd always shrugged it off as old-fashioned advice. Now she wished she'd listened.

"Who's Colin?" William asked.

Maggie looked at her hands. "My fiancé."

"Oh." He dragged out the word as he rose from the bench. "There was no ring, so I assumed . . ." He stood beside the garden and moved the dirt with the toe of his shoe. "Is he in the war?"

"He was taken prisoner on Wake. We're not sure where he is now."

"That must be very hard for you."

Maggie said nothing.

He gazed at the stars, bright in the cloudless sky, and sighed. "I'm going to miss this place."

"How long will you be gone?"

"Hard to say. Six months or more." He stepped over to Maggie. "Thank you for letting me stay. I hope you hear from your fiancé soon."

They walked slowly, very slowly, to the front of the house, where William paused, rubbing his chin. He turned toward her, removing his hat. "I hope this doesn't seem inappropriate. But I feel like I know you, Maggie. I've felt that way since we first spoke last winter on the street. Would you mind if I wrote to you from Seattle?"

"I don't know that you should."

"I understand. I only thought it would be nice to hear from someone from home. So many of my friends are gone now. Joined the service or took government jobs in other states." He smiled. "Or they've married soldiers and moved away." He looked somewhere past Maggie, his eyes betraying his sadness.

She knew what he must be feeling. For a man to be 4-F, to be left out of the war, must be such an isolating experience. So he was like her, alone, and she desperately wanted to reach out to him.

Agnes's shadow darkened the front window. Maggie hurried toward the porch steps, but she paused with her hand on the railing and turned to William. "Write," she said clearly and went inside.

Agnes was waiting on the other side of the door, along with Eddie, whom Maggie was surprised to see visiting so late.

"Who brought you home?" Agnes asked, trying to look past her. "That's a fancy automobile."

"That fellow looked familiar. Do I know him?" Eddie said.

"You probably know his father, Roger Preston." Maggie moved past them to stand at the foot of the stairs.

Eddie's eyebrows shot up. "Roger Preston? I certainly do. He's a banker from back East," he explained to Agnes. "Quite wealthy."

"How nice." Agnes beamed at Maggie. "It was kind of him to bring you home. Will you be seeing him again?"

"No. He's leaving for Seattle."

"Will he be back soon?"

"How should I know?" Maggie resented the excitement in her mother's voice and the way Eddie was watching her from the corner of his eye. "I'm going to bed." She climbed the stairs, stopping on the landing to listen to Agnes and Eddie whisper as they walked back into the parlor.

"I should have told him not to write," Maggie chided herself. "What was I thinking?" She dragged the backs of her fingers along the blue-striped wallpaper and turned into her room. Going to her open window, she gazed out over the garden. "No. I've done nothing wrong," she said aloud. "It's only a favor. No different from Gwen writing letters to the soldiers overseas."

Outside, a chorus of crickets had joined the first, and the

aroma of roses drifted up to her room. She rested her head against the window frame and hummed "I'm in the Mood for Love," an old love song Colin always sang to her.

The lamplight fell across a polished silver frame on her nightstand. It held a picture of Colin smiling at Maggie, gripping her hands between his. She picked it up, stroking the glass above his face and wondering if he was thinking of her. Though she'd never meant to betray him, she realized she should have told William about him from the start. Well, she'd tell him now—tell him all about Colin in the letters she would write.

Chapter 21

China, 1942

Outside the camp gates, Colin stood in a line of thin, exhausted men. His arms were folded low across his middle, and sweat rimmed his eyebrows. He was returning from a forced work detail in the Japanese army's truck repair shop a few miles from camp. It was August 12, Marty's birthday, and Colin was smuggling in a gift—alcohol used in the shop for cleaning grease from tools. When the guards stopped for lunch, Colin had taken a piece of truck tire inner tube, sealed one end and filled it with alcohol, sealed the other end and tied it around his waist. Then, feeling the charge of adrenaline, the surge of bravery, he pulled wires loose below the dashboard of the truck he was supposed to be fixing and put valve-grinding compound atop one of its cylinders before replacing the head. He smiled to himself, knowing he'd see that truck back in the shop within a few days.

But that cockiness had worn off as the hours wore down,

replaced by pure terror. Several men had smuggled alcohol into the camp using similar methods, but knowing that didn't help alleviate his fear when he felt Ape's eyes on him. Ape wore the red and white officer-of-the-day sash. He was a stocky Japanese guard, who stood with his head and neck sunk down between bulging shoulders and his bowed legs spread wide apart. He eyed the men suspiciously through large, round glasses and motioned them forward with his long arms. Colin passed without incident, releasing the breath he hadn't realized he was holding.

"I'm in the clear," he thought, letting his shoulders relax. But a hand stopped him, strong fingers digging into his bony chest. He stared at Ishihara's black boots, his stomach burning, and for the first time, Colin was glad to hear Ape's shrill voice as he called out to Ishihara to come examine a prisoner. The interpreter gave Colin an amused look, then roughly shoved him out of the way.

Colin's heart beat in his throat. He kept his head low and took a step toward the barracks, thinking it best to get far away from Ishihara. But he heard someone cry out and couldn't help looking back. Ape forced a young British soldier to his knees and handed Ishihara a couple of tools he'd confiscated from the man. Colin shook his head. The soldier sputtered apologies, saying the Japanese at the shop had given him permission to borrow the tools to make repairs to the barracks. A lie, and Ishihara knew it.

The interpreter's eyes narrowed. He took a club from one of the guards and held it with both hands. He knocked the soldier to the ground, grunting, the right side of his face twitching as he beat the man unconscious. Colin turned and walked away, but he couldn't close his ears to the thuds or the soldier's cries, and he couldn't stop the pounding of his heart. The soldier's misfortune had spared him, and he should feel sorry for that, yet all he could think was that he was glad it was the soldier and not him. He hated himself for that.

Patrick waited at the entrance to Barracks Four, his shaved head glistening with sweat. "Did you get it?"

Colin nodded, stepping into the barracks. He dropped down onto the sleeping platform and lowered his head between his knees, thinking for a moment he might be sick.

"Whatsa matter with you?"

"Ishihara may have just killed a man sneaking in tools. Shit. This crap's not worth dying for."

"Thought you was the one that said we hadda do these things to show 'em they couldn't break our spirits."

Colin lay back, his arm over his eyes. The air, heavy with heat, humidity, and insects, pressed him against the hard wood of the platform. Bedbugs leaped from the straw mat onto his exposed skin.

"Got any cigarettes, Patrick?"

"Nope. We can get one from the Japs if we bring 'em a hundred dead flies today."

"It's a hundred now?"

"We could get 'em by the *benjo*. They're thick as molasses there."

"I'm too tired to chase flies." He closed his eyes and tried to remember the last time he'd been alone—not since the night of the Japanese invasion on Wake, since Red and Chaplain had arrived at his dugout before the battle. He cut his thoughts short rather than think of his old friends. He saw enough of them in a nightmare, recurring lately with more frequency. In it he was running toward the beach on Wake, the Japanese firing at him from somewhere deep within the dense underbrush. He'd trip over Frank, lying motionless on the sand, and beside him lay Red and Chaplain. Their stomachs were laid open, their guts spilling out. The crack of a single rifle could be heard. He'd back away toward the waves, now fiery orange and leaping high into the air like flames, as the Japanese emerged from the brush. He'd awaken, terrified, to find himself in the only place that could be worse.

"Get Arthur and Marty."

Patrick whooped and limped from the barracks, favoring the ankle that sported a painful boil. A foursome in the corner threw him a curious glance as he left.

Colin waited until they folded back into their circle to slide Maggie's picture from between the platform planks. The crease that cut her off at the shoulders threatened to rip apart when he opened the picture. He gazed into Maggie's eyes and touched her hair with his blackened fingertip. He refolded the picture and replaced it between the planks before his friends arrived. Though he'd told them about the photograph months ago, even shown it to them on occasions when they couldn't stand the homesickness, these moments—alone with the memory of Maggie's body against his—he would not share.

"Found 'em."

"What's going on?" Marty asked.

Colin patted the inner tube. "Got a present for you."

"What about them?" Arthur asked, nodding toward the foursome.

"Hey, Randall. Beat it, will ya?"

"Jesus, Patrick, you're such an idiot." Colin groaned as the four civilians rose and headed toward them.

"What d'ya want us to leave for, Gulley?" Randall asked.

"'Cause I said so."

"Let it go, Patrick," Colin said. "There's plenty for everyone. It's not going to take much on empty stomachs."

Randall's good eye twinkled. "You fellas got booze?"

"If you wanna call it that. Deal is you have to keep watch."
Randall sent two of his men shuffling out of the barracks,
promising to relieve them shortly. Colin worked the seal loose on
the inner tube, careful not to spill a drop of alcohol. He offered
the tube to Marty. "Happy birthday, buddy."

Marty coughed as the alcohol burned his dry throat. He
passed the tube back to Colin.

"So how old are you?" Arthur asked.

"Twenty-five."

"Geez, you're that old? I'm only twenty-one."

"But you act like you're fifty," Patrick complained, and Marty
and Colin laughed.

When they and Randall's men had drunk all the alcohol, they
tied the tube around Colin's waist again. He would smuggle it
back to the shop tomorrow morning. The sleepy guards rarely
conducted searches on prisoners leaving the camp for work
details.

"Let's get out of here," Colin suggested. "It's too damn hot
in this box."

Randall and his friends shuffled off, their feet raising the dust
in the compound, while the others rounded the corner of the
barracks with Colin in the middle to shield him from the guards'
attention. They stopped to sit in the shade, their backs against
the barracks wall. This was Colin's spot, though not even Patrick
knew why. He sat with his palm on the warm earth, over the
place where his father's watch was buried, and rested his head
against the wall, enjoying the tingling in his hands and legs.
Though his shirt stuck to his back and the sweat rippled down
his face, the alcohol somehow cooled him, and he couldn't keep
a lopsided smile from spreading across his sunburned face.

"I sure could use a woman," Arthur said.

"You wouldn't know what to do with one." Patrick said.

"Well, I would," said Marty. "And I'd do it over and over."

It felt good to laugh again. Colin closed his eyes and swam in the bliss of the alcohol. He was far from the camp, somewhere above it. From far away, he heard Marty speak again.

"Look at those scrawny Japs. Sometimes I almost feel sorry for them—so stupid they think their emperor is a god. Trained monkeys. Sad, pathetic slaves." Marty was slurring his words now.

"Not all of them," Arthur said.

"Take it easy, Art. I wasn't talking about your grandma."

"I'm talking about the peasants," Arthur said. "They're all right. And the folks that speak out against the army. The army's got all the power, you know? How are country peasants going to fight back against that?"

Colin rolled his eyes open. "Face it fellas, we're looking at the bottom of the barrel here. They send the old geezers like Useless and the sadistic, crazy bastards like Ishihara and the dumb-as-dirt farm boys out here to run these camps. Sometimes I think the Jap soldiers might actually like us to win. Their officers treat 'em like shit."

"I've wondered about that too," Marty said. "They send us on these work details, and we bang up shells we're supposed to be polishing or break parts off trucks, and they just call us clumsy and whack us around a little. They've got to know we're doing it on purpose."

Arthur shrugged. "We're white. They expect us to be stupid and clumsy. That's what they've been told."

Patrick spit on the ground. "Seems simple enough to me . . . They hate me, I hate them. What's there to yap about?"

"What about Dr. Shindo?" Arthur asked.

"A Jap's a Jap."

"Not Dr. Shindo," Colin insisted. "He stands up for us. Tries to get us medical supplies. And I'm never going to forget how sorry he looked when Frank died." He stretched his legs out and crossed his ankles. "Then there are the kids we see running beside us on the way to the work details. How am I supposed to hate kids?"

"Easy. Kids grow up."

Colin shook his head. "My father always told me never to hate a man unless he'd done me some personal harm. I've always tried to live by that."

"Oh that's beautiful." Patrick clapped. "What a load of crap."

Colin fixed him with an angry glare.

"Believe what you have to believe, Colin," Arthur said. "We all have to get through this in our own way."

They sat in silence for a moment, Colin slipping further into the comfortable fog. "Hey, Marty. Read your letter again."

"Come on, Colin, you've got the damn thing memorized," Patrick moaned. "There ain't but fifteen words on the whole page what weren't cut out. It says his ma went to church, his dad had a cold, and the weather's fine. Fuckin' boring."

Marty sat up. "Take that back, Gulley."

Patrick raised his hands defensively.

"Knock it off, you two." Colin held his arms out to keep them apart. He waited while both men slowly settled back against the wall.

After a moment, Arthur continued. "Do you think any of our letters have made it home?"

"Hell, no. 'Sides, what's the point. You can't say shit in the twenty-five words we're allowed."

Colin leaned forward, drawing up his knees. "I don't feel so good."

"Don't stand up," Arthur warned. "It'll just make you dizzy.

We're going to have to wait until this works its way out."

Marty groaned and crawled to the end of the barracks to vomit.

Colin wrapped his arms around his knees. The heat shimmered above the earth, and men milled around with their heads low, swatting at buzzing flies.

"I don't care if I'm sick for the rest of the day," Colin said. "It was worth it. For just a minute there I almost felt like I wasn't here—like this whole stinking camp just faded away."

"Sometimes I think it's me that's fading away," Arthur said.

Colin wrapped an arm around his shoulder and glanced at Patrick, who looked quickly away. "Nobody's going to let that happen, Art. We're going to look out for each other."

"Fat lot of good that did Frank." Patrick snorted.

Colin let his head drop back against the barracks wall and closed his eyes. He remembered now that Patrick could get mean when he drank, and he decided not to let him spoil his mood. He was glad he'd taken the chance with the alcohol, though his stomach still burned, and he knew he wouldn't feel at peace until he'd returned the inner tube. But it had been worth it to experience that one fleeting moment of freedom. For that he might be willing to risk anything.

Chapter 22

China, 1942

"Your friend is very sick."

"Is it pneumonia?"

Doctor Shindo nodded. "Both lungs. I take him to infirmary."

"No," Arthur insisted. "The guards will only give him half rations there. He stays here. I'll take care of him."

"What about *tenko*?" Colin asked. "If he doesn't show for that they'll come for him anyway."

Arthur looked nervous, but his voice was firm. "I'll get him to *tenko*. I tell you, I can do this."

Dr. Shindo frowned, and Colin knew he doubted Marty would pull through. "Okay. He stay. But I must draw fluid from lungs. You hold him down. Keep from moving."

Marty lay on the sleeping platform, chest expanded, face strained, fighting for each short breath, sweating though the weather had turned cold again. Dr. Shindo opened his black bag and produced a trocar, which looked to Colin like a large syringe with a needle the size of an eight-penny spike. They opened Marty's overcoat and the two shirts he wore beneath it and pinned him down.

"Aren't you going to give him something for the pain?" Colin asked.

"I have nothing. Not even at infirmary."

Colin tightened his grip on Marty's arm and buried his face in the big man's shoulder as the needle punctured flesh.

Marty screamed once and murmured something about the blood rippling through the hair on his chest. Then he passed out. When he came to several minutes later, the fear began to leave his eyes as he breathed easier.

When it was over, Colin rushed outside and breathed deeply, his own lungs coating with moist, frigid air. He coughed the throaty hack of a sick man.

Patrick hunched over beside him, hands on his knees, trying not to be sick, while Arthur appeared in the doorway, shivering, his arms crossed against his chest, holding tight to the corners of his blanket.

"Marty's going to need extra rations if he's going to get strong again," Colin said. "Especially as big as he is."

"What'd ya have in mind?" Patrick said.

"I could get in on the game those two fellows from Wake run at the corner table in the mess hall."

"Don't be a chump, Colin. Everybody knows they fix that game. They say the one fella counts cards."

"You got a better idea?"

"Yeah, we could run a rat game. Least then we'd stand a chance of winning."

Colin wrinkled his nose. He'd almost bet on one of those

games once. A rat would be thrown into one of the "honey buckets" used to carry human waste from the *benjo*. They'd fill the bucket with water and bet on how long it would take the rat to drown. The guards knew about the game but let it go. The fewer rats, the better.

"We could get three other fellas then close the game. That way we'd stand a fifty-fifty chance of winning, and if one of us loses, the other two could cover his meals."

"We'd be no worse off," Arthur agreed. "I know two fellas in my barracks to bring in. They're down to skin and bones. Gambled away all their rations or traded them for cigarettes. They won't last the winter."

"All right," Colin said. "Tell them you know a contractor taking bets on a high stakes game—a full day's rations. Bring those two men and one other, and meet Patrick and me behind the *benjo* before chow. That way we can get their evening meal."

"Or they can get ours," Patrick said.

Colin ignored him. "Remember to keep this quiet. The more people we let in, the less chance we have to win."

Arthur nodded, turned up the collar on the dress greens he'd gotten from a North China Marine desperate for Arthur's ration of cigarettes, and hobbled away on wooden clogs wrapped with rags.

Colin watched him go then took a deep breath. "Come on, Patrick. Let's catch us a rat."

A cold wind pierced his clothing as Colin stood at attention outside the barracks a week later on December 6. Ishihara was screaming about stolen loaves of bread from the storeroom, the kind filled with sawdust and wood fiber that burst into flame when toasted. He produced two suspected thieves, middle-aged men from the merchant ships. They had obviously been beaten severely and could barely stand.

"No one move until these men *confuse* they stole bread," Ishihara ordered. "Anyone move, I shot you." He brandished a pistol taken from one of the guards. Colin groaned. The men ridiculed Ishihara's mispronunciations but also feared them. The mangled words usually signaled a dangerous shift in the interpreter's unpredictable moods. The more sadistic he became, the worse his English. He turned, striking the man nearest him with his pistol as a warning, and stormed away to the guard station, leaving the prisoners to freeze in the brittle winter air.

For two hours they stood, their breath turning to ice in the beards they'd grown to keep their faces warm. One of the accused thieves collapsed and was beaten to his feet. The other slouched to one side, his bluish hand protecting what was probably broken ribs. Colin worried about Marty, who had stood unassisted yesterday for the first time since Dr. Shindo saved his life.

The extra day's ration Patrick had won in the rat game had made a difference. So had food Colin and the others had shared with Marty, pinches of gritty rice gruel and bread and sips of a greenish, watery vegetable soup they'd nicknamed Tojo Water after the Japanese Prime Minister. But giving up those tiny portions of food had left Colin weaker, and today's punishment had robbed him of the tea and stripped wheat brimming with weevils, which would normally have been his morning meal.

When the accused thief collapsed again and this time failed to rise despite the guards' blows, the other broke down and confessed. They were dragged to the door of the guardhouse, where Ishihara waited. Colin knew they had probably stolen the bread. Hell, every man in camp had stolen something, but these men had been careless, or maybe just unlucky. They'd been caught. If they were fortunate, if Ishihara's mood had cooled, they'd be beaten again and released. If not, they'd disappear to one of the prisons in Shanghai for a few months to return broken and barely alive—if they returned at all.

The men waited, stirring impatiently, and Colin wondered why the guards hadn't released them. Ishihara reappeared, his hands behind his back, the bloody riding crop dangling behind him. He was followed by a short, squinty-eyed guard whose upper teeth protruded grotesquely. They called him Mortimer Snerd, after the wooden dummy of ventriloquist Edgar Bergen. The guard had enjoyed the name at first, after they told him Mortimer Snerd was a handsome movie star, but when he'd learned the truth, he turned the full force of his hatred on the Wake contractors whom he blamed for his humiliation. He glared at them now as he took a folded list from his breast pocket and handed it to Ishihara.

"Today some of you go to new camp—better camp," Ishihara said. "I read your name, you report one hour. We march to new camp."

Colin's eye twitched as he looked over his shoulder at Patrick standing several rows back. He faced front again, the pressure growing in his forehead. Ishihara called men by their last names and *tenko* numbers. When Colin heard his own name he sputtered, doubling over as a coughing fit racked his body. He pulled himself upright, but Ishihara had moved on to the next group of men gathered outside Barracks Five.

Patrick called to Colin urgently, his voice a raised whisper, but Colin did not turn. He stared straight ahead—at the snow-dusted spot where Ishihara had called his name, the spot where the thief had collapsed—and he tried to figure out what all of this meant. He knew better than to believe Ishihara. He hated

Woosung with what little strength he retained, but the thought of leaving terrified him. What was it that Eddie always said? The devil you know is better than the devil you don't.

Colin never heard the order to dismiss, only the soft breathing sound of snow falling.

"What are we gonna do, Colin? They didn't call my name," Patrick said.

Colin roused himself and looked into his friend's worried eyes. "Are you sure?"

"Course I'm sure. You was standin' right here."

Colin looked around for an idea, his gaze settling on Mortimer shuffling through the compound, smirking at the stunned prisoners.

"Wait here," Colin said.

Patrick reached for him, but Colin sidestepped and hurried into the barracks. He returned quickly with the photograph of Maggie curled in his hand, and nodded toward Mortimer.

"That crazy runt collects pictures of the prisoners' families, right? Steals them right out of the mail we never receive. I'm going to make him a deal." He walked casually toward Mortimer, Patrick tagging behind.

"I have a trade," Colin said when he'd caught up to the guard.

Mortimer stopped, turned his back to the guards walking the fence, and put his hands in his pockets. "What you got?"

"Picture. American girl. Very pretty."

Mortimer glanced around and motioned the men between two barracks units. "Show me picture. Ah, yes. Very pretty."

"Take my name off the list," Colin said.

"No name off list. No trade."

Colin frowned. "Then put *his* on. No one will question one more name."

Mortimer tapped his fingers against the breast pocket that held the list. "Okay, deal."

"His name's Gulley, number 191," Colin said.

"1-9-1," Mortimer repeated. "I'll write later. Give me picture."

Colin shook his head. "Not until you put his name down."

Mortimer stretched up on the toes of his clunky, hob-nailed boots and leaned into Colin's face, his breath stinking of Japanese daikon radishes. "No picture, no deal."

To think of this ugly Jap fingering Maggie's picture turned Colin's stomach, but he forced his hand out, thrusting the picture toward Mortimer before he lost his nerve.

"This your girl?"

Colin nodded.

Mortimer sneered, bringing the photograph to his lips for a prolonged kiss.

Colin lunged forward, but Patrick held him back.

Mortimer laughed and turned away.

"That little shit better put my name down," Patrick said.

"He will. He doesn't have the balls to cheat on a deal." Colin turned and slammed his open palm against the barracks wall.

"Really 'preciate you givin' that up, Colin," Patrick said, his eyes on the ground. "Never know what he does with those pictures."

It was the wrong thing to say, but then Patrick always said the wrong thing, Colin thought. "You owe me one," he said, shoving Patrick out of his way. As he walked he shook his head to clear the memory of Mortimer kissing the photograph. He paused on the steps to Marty's barracks and did his best to release his anger and disgust before he stepped inside. He stomped his feet to warm frozen toes and motioned for Arthur, who rushed over.

"How's Marty?" Colin asked.

"He fell down once while we were standing out there. They beat him, and he got up. I didn't think he would. He's a tough son of a gun." Arthur paused. "They called my name."

"Mine too. And Patrick's."

"Not Marty . . . Maybe it's just as well. He'd never make it on a march." Arthur's eyes filled with tears. "How am I supposed to leave him here sick? Who's going to watch his stuff? Without me, he won't hold onto that overcoat for long."

"Everybody likes Marty. Isn't there someone who will watch out for him?"

Arthur stopped to consider. "I could ask Tommy Ramirez. He wasn't called up, but his best buddy was. We were at boot camp with Tommy, and we helped him through his malaria last summer. Maybe he and Marty can look out for each other. I'll go find him."

Colin went to Marty's sleeping platform and took the big man's hand.

"Are ya leaving, Colin?"

"Yeah. Patrick too."

"Then I guess I'm on my own."

"Hey, don't worry. Soon as you're better, they'll probably send you to the new camp. We'll all be together again." He squeezed Marty's hand. "Remember high school? You were the toughest damn player on the football team."

Marty smiled. "Long time ago."

"You're gonna make it." Colin took a half cigarette from his pocket and pressed it into Marty's hand. "Here. I've been saving this for an emergency. Trade it for a meal."

He rose to leave, but Marty pulled him back down.

"My girl's name is Becky Savick."

"I know. You've told me a million times."

"She lives with her parents on Eighth Street north of the Capitol Building."

"Yeah, not far from where I live."

"If you get home before me, would you ask her to wait for me?"

"You bet I will. And I'll tell her you talked about her all the time."

Marty released Colin's jacket, his arm dropping hard onto the bed. Colin could feel the weight of his friend's eyes upon him as he turned to walk away.

"See ya in the States," Marty called.

"Nah, I'll see you sooner than that."

Colin thought of what he'd done for Patrick and cursed himself for not waiting to find out about Marty and Arthur before approaching Mortimer with the deal. "I had to act when I had the chance," he told himself. But he knew if Marty died it would be one more person he could have saved. He'd let his father die and then Chaplain in the battle. Frank was gone and maybe Red. He stopped in the road and groaned loudly, holding his head between his hands. A guard turned to look at him, and he pulled himself together, staggering against the wind toward Barracks Four.

The compound was nearly empty. Most men were resting for the march, but Colin had one more thing to do. He removed from his pocket the bent spoon he'd retrieved while getting Maggie's picture, and dropped to his hands and knees outside his barracks. The guards glanced his direction as he wretched his body, pretending to vomit. Then they looked away. He gouged at the hard earth, digging fiercely until his spoon broke and he had to scratch the earth with bleeding fingernails. He scooped his father's watch from the ground and put it in his pocket. Only then did he notice a couple of prisoners leaning against the corner of the barracks, watching him.

"What are you looking at?" he demanded.

They looked him over and moved slowly away.

He picked up the pieces of spoon as Patrick rounded the corner, stopping when he noticed Colin.

"I was comin' to find ya. I'm sure sorry 'bout your picture."

"Forget it. You'd have done the same for me," Colin said, but he found he could not look at Patrick.

"You think this new camp will be worse, Colin?"

"How would I know?"

"You still sore at me?"

Colin shook his head wearily. "No. I'm just worrying about the same things you are."

Patrick backed against the barracks. "Wish I'd had the sense to sneak in a picture of Ellen. Sometimes I'm not sure I'm remembering her right. Hell, now that I'm here, I can't figure how a girl like that ever took to a fella like me."

Colin leaned up next to him. "You know, I've often wondered that myself."

"God Almighty, I miss that woman."

Colin pushed himself off the wall. "We better go rest up a bit before the march."

Patrick nodded and forced a laugh. "Hope it ain't too far. My boot's fixin' to split down the middle as it is." They walked a few paces until Patrick caught Colin's sleeve. "I don't mind tellin' ya, I'm scared."

Colin looked away toward the guardhouse, where Ishihara stood in the doorway surveying the compound and Mortimer arrived to hand him the list. "I'm scared too." Colin said. "But what choice have we got?"

Chapter 23

Boise, 1942

William had written from Seattle and asked Maggie to spend New Year's Eve with him at his parents' party. She wrote back to turn him down, telling him she had plans to meet Gwen for dinner at the Up-to-Date Café in the Idanha Hotel, but she mentioned they would be going to a dance later at the Miramar Ballroom and invited him to join them, explaining that her favorite orchestra would be playing. He wrote back to say he'd meet them after dinner, as soon as he could break away from his parents' party. And he added that he was looking forward to the dance, just as he'd always looked forward to her letters.

Now that the night had arrived, Maggie was in the mood to forget her troubles for an evening and enjoy herself. She sat at a drafty window table with Ellen, finishing a piece of hot apple pie. Ellen had initially turned down Maggie's invitation to dinner, content to spend the evening in front of the radio with her in-laws, knitting socks for the soldiers overseas. But Maggie had prodded her into coming, and now she was glad she had. Gwen was over an hour late, and Maggie would have hated to sit alone on New Year's Eve.

"Maggie, I'm sorry to ask," Ellen said, "but can I borrow a ration stamp for sugar? Next week is my father-in-law's birthday, and he's always been so fond of sweets. I thought I'd try to make him a cake with real sugar instead of a substitute."

"I'm sorry, Ellen, but Mother donated next month's sugar ration to the church for their fund raising dinner. But we could probably spare some molasses."

"No thank you. We have plenty." Ellen scooped her vanilla custard with the tip of her spoon while Maggie stared out the window, watching for the dark Chesterfield overcoat she remembered William wearing the first time she talked to him nearly a year ago outside the phone company.

"Where could Gwen be?" Ellen asked. "When she took that job at Walgreens to help support her mother, I thought she was finally growing up. Then she does something like this."

Maggie propped her elbows on the table and folded her hands under her chin. "When I first met Gwen, she was twelve. She was giddy and talkative and hung on my arm the whole evening. It drove Colin crazy. But there was something about her eyes, something *knowing*. I agree Gwen can seem quite flighty, but I believe everything she does, she does for a reason."

Ellen tilted her head, looking unconvinced, and went back to her dessert. "I've found out about some of the other Wake wives."

"Really? How?"

"I've been asking around, and I've found relatives who've told me how they are getting along. One woman took her children and went to California to work in a factory. She makes eighteen cents an hour and lives in a trailer park overrun with ants. She had to stand her daughter's birthday cake in a pan of water to keep the ants from getting to it.

"Another left her children with her parents and joined the Army. I guess she needs the money and the job training in case . . . well, in case her husband doesn't return. The Army sent her to an Indianapolis hospital to learn x-ray procedures. I don't know how she can stand to be so far from her children."

Maggie tapped her fork against her plate. "I'm sure we'll hear many more stories like that before the war is over."

"What do you mean?"

"I mean everyone's suffering, Ellen. At least those wives have options, like you, like me. It could be worse, you know?"

Ellen looked at Maggie as if she didn't recognize her. "*How* could it be worse? We don't even know if our men are alive."

Maggie stiffened. She hated feeling reproached. "Is it so wrong to want one night without thinking about the war, without wondering if I'll ever see Colin again?"

Ellen pushed her custard dish away. "I'm sorry, Maggie, but I can't stop thinking about it."

Maggie frowned at her friend. Maybe she would have been better off if Ellen had stayed home. She glanced at the door, and her spirits lifted. She smiled and waved at William, who was crossing the room in overcoat and polished black Oxfords. He was more handsome than she remembered.

"Who's that?" Ellen asked.

"Will Preston. He's a friend from Seattle."

Ellen frowned. "What's he doing here?"

"I asked him to join us." She lifted her handbag from the seat she'd been saving for Gwen and beamed at William.

He nodded to Ellen as Maggie introduced them, removing his hat and coat to reveal a white dinner jacket and black pants.

His smile flashed as he beheld Maggie, her hair pulled back in a net snood, her black, ankle-length dress clinging to her attractive figure.

"How was your parents' party?" Maggie asked eagerly.

"Boring. You didn't miss much."

"So are you back in Boise for good?"

"Not quite. Father's asked me to stay on in Seattle for a few more months. Guess I will. There's nothing to keep me here." It sounded almost like a question.

Ellen cleared her throat and dropped her spoon into her dish.

William pulled his eyes away from Maggie to glance at her and rose to his feet. "Can I get you ladies some tea? I have to say, I miss coffee since they started rationing."

"None for me, thank you," Ellen said, without looking at him.

"What's the matter, El?" Maggie asked. "You love tea."

"I should be getting home."

"It's New Year's Eve. Wouldn't you like to stay and celebrate?"

"What's to celebrate, Maggie? Another year without Patrick?"

Maggie stared at her plate.

"Well, I'll go get that tea." William backed away.

When he'd gone, Maggie looked up. "You needn't have been so rude."

"I'm sorry, Maggie. But 1943 holds little promise for me. The war shows no signs of ending soon, and Patrick's mother is getting worse. All that keeps her alive is the hope of seeing Patrick again. Thank God his brother is safe, stationed in San Antonio. I don't think she could handle having two sons overseas."

This was not what Maggie wanted to think about tonight. She

glanced at William chatting with a waitress by the horseshoe-shaped bar.

Ellen rose, buttoned on her coat with her small, delicate hands, and wrapped a scarf around her neck. "Be careful, Maggie. It's not difficult to see how he looks at you."

"I know what I'm doing, El."

Ellen paused, then reached out to touch Maggie's hand. "I'm sorry I've been such poor company. Why don't you and your mother come by tomorrow." She turned and made her way through the tables, choosing a route that would take her farthest from William as he walked back to join Maggie.

William set two cups of tea on the table. "Where is your friend going?"

"Home." She took a deep breath and vowed to forget about Ellen. She held a cup to her lips. "How long will you be in Boise?"

"A week or so." He paused, leaning toward her. "I'd forgotten how beautiful your eyes are."

She tried to look unaffected by the compliment, warming her hands over the teacup. "There must be lots of pretty girls in Seattle," she said.

"Prettier ones here."

Maggie looked out the window. William changed the subject to the weather and Christmas celebrations, and Maggie relaxed again. Then Gwen appeared, her cheeks scarlet from the cold, her red curls scattered around her head. She barely acknowledged William, who rose to greet her. Taking his chair, Gwen seized Maggie's hands, leaning in close.

"I'm getting married. *Tonight!* Please, you must be my maid of honor."

"Slow down, Gwen," Maggie laughed. "You're not making sense. Who would you marry?"

"Gray Skinner, of course."

Maggie's smile faded as she realized Gwen was serious. She rubbed her forehead, turning the name over in her mind. "Which one is Gray?" she asked gently.

Gwen looked hurt. "Captain Skinner. Tall, dark hair. He's stationed at Gowen Field. We met him here earlier this month."

"Gwen, you hardly know him," Maggie said, looking helplessly at William.

"I know him well enough. We've been together every spare minute for the past three weeks. I know he's brave and smart. He's from Missouri and says he's never seen anything as beautiful as our mountains, except for me. I know he loves me and . . . he's shipping out to Europe in less than a week."

Maggie knew from the angle of Gwen's brow that her mind was set. So she said the only thing she could think of. "What about the dance? Couldn't you wait till tomorrow to get married?"

Gwen burst into laughter, and the couples at the next table turned to stare. "Oh Maggie, who cares about a dance?" She jumped up and pulled Maggie to her feet. "Come on, get your coat. The chaplain at the base is a friend of Gray's. They're waiting for us, and we still have to get my mother."

"I'll drive you," William offered.

Gwen seemed to notice him for the first time and for a moment looked puzzled, but she quickly accepted his offer.

"Do you have enough gasoline to get us all the way to the base?" Maggie asked, hoping he'd say no. It might buy her a few minutes to reason with Gwen if they had to wait for a taxi.

"I think I have enough." He dropped several bills on the table and excused himself, saying he'd pull the car around front, but Maggie noticed he exited the café into the hotel lobby.

Gwen stood in the doorway debating which dress to wear

and how to fix her hair, and she wondered where they could get flowers this time of year. Maggie stood to the side and tried to see Colin in his younger sister. They resembled each other only in their smiles, full of confidence and good humor. What would Colin say when he came home to find Gwen married to a man she barely knew? Nothing made sense anymore.

Outside, William blew the horn, and Gwen took Maggie's arm, drawing her away from the café and the busy revelers readying to welcome the New Year.

———

Gwen looked beautiful. It wasn't the cream-colored, floor-length dress or her mother's crinkled veil or the golden glow of the candles in the small chapel at Gowen Field Air Force Base. It was the sparkle in her blue eyes, the tremor in her body, and the way she wrapped her arms tightly around the clean-cut, uniformed Captain who bent to kiss her. Maggie smiled and hugged Colin's sister, until Gwen pulled away to rush into the arms of her dazed mother as the groom's friends clustered around the couple to offer congratulations.

William came to stand at Maggie's side. "Are you all right?"

"Colin should be here to see this," she said, but she knew that wasn't what was really bothering her. This should have been her wedding. She should have been the glowing bride and Colin the groom. She felt guilty that she couldn't feel happy for Gwen.

Gray's best man produced a flask and held it high. "I'd like to propose a toast. To Gray and the prettiest girl in town. May the war end soon and their love last forever." Gray's friends cheered and passed the flask around. Laura Finnely began to cry, and Maggie moved to put an arm around her.

William stepped forward, pulling an envelope from his jacket pocket. He offered it to Gray. "This is for you. It's a room at the Idanha for tonight."

Gray regarded William, perplexed.

"It's from Maggie and me," William explained. "I hope you'll be very happy."

Maggie stood stunned while Gwen and her mother turned to stare at her. She reached out to grasp both of their hands and glanced over her shoulder at William. "What a generous thing to do, Will." She looked at Colin's mother. "He really is a good *friend*."

Gwen shrugged and turned back to her new husband, but Laura Finnely continued to watch Maggie as William stepped forward to hold her coat.

"I suppose I didn't handle that well," William said, drawing her aside. "I only wanted you to be able to give them something. I never meant to embarrass you."

"Take me home please, Will. All this excitement has made me very tired."

He went to get the car while Maggie said a final good-bye to Gwen, avoiding Laura's eyes. She retreated down the narrow aisle of the chapel, pausing in the doorway to watch Gwen rise on her toes to kiss her new husband. Maggie dropped the tickets to the dance in a wastebasket by the door and walked out into the cold.

They drove home in silence, but when he parked in front of her house, William reached out to take Maggie's gloved hand. "You're angry with me—"

"It was a sweet gesture, just somewhat awkward for me. It's not you, Will. It's me. I better go."

"But it's not midnight yet," William said, still holding her hand. "Can't we at least wait for that?"

Maggie slumped against the seat. The thought of ringing in

the New Year while her mother and Uncle Eddie assailed her with hollow promises of better times to come simply didn't appeal to her. "All right, Will. Till midnight." They were silent again.

Finally William spoke. "Maggie, come with me back to Seattle. I could get you a job in the bank. It would do you good to get away from here for a while. See some of the world."

Maggie smiled. "From your letters Seattle sounds wonderful. So much more exciting than Boise. So much more dangerous! To think you must actually worry about an invasion, that people are constantly scanning the ocean for signs of ships, watching the skies for planes. Uncle Eddie's an air-raid warden now, you know? You should see him strut about in his white helmet and armband waving that ridiculous whistle. He takes his job so seriously, but enforcing blackouts in Boise sometimes seems ludicrous. Think how much more important Eddie would feel in Seattle."

William nodded politely. "I wasn't talking about Eddie, though. Don't you want a change, Maggie? So many women are doing things they never thought possible. Flying planes, joining the service, building tanks."

"I do things for the war effort, Will. Just last month I helped with a scrap metal drive."

He chuckled and took her other hand, turning her toward him. "I know you help, Maggie. But I'm talking about doing something for yourself. Come to Seattle. My secretary's mother owns a boardinghouse. You could stay there. Someone like you would come alive in Seattle."

Maggie looked at her hands in his. "I see." She slowly withdrew her hands. "You're really not that different from everyone else. You think you know what's best for me." She held up a hand. "No, I'm not chiding you, Will. I don't disagree that I *could* do more with my life, be more than I am, and I won't say a part of me doesn't desperately want to accept your offer, to live in a wonderful city, to meet new people, to leave all this behind. I've thought about it. Gwen and I talked once about going to California to work in the munitions factories." She laughed. "I even thought about joining a traveling USO show. I'm not a half-bad singer, you know?"

She looked out the windshield, wrapping her arms around herself. "But every time I think seriously about leaving this place, a coldness settles over me. I know Boise is a backwater town, but it's home. The only home I ever wanted." She pointed down the street. "In one of those small houses, that's where I always planned on raising my kids, just down the street from Mother and Uncle Eddie. We'd picnic in the foothills in the summer, go sledding in the winter." She shook her head. "My dreams are simple, Will. I watch the newsreels and see what women are doing now, and I'm impressed. But that's not me. Working a switchboard—that's me. Serving drinks to soldiers from Gowen Field, listening to their stories of home, to their hopes and fears—that's me." She shivered and rubbed her arms. "I guess I'm too old-fashioned for this war."

William smiled. "You've figured out what you want, Maggie, and you're reaching for it. That's more than most of us will ever accomplish. There's no shame in that."

"You always say the right thing, don't you Will?" She smiled.

Just then a gun started firing, a few shouts followed, and someone rang a cowbell. Maggie brushed her hand across the window to clear the fog. She laughed. "It's Mr. Newell and his wife. They do this every year."

William leaned close to Maggie to see. When she turned she found his face near hers, and she felt this was a man she could trust, a man who would always be there for her, as Colin was supposed to be. She closed her eyes for a moment.

He kissed her tenderly on the cheek, though near enough her mouth that she could clearly imagine his lips on hers. "Happy New Year, Maggie," he said.

"I'll miss you, Will." She got slowly out of the car and went to open her front door, ignoring her mother's calls and heading straight for her bedroom. She covered her eyes with her hands and willed herself not to cry. She tried to think about Colin, but couldn't bring herself to wonder what a new year in captivity might bring to him, if he were still alive. Too much had happened tonight, too many emotions had surfaced, and she was tired. In the morning she'd think about what it all meant, sort out how she felt. Right now, she just wanted to sleep and not dream about Colin or Will or Gwen or anything that had to do with this damn war. Tomorrow she'd go to Ellen's and act as if nothing had happened tonight, for she was already convincing herself nothing had.

Chapter 24

China, 1943

Colin studied the newly arrived prisoners shivering inside the compound of Kiangwan Prison Camp on a frigid morning in March. He scanned their faces looking for Marty. Most of the prisoners from Woosung had been transferred to Kiangwan by now, and Colin desperately wanted to know what had become of his friend. Tommy Ramirez had arrived over a month ago saying Marty was sick but alive when he'd last seen him. That was all Colin had been able to discover.

The new prisoners stood with heads down, except for two robust boys, dressed in clothes without holes or tears, their frightened eyes taking in every fence post, every loose board, every skeleton face peering at them. Colin made eye contact with one. The boy, horrified, looked away. Colin shook his head and sniffed loudly. "Green as grass," he muttered.

He followed the boy's gaze out across the camp, remembering

what it had been like to see it for the first time. They'd marched out the gate of Woosung that snowy December morning without looking back, partly because to turn would have taken too much effort, partly because no one really wanted to remember the place.

For the first several miles of the march, Colin worried about Marty, picturing the big Swede as he'd looked leaning in his barracks doorway watching the ghosts parade past. But after a while, he stopped thinking of Marty, stopped thinking of anything but the rhythmic thump of footsteps on the frozen road.

Patrick marched beside Colin, but Arthur was ahead with his battalion under orders from Major Devereux, who'd been left behind at Woosung that day. That had been the one good thing about the move as far as Colin was concerned. Rumor had it Devereux compiled the transfer list, getting rid of as many Wake contractors as he could. It was no secret that the Major, holed up in his officer's quarters, disliked the contractors because they refused to follow orders, salute his officers, or maintain military discipline. He seemed to have forgotten that the civilians had asked to be recruited into the Marines back on Wake to afford them the status and protection of the military, and Devereux had turned them down. Colin was glad to leave him behind. He'd come to abhor the look of the man's face.

They'd marched south for ten miles, accompanied by Dr. Shindo, Ape, Rocky, Mortimer, and a dim-witted guard they called Tiny Tim, who actually seemed fond of the Americans. Ishihara strode along, flicking prisoners with his riding crop, kicking them when they stumbled on the ice. Colonel Yuse was not among them. The old man had died of a heart attack a few months earlier and been succeeded by Colonel Otera, called Handlebar Hank because of his thick mustache.

Ape, cold and tired, had thrust his rifle at Colin for him to carry. Colin took it without thought of turning it against the guard. To do so would have been suicide, though it might have been worth it. They passed through villages, but Colin barely noticed; he was watching his boots to be sure his feet kept moving. He was constantly aware of his gold watch bumping against his testicles. He'd hidden it in his cloth g-string beneath his pants and was praying there'd be no strip-search when they arrived at the new camp.

Kiangwan wasn't much different from Woosung. There were six barracks units—somewhat newer and better built than the ones at Woosung—a hospital unit, and an officer's garden. Beyond a wire fence were the kitchen, woodshed, guardhouse, office, garage, and utility buildings. An eight-foot-high brick wall topped with an electric fence encircled the camp.

Outside the wall were two large horse stables, a mule barn, and the Japanese barracks. A dirty creek ran along the west side, and the war-torn city of Shanghai lay only a couple of miles to the south. On either side of the camp were two Japanese airfields.

Nearby was a flat piece of land on which the prisoners had been ordered to raise a "mountain" six hundred feet long, two hundred feet wide, and forty-five feet high. They worked with picks, hoes, and shovels, carrying dirt in baskets hung from bamboo *yo yo* poles slung over the shoulders of two men. They poured the dirt into metal cars and pushed the cars up a short railroad track to dump them atop the mountain. The men slaved ten to fourteen hours a day, and when it rained and the field was muddy, they were ordered inside to shine artillery shells until they could get back out into the dirt.

They'd been told they were building a playground for Shanghai children or a monument to the Japanese war dead, but Colin had begun to suspect it was really a rifle range for the

Japanese army, and again he cursed the Japanese for not signing the Geneva Convention. It would have forbidden them to force prisoners to perform war-related labor. Mount Fuji was Ishihara's pet project, so Colin hated it even more. Maybe that was a benefit. Near starvation, most of the men could barely lift the buckets, barely push the cars up the hill, but Colin's hatred for Ishihara kept his blood racing, his muscles moving.

He had never wondered what it would be like to kill a man until he encountered Ishihara. Now he fantasized about it often, imagining the Allies winning the war and the prisoners going quietly to the guardhouse, without cheers or laughter, but with menace in their eyes. They'd take Ishihara, calmly strip him naked, and rope him to a post, his bare feet standing in a round wooden tub. A broken bottle would be tied around his neck, preventing him from lowering his head. They'd let him shake for a time in the freezing winter air. Then they'd pour water over his body and wait until the drops had frozen to his skin. Then they'd do it all over again. It was a favorite torture of Ishihara's, performed especially on the Chinese coolies, who were hated by the Japanese even more than the Allied prisoners.

But in Colin's other fantasies, Ishihara died an equally brutal but much quicker death, pulverized with clubs and rifle butts and that goddamn riding crop.

Arthur shuffled over to Colin on his makeshift clogs, pointing anxiously at the new prisoners.

"Nope." Colin said. "Marty's not with them."

"I thought for sure he'd be with this group. God, I hope he's okay."

Colin looked up to watch a Japanese fighter drop in altitude toward the nearby airfield. He felt his anger grow. "Sneaky bastards. I figure they brought us here thinking our boys wouldn't bomb those airfields for fear of hitting our camp."

"That'd be my guess."

"Well, sometimes I wish they'd take the chance. Blow those airfields sky high. At least we'd take a few Japs with us." Colin rubbed the back of his hand across his nose. "I'm so sick of the smell of shit around here."

"You're in a cheery mood today," Arthur said.

Colin stuffed his hands through the holes in his pants pockets and stared at the smoky, gray sky. "Sometimes I hate the thought of dying in this place. Today . . . I just don't care . . . Except for one thing."

"What's that?"

He rubbed his blistered palm. "I want to see *him* dead first." He nodded toward Ishihara, who was crossing the compound toward the new prisoners.

Arthur followed his gaze. "Only one problem with that."

"What?"

"You can't kill the devil." Arthur doubled over suddenly, grabbing his right side.

"What's the matter, Art? It's not your appendix, is it?" Colin swallowed hard, thinking of the contractor who, without benefit of anesthesia, had his appendix removed by Dr. Shindo last month. The operation had saved the man's life, but his screams still echoed in Colin's ears.

"I strained something working on Mt. Fuji, that's all," Arthur explained.

"I'm surprised any of us are still standing with all the crap they make us do. Come on, let's get you back to the barracks so you can lie down."

Even after Major Devereux had finally been transferred to Kiangwan, Arthur had disregarded military protocol to bunk with his friends in the contractors' barracks instead of with the Marines. Since Arthur had kept mostly to himself on Wake, he'd really only had one friend in his battalion and that was Marty. With Marty gone, he seemed to feel most comfortable around Colin. Colin helped him over to the sleeping platform.

"What's with you?" Patrick asked, rising to help.

"Don't know. Pulled something maybe."

"How 'bout a game of cards," Patrick said. "Get your mind off your pain."

"Sounds good."

"Count me out," Colin said.

"Why? You got someplace to be?" Patrick demanded.

Colin scowled at him, but sat down with an exaggerated huff.

Patrick took out a hollowed-out book, which had been donated to the camp library by the International Settlement in Shanghai. Inside were playing cards made from the cardboard from cigarette packages and a half-eaten candy bar, all that remained from their Red Cross boxes that had, surprisingly, been distributed a few weeks earlier. Colin accepted a square of chocolate from Patrick, hungrily remembering the other contents of the box, canned milk, butter, dried fruit, cheese, coffee, sugar cubes, cigarettes, and something Colin had never seen before, a fatty meat called Spam.

"Think the guards will ever let us have another R.C. box?" Arthur asked.

"Doubt it," Patrick said.

Arthur turned his chocolate square over and sighed. "Then I guess I better make this last." He nibbled off a tiny bite and set it on his tongue to melt.

"Do you have any cigarettes left?" Patrick asked Colin.

"Maybe."

"Well, let's smoke one."

"Smoke your own."

"Already did."

"That's your problem," Colin snapped. "I'm saving mine to trade for food. If you had half a brain, you'd have done the same."

Patrick glared at him. "Who put a burr under your saddle?"

"Nobody. I just don't see why I have to bail you out all the time."

"Go screw yourself."

"That's enough, fellas." Arthur said. "Deal the cards." He lay back on the platform, staring at the ceiling and sucking hard at the slight smear of chocolate on his fingertips. "Know what I've been thinking about? My aunt's strawberry pie. Sweetest thing you've ever tasted."

"I like vanilla ice cream on pie," Patrick said. "Ma makes it fresh, just how I like it, real thick. Don't want it sloppin' all over my plate. Want it sittin' right on top."

"Can we not talk about food, for once?" Colin said.

Arthur seemed not to hear. "Every now and then I'm sure I catch a smell of white man's food drifting in from Shanghai, maybe sausage or ham."

"Ain't it funny?" Patrick said. "You never get used to being hungry. You get used to the bugs, and the sores all over your body and the Japs, but never the hunger."

"I said quit talking about it," Colin growled.

"Okay, okay." Arthur studied his cards for a moment. "I can't concentrate," he said. "Some days my mind's just dead. Know what I mean? I can't hold a thought to save my life." He lowered his cards. "Like the other day. I go to Ramirez's Spanish class and can't remember a word he taught us by the end of the day. I can't figure how some of these fellas are rigging hot plates and bed warmers and compasses. I hear an officer is even making a radio. Wish I could get my thoughts together to do something like that."

"If I was smarter, I'd figure how to outwit the hustlers and traders," Patrick said. "Get my hands on some of their extra rice or cigarettes. Seems like them fellas got a bit more meat on their bones."

"They also get the shit kicked out of them when they're caught or when someone's looking to pirate their stuff," Arthur said. "They can't trust anyone. You don't want to be like them, Patrick."

"Maybe I do."

"Play your goddamn hands," Colin said.

"Don't get yourself into a lather," Arthur said. "We're just talking."

"Talk is cheap. Especially in this place."

"Well, it passes the time."

"What's the good of that? When you're done yapping we're still here, aren't we?" He looked from Arthur to Patrick, hating the patronizing expressions they wore. "Oh forget it."

He threw his cards down and stormed from the room, furious with his friends, and Ishihara, and Marty for being left behind; the Japs and the war and the people back home gorging themselves on steak and potatoes; the U.S. Army for being too slow and the bedbugs and hustlers and officers with their extra rations and exemption from work; the cold and China and the lice and the rotting smell of the creek and the tasteless rice and tasteless soup and tasteless tea.

Outside he slammed his shoulder against the barracks wall, cussing, yearning to hit someone, to tear the numbness from his arm, the ache from his belly, the sting from his bowels.

Yearning to be home.

Chapter 25

Boise, 1943

Maggie slipped out of her raincoat on a wet morning in May and hung it in the closet at the Mountain Bell office. She deposited her dripping umbrella into the umbrella tree, ducked into the bathroom, and removed her scarf to check her hair. It was Monday, and she'd splurged over the weekend to have her hair parted on the side and permed. She'd even had her eyebrows tweezed and penciled like Gwen's and she was anxious to hear the opinions of her coworkers.

She left the bathroom and stepped self-consciously down the long row of switchboards, accepting nods and remarks of approval from the women. Mrs. Quintan, a middle-aged lady with three sons in the war, was finishing up her shift at Maggie's switchboard. She smiled. "Your hairstyle is very fetching, dear."

Ida Gardner turned and whistled. She was a platinum blond who did her hair in the peek-a-boo style of Veronica Lake. She wore red lipstick and short skirts to show off her shapely legs. Though she sat at the switchboard next to Maggie's, that was all they had in common.

Ida covered her mouthpiece with both hands. "You really should try it as a blond, Maggie."

Maggie was about to snap off an answer when someone caught her arm. She turned to see Ellen and quickly forgot about Ida. Ellen's usually calm grey eyes were alight with excitement.

"What is it?" Maggie asked.

Ellen held up a Red Cross postcard, wrinkled and smudged, with one corner torn away. "It's from Patrick."

Maggie stared at the postcard, unable to bring herself to touch it. "You sure?"

Ellen laughed, and a few of the women turned to notice. She laughed so seldom these days. "Of course I'm sure. He signed it, and I'd know his terrible handwriting anywhere. I stopped by your house, but you'd already left, so I showed the letter to Eddie. He thinks this prison camp might be one of the ones near Shanghai." She paused, and her smile stretched her thin, pink lips until they seemed to disappear. "He mentions Colin."

"Here, dear." Mrs. Quintan directed Maggie into the chair. "You look like you need to sit down."

Ellen placed the postcard in Maggie's hand. It came alive, twitching on her shaky palm. She read carefully.

Dear Ellen,

How are you? I'm feeling good. Colin, too. Been keeping busy. Trying to -------. Yesterday my ----------------. Love to family. Patrick

Maggie's eyes focused on two words, while the others swam around them on the page. *Colin, too.*

He was alive.

She held the postcard to her heart and beamed at Ellen.

"I called Gwen," Ellen said. "She was so excited she hung up on me to find her mother."

"I can't believe it," Maggie said, reaching for Ellen's hand. "They're alive."

Ida took the postcard from Maggie and looked it over. "My husband writes me once a week from England," she said, studying the markings. "Did you notice this postmark is over six months old? Gee, a lot can happen in six months. Why, I knew a lady in my neighborhood who got a letter from her husband in Europe one morning and by afternoon got a telegram saying he was dead. And her standing there holding that letter from a dead man."

"Ida, hush," Mrs. Quintan scolded.

"What did I say? I got a man in the war too, ya know." She shoved the postcard back at Ellen.

"How could I not have noticed how dated it was?" Ellen said, bewildered.

The lights on Maggie's switchboard blinked impatiently, but she couldn't move. She sat staring at Ellen.

"I'm sure your boys are fine," Mrs. Quintan said. "We must keep faith." She gave Maggie a quick hug, her perfumed hair stiff against Maggie's cheek.

Maggie picked up the earphones and placed them over her ears. She closed her eyes for a moment, appreciating the silence. Slowly, she plugged the long cord into a hole, receiving a slight shock from the perspiration on her fingertip. "Number, please," she said mechanically.

She tried to lose herself in her work, but as the moments passed, her hands felt heavy, and she choked back sobs. She needed to talk to someone who wouldn't judge or advise her, someone who wouldn't be overly cheery. She glanced around for Miss Achurra, then rang the long-distance operator and asked for William's number in Seattle. She was about to disconnect when he answered.

"Hello, Will."

There was a pause, and Maggie pictured him dropping his fountain pen, leaning back in a high leather chair.

"Maggie? I'd almost given up on you. I've barely heard from you since New Year's Eve."

She twisted the cord between her fingers, remembering her New Year's resolution to taper off her correspondence with Will. She could no longer deny she felt a certain attraction toward him, and she'd begun to feel concerned about the way she felt in his presence—protected, admired. She had begun to feel his love and, though it comforted, even excited her, it could not be fair to Colin. "I'm sorry I haven't answered your letters. I've been . . . busy."

"You don't sound well. Is something wrong?"

The tears fell freely now. Though the guilt was returning, she needed Will to help her feel strong. "Ellen heard from Patrick," she said. "He's in a prison camp in China."

"My God."

"He mentioned Colin in his letter."

William paused again, his voice coming back flat. "You must be very relieved."

"You would think so, but I'm not. I can't stop imagining how horrible it must be. Patrick tried to tell us more but it was blacked out by the censors." She was wringing her hands now, her breath coming in ragged spurts.

"Maggie, are you still there?"

"All these months I've prayed for a letter from Colin. Or any news that would tell me how he is. Sometimes I've even hoped for a telegram saying he's dead . . . at least then I would know."

She choked back sobs. "Well, I got what I wanted, Will. I heard about Colin, but I don't feel any *better*. I still don't know if he's cold or sick or how the Japanese are treating him. Part of me is convinced this is a cruel trick meant to give me hope when there is none." She shielded the left side of her face so Ida wouldn't see her cry and fought the hysteria she could hear creeping into her voice. "Everyone here will expect me to be strong, to look on the bright side and be glad I heard something. But it's been a year and a half since Colin was captured and more than two years since he left for Wake, and I'm so tired. I just can't *take* it anymore."

"Why don't I come home for a few days?" William sounded concerned. "We could talk. I could catch the next train."

She wanted to tell him not to come, that she hated how desperate she sounded and she'd pull herself together and be fine. She hadn't even told him that Gray Skinner had been reported missing in action from his third mission over Germany. That Gwen was three months pregnant and convinced she was having a boy, whom she would name after his father. That Gwen was handling everything so bravely, with so much more strength than anyone would have expected from her. And that Maggie was ashamed because she still resented Gwen for being married at all.

She tried to convince herself to refuse his offer, to insist he stay in Seattle. She hated herself for knowing this is exactly how he would respond, and hated herself even more as she leaned forward and spoke directly into her mouthpiece. "Don't tell anyone you're coming to see me, Will. They wouldn't understand. Call me when you get in."

Chapter 26

China, 1943

"I'm worried, Patrick. He's getting worse."

Patrick nodded, scratching a swollen mosquito bite on his bare, tanned chest. It was August again, and the hot China summer was raging, drying up the creek, weighting the air with humidity, insects, and the smells of human waste, infected wounds, and rotting bodies buried in shallow graves. Arthur was shaking terribly, bathed in sweat, lost in the inside-out reality of a malaria fever. His eyes were shut tight, and his lips formed words no one could understand.

Colin cocked his head and pointed. "There, I think he said *obaa-chan*. That means grandmother. He's talking to his grandmother in Japanese."

"Well, he better knock that off. The Japs hear him talkin' like that, and he's a goner."

"We need Dr. Shindo. He's *got* to get us more quinine."

"Air bedding." Someone said, sounding the secret warning from outside the barracks door.

Colin tensed like a runner before the pistol fires, only he hadn't the strength to run. His eye twitched, and he rubbed his palms together. "Give me something to put in his mouth," he urged, but it was too late.

Ishihara burst into the barracks, his eyes taking in every movement as the men scrambled to ready for the surprise inspection. Ever since he'd discovered the rumor of a radio in camp, Ishihara had become obsessed with finding it and any other contraband. The ingenuity of the Americans seemed to infuriate him.

Rocky and Ape went to work throwing bowls and utensils, books and spare clothing, about the floor.

Colin sat down beside Arthur, gripping his arm. "Come on, Buddy. Pull it together," he whispered.

As Ishihara approached, Colin bent low over Arthur, shielding him from the interpreter's view. He wiped Arthur's face with a damp, smelly rag. Patrick, for once, did the smart thing. He stood off to the side, observing the guards tearing the room apart, drawing no attention to Colin and Arthur.

Colin panted softly, the sweat rolling off his face. Ishihara flicked Colin's shirt with his riding crop. "Get him up," he ordered, indicating Arthur.

Colin kept his eyes down and bowed his head low to show respect. "Very sorry, Captain," he said, knowing Ishihara insisted on the title though he held no real rank. "My friend is sick. He cannot move."

Ishihara jabbed the crop at Patrick. "You. Help move this man. Now!"

They grabbed Arthur under the arms and strained their muscles to lift him, though he could not have weighed much more than a hundred pounds.

Arthur opened his eyes and began shouting in Japanese. Ishihara gaped at him and the room grew quiet as all eyes fixed on Arthur. The color rose in Ishihara's cheeks, his jutted jaw beginning to quiver. He turned his searing stare on Colin and struck his riding crop against Arthur's chest. "This man speak Japanese," he growled. "He is American spy."

"He's not a spy," Colin insisted. "His grandmother was Japanese."

Ishihara raised his crop and sneered at Arthur. "Take him to guard station," he ordered the guards. They seized Arthur's arms, tearing him from Colin's grasp.

"No!" Colin cried. He wasn't about to lose another friend. Ishihara slid the riding crop along Colin's cheek, raising a thin black eyebrow. "Maybe you know something, hmm? Know why your friend was sent to spy on Japan?"

"I don't know anything."

"We shall see. You come, please." He took Colin's arm with mock politeness.

Patrick stepped forward, hands tightly fisted.

"No, Patrick. I need you to watch my stuff," Colin said to him quickly, indicating his work boots on the floor. He'd hollowed out the heel of his right boot with a contraband knife, and that's where he'd hidden his father's watch.

Colin glanced over his shoulder as Ishihara pulled him from the room and saw Patrick move to stand over Colin's boots, his body trembling with anger and fear for his friend.

Colin was surprised to feel nothing as Ishihara dragged him from the barracks, nothing but a luxurious emptiness, and he guessed it must be the shock, the same thing he'd felt when the shrapnel first hit his arm back on Wake. He knew his feet were moving, he could feel his heart beating against his bony chest, but in all the camp there were no sounds and, oddly, no smells. His head rolled from side to side, his eyes meeting the gaze of every prisoner who lined the way to the guard station. He saw their mouths moving but understood nothing until the wooden door of the guard station swung open. Only then did he resist, but Ishihara thrust him through the doorway. He fell to his knees as the door swung shut and the shadows surrounded him.

It was hot already when the sun rose three days later. Colin moaned, writhing on the sleeping platform as he relived the torture in a dream.

Inside the hot, dusty guardhouse, he was strapped to a plank, his head angled down, a heavy wet towel over his face. He could hear Ishihara chuckling as the guards poured water over the towel again and Colin struggled against the straps, needing oxygen, breathing deeply until the water reached his lungs. Again and again they soaked the towel, and Ishihara asked Colin inane questions about Arthur. Colin would shake his head desperately, move his shoulders, do anything to convey there was no answer to Ishihara's question. Then they'd pour the water again.

Still dreaming, Colin clawed at the towel covering his face, Patrick chasing his hands to pin them to his chest. He opened his swollen eyes and pulled his hands free, rolling away from his friend. Holding his bruised ribs, he lowered sore legs over the side of the sleeping platform.

"Are you okay?" Patrick asked. "You was havin' one hell of a nightmare."

Colin stared ahead.

"Can you talk about it yet? Please, I gotta know what they did to you."

Colin closed his eyes. He'd never forget how it felt to be suffocating, drowning, beaten with clubs, fists and boots. He'd live with the memory of the searing pain as the riding crop split open the back of his neck.

Patrick shook his arm. "Colin, tell me what happened to Arthur."

Colin saw, again, the hose in Arthur's mouth, Ishihara's foot above Arthur's swollen stomach, the water shooting out of the young Marine like a geyser.

"What was it like in the brig? Answer me, Colin."

Arthur had lain in the cell on filthy straw, and Colin had not been allowed to tend to him. In fact, he was ordered to stand at a distance. He watched from the corner of the cell as Arthur took his last breath, watched the flies and mosquitoes swarm to the feast, watched the body bloat until it almost looked healthy, the bones no longer protruding through the skin.

"Say somethin'," Patrick pleaded, his voice shaking. "What's wrong with you, Colin?"

Colin did not answer.

Patrick grabbed his shaved head and rocked back and forth for a moment, then took a deep breath. "We're shippin' out tomorrow, Colin. They say to Japan." He raised his head. "Do you understand? We're goin' to the Jap homeland. Some fellas been sayin' it'll be worse there. 'Least here we got the Red Cross and the foreigners in Shanghai. We got the Chinamen sneakin' us food on work details. We won't have none of that in Japan."

Colin looked at Patrick for the first time and marveled at Patrick's naiveté. His friend still didn't understand. It didn't matter where they died. China, Japan, even Wake. They were all going to die before the war ended. The Japanese would see to that.

"Jesus, Colin," Patrick moaned. "You're scarin' me." He lay

his head against Colin's shoulder.

Colin remained still and stared out across the room filled with men writhing in fitful sleep. He was looking for the woman again. She'd come to him in the brig on the second night, dressed in white, pink flowers in her dark flowing hair. He'd reached for her, but she'd only smiled sadly and turned and walked away. Her appearance had so haunted him, though, he had willed himself to live just for the chance of seeing her again. He was still looking for her now, but he could not wait much longer. He could feel his body growing weaker and his mind slowing. Soon he would leave this place, the same way Arthur had and Frank and maybe Marty. Maybe then he'd see his angel again. He smiled faintly.

"Jesus, Mary and Joseph," Patrick said. "You're really scarin' me, Colin."

Chapter 27

Boise, 1943

Maggie was quiet as she sat with William atop Camel's Back Hill overlooking Boise. They'd waited out a thunderstorm in his car before hiking to the top of the hill to watch the sunset. The storm had passed quickly, with little rain, and the wind had died down to a breeze, but the air still felt charged by the lighting and, far off in the distance, the thunder occasionally rolled. A jackrabbit bounded through the nearby brush, and a locust whirred close to Maggie's leg, landing near her foot. She scuffed the dirt, sending it back into the air.

"Did you help at the Red Cross today?" William asked.

She nodded.

"More rolling bandages?"

She smiled and nodded again.

"You must be good at that by now. What will you do when the war is over? It's kept you so busy. Two jobs, volunteer work, singing at the USO dances." He paused, studying his hands. "I've hardly seen you these last three weeks."

She wrapped her arms around her legs, and rested her chin on her knee. "Yes, I've been busy, but sometimes it still doesn't seem like enough."

"You've been awfully quiet tonight," he said. "Anything wrong?"

"I've been thinking about Colin. This is the hardest time of year for me. We met in the summer, you know? We were supposed to be married in the summer, too."

William leaned back on his hands, watching a hawk circle overhead. "So you still think of him often?"

"Of course I do. Why would you ask me that?"

"He's been gone a long time, Maggie. Another woman might have moved on."

Maggie rose to her feet and walked to the edge of the hill.

Will came to stand behind her and let a moment pass. Somewhere down the hill a couple of lovers laughed. William lay his hand on Maggie's shoulder and gently turned her toward him. "You never told me why you stopped writing to me earlier this year."

Maggie waved his question away.

"Please, Maggie. I need to know."

She turned to face him, looking away quickly when she noticed the earnestness in his eyes. "I guess I was angry after Gwen's wedding. Feeling sorry for myself. I thought it should have been me getting married that night." Maggie scooped up a pebble and tossed it down the hill. "Gwen looked so happy and so beautiful."

"So that's why you stopped writing?"

Maggie forced herself to look him in the eye. "My mother was hinting a lot about you and me, Will. It didn't seem appropriate to write anymore, especially after what happened that night."

"You mean the gift I gave Gwen?"

"No, although Colin's mother has looked at me differently since then." She glanced away. "I meant . . . the rest of it."

William turned to look out across the city. "I was so relieved when you called me in Seattle. I thought I might never hear from you again."

"I shouldn't have called," Maggie said.

"Why not?"

"Because it's not right. My being with you." She turned and wandered along the trail.

Will followed. "You're ashamed to be with me," he said.

Maggie stopped. "Will—"

"This whole summer you've never let me call for you at the house, we don't do anything with your friends, and we always come to places like this, where we're alone."

"I wouldn't want anyone to think I'm betraying Colin. Surely you can see how they might." He was looking at her so intently she felt it hard to breathe, and she knew that tonight her evasive answers weren't going to suffice. She stepped closer to him but found she could not meet his gaze. "You've been a good friend, Will. Ever since we first started writing to one another, I've felt a connection to you, like you understand me. And with you I never have to pretend to be something I'm not."

He took her face in his hands. "I do know you, Maggie— better than I've ever known anyone—but it's not your *friend* I want to be." His fingers were trembling now. "I could make you happy, if you'd only give me the chance."

He bent close, his eyes closed, his hands tightening on her face and, though she knew what he meant to do, she found she could not pull away. It was as if part of her needed to know, finally to know for sure. She felt his lips on hers, felt the distinct sensation of longing steal over her. To be touched again, to be desired, she hadn't realized how much she'd missed those feelings, but it was not the same as it had been with Colin. The pounding in her heart was not love, but a certainty that this was not right.

As William moved to put his arms around her back, she pulled away. "I should go home," she said.

He held onto her hand, and his voice shook. "Maggie, you're not a child anymore. Don't run away from me. If you don't want me, then stand here and tell me. Tell me you don't think of us together, that you don't think of what I could offer you, what we could have. Tell me you'd rather keep waiting for something that might never be."

"Yes, I've thought about us. How could I not?" She squeezed his hand tightly, hating to hurt him. "But I'm still in love with Colin. I have no choice but to wait for him."

"And if he doesn't come back?"

"I can't think of that, Will. You mustn't ask me to."

William lay his hand on her cheek then fisted his hand and turned away. "I'll be your friend for now, Maggie, since that's what you want, but I can't stop feeling what I feel for you. I've tried." He turned back to face her. "And I won't give up hoping."

The sun had nearly set. Maggie glanced down the hill at the view of Boise. Of all the ways she'd imagined her life turning out, she had never pictured this. When she'd first fallen in love with Colin it had all seemed so simple. Nothing had turned out as she'd planned. She wished she'd never come here tonight. "Take me home, Will," she said softly.

They walked to the edge of the steep path, and William offered his hand. She hesitated.

"It's all right, Maggie. Let me help you."

Maggie blushed. For a moment they watched lights come on

in windows as dusk settled over the town. Then Maggie took William's hand and together they started down the hill.

Chapter 28

Japan, 1943

At bayonet point, they marched through the streets of Osaka—
Wake Island civilians and soldiers, Guamanian workers from
Pan Am's hotel, and a few North China Marines. Painfully thin,
reeking, doubled over with disease, they marched in bare feet,
clogs, or worn boots. They wore tattered shirts, shorts, trousers
or g-strings made from rags. Draped over bony shoulders, their
filthy linen sacks contained only threadbare blankets, an extra
piece of clothing, a favorite book, a razor with dull bits of blades,
a pencil, a toothbrush, a sliver of soap, a dirty rice-husk pillow.
Ramirez carried sketches of camp life hidden in an empty shaving
cream tube. Lockman had a journal written on scraps of paper
that had blown over the fence. Ford carried a Bible with the
names of the camp's dead recorded in code in the margins. Colin
still had his watch, concealed in the hollowed-out heel of his
boot.

They'd left Kiangwan to travel in a fishing boat along the coasts of China and Korea, darting across the Sea of Japan to avoid American submarines. They'd reached Osaka in the middle of the night and been forced to unload their own stock of food—fish eggs and rice. Japanese civilians ignored air-raid sirens to gather at street corners to glimpse these white devils, but the men could never have summoned the energy to look proud or defiant. They tried only to remain on their feet, to keep from stumbling and being kicked by the guards, to stay one step ahead of the bayonet points.

They boarded an electric train, which took them across Honshu Island, the largest of the four islands of Japan, past tangerine and orange groves, neatly plotted vegetable gardens, green landscaped countryside. Colin looked up for the first time in hours and, dazed by the beauty of the area, he almost smiled.

They were taken from the train and transported, standing in trucks, to Kawasaki Camp 5, known as Dispatch Camp. It was located between Yokohama and Tokyo in an industrial area where the local population toiled to make heavy electrical equipment, chemicals, and aircraft. The camp was connected to a sprawling steelworks.

No sooner had they arrived than they were put to work alongside thousands of Japanese and Korean men and women and other Allied prisoners from this new camp. For twelve hours a day, they lumped brick-like steel billets. With giant tongs, they turned the billets, searching for imperfections to be chipped away with air hammers or billets so flawed they would be ground down to a metal dust that would jam Colin's nostrils and fill his lungs. The noise in the steelworks was deafening.

It was exhausting work, a mind-numbing routine, but Colin didn't seem to notice. He worked, ate, slept, rose, and worked again. Patrick tried everything to get him to talk, to raise his head, to stop looking so hunched over and defeated.

"Honest, George, he didn't used to be this way," Patrick said one evening.

"Maybe he's just too tired to talk," the other man answered.

"Nah. He ain't been the same since they worked him over in Kiangwan and killed our friend."

Lying on his bunk with his eyes closed, Colin could hear every word they were saying, but they sounded to him no different than the creak of the floorboards or the coughs of the sick men.

"He keeps this up, he's gonna die. I've seen it happen many times," the man named George said.

"He ain't gonna die. Are ya, Colin?"

Colin remained still.

"What am I gonna do?" Patrick said. "He's my best friend. I can't let him go."

Colin felt someone sit beside him and recognized the stench of dysentery. "You said he's got a girl back home?"

"Yeah, Maggie."

"Any family?"

"His ma and sister. He's real close to them. So you said you had somethin' might help?"

"Yeah, I think I've got somethin'," George said. "What can you trade for it?"

"Half my next ration," Patrick said.

"No dice. Gotta be the whole thing."

Another pause. "You got it."

"The Japs gave me this paper. It has a number on it," George said. "I'm supposed to go to town tonight to record a message home. They play the messages on Jap radio so the people in the States can pick them up over shortwave. It's some kind of propaganda ploy for the Japs. There's not much use in me going.

I only got one brother, but I haven't spoken to him in years. I've got an aunt in Chicago, but that's it."

Colin felt something crammed into his fist. He heard George's voice close to his ear, smelled his sour breath. "You take this number, Finnely. Let your girl know you're alive."

"Hear that, Colin?" Patrick said. "You can get through to Maggie."

Colin concentrated on the slip of paper in his hand and Patrick gripping his ankle. In his mind, he struggled to form a clear thought, to understand what it was he needed to do, and which muscles he needed to move.

"Well, she must not be anything special," George taunted. "'Cause he doesn't seem too interested." He pried at Colin's fingers to take the paper back, but Colin's fist was closed tightly around the slip. He forced his head to turn and fixed his eyes on George. Slowly, he recognized him to be George Tanner, an electrician from Wake who had been short and slightly overweight, with a prominent nose and a thick head of curly brown hair. Back on Wake, he'd been known for his quick wit, his way with a punch line and his talent for pranks. Now his stomach curved in below his bulging ribs, much of his hair had fallen out, and the hunger had slowed his mind so the jokes came infrequently. He'd worn glasses on Wake, but they had long since been lost.

"Well, look who's back," George said. "Do you wanna talk to your girl?"

Colin forced himself to nod. He heard Patrick exhale in relief.

"Then you gotta snap outta this. Sit up," George ordered.

Colin glanced at Patrick, but he still could not move.

"I said sit up, damn it." George reached for Colin's shirt, and Colin sat up slowly.

"Good," George said. "Now. Say something. For some reason your friend here wants to hear your voice."

Colin's lips parted, but no sound came out.

George snatched his wrist, pried the paper from his fingers. "Deal's off. I'm not letting you blow this chance. I'd rather trade it to someone who'll use it." He rose to leave.

Colin gripped his arm. "I'll use it."

George smiled briefly, then looked serious again. He held out the paper, tempting Colin. "How do I know you won't clam up again?"

"I won't."

The corner of George's mouth edged up. "Attaboy." He gave the paper back to Colin. "Mention me if you can. Maybe my aunt will hear." He winked at Patrick and turned away.

Colin held the paper close to his eyes. Written on one side was the *kanji* character for six.

"Can I see it?" Patrick asked softly. "Whatcha gonna say?"

"What they tell me to say, I guess."

"I been so worried 'bout ya, Colin. I thought you'd gone off your nut for sure. I just knew I couldn't make it through this war without you." He gripped Colin's forearm.

"Did you see the orange groves, Patrick?"

"What orange groves?"

"The ones we could see from the train."

"Jesus, Colin, I wasn't doin' no sightseein', I was just tryin' to stay on my feet."

"They were beautiful. If I close my eyes I can see them, smell the oranges. How could something so beautiful be just out of reach?"

"Is that what you been thinkin' 'bout all this time?"

"I thought maybe I'd stop fighting to live . . . just float out over those groves." His hand floated across the air. He sighed, taking the paper back from Patrick. "But I can't leave her. She won't let me go."

Patrick shook his head wearily. "You think too much," he said. "That's always been your problem."

"*Ki o tsuke,*" a guard shouted from the doorway.

Patrick helped Colin to his feet.

The guard called for prisoners with numbers for the radio program and told them to form a line by the door. Colin nodded to George as he marched with the others out into the mild September evening. The air was muggy, filled with smoke and the thick, metallic smell of industry. He clenched his fist around the scrap of paper. Nothing he'd ever touched had seemed so important. In the back of his mind, he knew George Tanner had saved his life.

They came to stand in front of the high stockade fence. Somewhere beyond it, beyond the camp, lay the groves, green and silent and beautiful. He was beginning to want to live again, to taste an orange, to hold Maggie in his arms. "I didn't listen, Red," he whispered. "I let them get to my mind."

He pulled his shoulders back with great effort. If he was going to die, he decided, it would have to be at the hands of the Japanese, not by his own doing. He owed that much to Red and Maggie and his mother, to Patrick, and now to George.

He owed it to himself.

Chapter 29

Boise, 1943

A cup of Earl Grey tea with cream steamed in Maggie's hands. She draped a brown afghan over her legs and laid her head against the high back of the stuffed chair to watch Agnes crochet a baby blanket for Gwen's child. Eddie reclined on the sofa, alternately dozing and reading a newspaper. They were listening to a shortwave radio broadcast voices of prisoners from across the sea, but Maggie was thinking of William. He'd taken a sudden trip to Seattle a few days after their talk on the hill and she'd received only one letter from him since. She was surprised by how much she missed him and found it disconcerting how much she'd grown to rely on him.

The announcer on the radio was a Japanese woman speaking in English. She taunted the Allied Forces, challenged them. Maggie hated her and did her best to tune her out. That wasn't hard to do tonight. Her busy routine was catching up to her and it was hard to keep her eyes open, so when she heard his voice, she at first thought she might be dreaming. He said his name and hometown and then paused for a second. Maggie slammed her teacup down on the coffee table and dropped to her knees before the radio. Eddie sat up and Agnes dropped the baby blanket into her lap. It was definitely Colin.

Maggie had always imagined Colin's voice coming in clear and rich, transcending the static, sounding stronger and more assured than the other prisoners. Instead, she heard weakness, desperation, a forced cheerfulness.

Eddie snatched up a pad and pencil and began scribbling Colin's message: *Japan is wonderful—like Fox Canyon back home. I'm fine. I weigh as much as Whinny now. The food's good here. Like the garden my mother grew. Patrick's okay, George Tanner, too—*

The Japanese announcer cut him off.

"No!" Maggie cried, pressing her hand against the speaker, as if she could touch Colin through the radio.

"Did you hear that?" Eddie said. "He's alive! I knew that boy had pluck."

Maggie bit her lip to keep back tears.

"What did his message mean, Maggie?" Agnes asked.

Maggie turned down the volume on the radio, and the voice of the next prisoner faded away. She took the paper from Eddie and raised a shaky hand to her forehead. "Let's see. Fox Canyon . . . I think that's where his father died."

"Then he must have been trying to tell us how bad it is for him." Eddie said.

"Or maybe that many men have died," Agnes said.

"Maybe," Maggie said, her voice breaking. "I don't know what it means. I don't know."

Agnes held out her hand to look at the paper. "Who's Whinny?"

"Gwen," Maggie said. "It was his nickname for her when they were children."

"Did he mean to say he weighs as much as a child?" Agnes asked Eddie.

"I suspect so. But then why say the food was good?"

"I don't think that's what he meant," Maggie said. "He compared it to his mother's garden, but Mrs. Finnely planted a garden only once that I know of. We had an early frost that year, and there was very little harvest."

"So he must have meant there's little food," Eddie said.

"Or that it's spoiled," Agnes offered.

Eddie nodded. "Very clever, very brave. They were likely holding a gun to him, ordering him to say only good things about the camp."

Maggie turned her gaze back to the radio and touched the speaker again lightly. "It was like I had him back for just a moment and then . . . he was gone again. If only I could have spoken to him. If only . . ."

Agnes picked up Maggie's teacup. "Here, drink this, Margaret. It's still warm."

"I don't want it, Mother."

"Then come and sit down."

Maggie glared at Agnes. "I don't want to sit, Mother. Can't you stop babying me for once?"

"There is no need to raise your voice."

"I have every right to raise my voice. I may have just heard from Colin for the last time." She leaned in closer to Agnes. "But then you'd be glad if Colin never came home wouldn't you, Mother?"

"What a thing to say."

"You've never liked him."

Agnes rose and dropped the baby blanket on the chair. "He

would not have been my choice for you, but I would never wish him harm."

Maggie rose too. "Who *would* be your choice for me? William?"

"William Preston is a fine man."

"But he's not the one I love."

"Love isn't everything, Margaret." Agnes turned away.

"Didn't you love my father?"

"Of course I did."

Eddie took Maggie's arm. "This may not be the time, honey. You're upset."

She shook him off. "I want to know where Colin and I stand with both of you. I want the truth."

"Sit down, please," Eddie said. "Your mother and I are concerned, that's all."

"Concerned about what?"

Eddie hesitated.

"Tell me."

"All right." He looked at Agnes strangely.

"Edward, don't you dare."

"It's time, Ellie," he said. "Maggie's a grown woman now. She has a right to know."

Agnes turned away, steadying herself with a hand on the back of her chair.

Eddie looked at Maggie. "You've never seen what war can do to men, but we have, honey. We were there, during the Great War. It leaves men crippled, broken—inside and out—scars on their bodies, and on their minds. Your father was tormented by nightmares from the war. He was forever seeing the face of a German boy he stabbed with his bayonet, right after that soldier shot your father's friend. Kurt always blamed himself for his friend's death. In the end, that's what killed my brother."

Maggie shook her head. "I don't understand. I thought Father died of influenza."

Eddie glanced at Agnes, who remained with her back to him. "No. Kurt was quite sick. He suffered a chronic cough from the mustard gas he'd breathed in the trenches. The pain and memories were too much . . . He killed himself."

Maggie caught her breath. She looked from Eddie to her mother. "Why didn't you tell me?"

"Your mother thought it best to keep it from you."

"I didn't want to hurt you," Agnes explained.

Eddie lit a cigarette, watching Maggie carefully as she sank back into her chair. "It's important that you realize, Maggie, even if Colin comes back, he may never be the man he once was."

Maggie lifted her chin. "That doesn't matter."

"I said the same thing when Kurt came home," Agnes said. "But it did matter—very much."

"You need to think about what lies ahead," Eddie said. "Be sure it's what you really want."

"No one will blame you if you choose another route," Agnes said. "Not even Colin."

Maggie shuddered. "Would you have chosen another route, Mother?"

"That was different. We were already married."

"What if you hadn't been? Would you have abandoned Father?"

Agnes reached toward Maggie, but pulled her hand back. She glanced at Eddie helplessly, then took a deep breath. "No, Margaret. For me there was no other route, but for you—I would choose to spare you the pain."

"It's your decision," Eddie said. "Just promise us you'll think about what we're saying."

It was the first time Maggie had seen her mother cry. It

softened her hurt and anger, but not entirely. She rose from her chair, her mind made up. "There's nothing to think about," she said. "I'll never turn my back on Colin. You didn't trust me enough to tell me the truth. Well, I'm stronger than you think." She snatched up the pad of paper and stormed from the room, pausing in the doorway long enough to see Agnes lay her head against Eddie's chest.

She rushed to her room, where she threw herself on the bed and reread Colin's words over and over, struggling to hear his voice, closing her mind to the news about her father. She couldn't think about that now. All she could do was tell herself that Colin was alive, that he'd reached out to her, that his voice didn't sound weak, only soft, like when he used to whisper his love to her on the front porch before she went inside for the night.

There was a firm knock on her door and Eddie called her name.

"Go away, Uncle Eddie." She clutched the slip of paper.

"Open this door, Maggie," Eddie said.

Maggie hesitated, then went to the door.

"Let me in," he said, and she stepped aside.

He sat down on her bed. "I don't want you taking this out on your mother," he said. "I may not always agree with Agnes, but I trust that she does what she thinks is right."

"You mean Ellie?" Maggie said.

"What?"

"Ellie. That's what you call Mother sometimes. Why, Eddie? What else haven't you told me?" Maggie crossed her arms and fixed him with a steady gaze.

Eddie took a cigarette and lighter from his shirt pocket. Maggie considered asking him not to smoke in her room, but changed her mind when he began to talk. "Your mother and

213

I are more alike than you think," he said. "For one thing, we both loved your father and we both love you. But you're right. There is something else." He lit the cigarette and watched the end burn for a moment before continuing. "Kurt had always wanted to be a soldier. When England entered the Great War, he enlisted right away. Since our parents had moved to England from Germany before we were born, there was pressure on our family to prove we were loyal. That just gave Kurt more incentive to get involved, not that he needed any. I loved my brother, but he had a wild streak in him that scared me sometimes. Just before Kurt signed up, he started seeing a young woman he met in a pub. Her name was Agnes Eleanor Pritchard, but she went by Eleanor at the time." Eddie chuckled. "In fact, she hated being called Agnes back then."

Maggie joined Eddie on the bed. "Father and Mother met in a pub? I don't believe it."

"Well your mother was a different woman then. She'd moved to London on her own to live with a cousin, and her parents were furious. She was working as a seamstress and saving her money to travel around Europe, but then the war started. She threw herself into war relief. If she'd been a man, she'd have been one of the first to join up."

Maggie shook her head. "I just can't picture that."

Eddie squeezed her hand. "Your mother's had a hard life, Maggie. When your little brother was stillborn it almost killed her, and then only a few months later she lost Kurt. Hard times change people."

Maggie looked away. "So my father called her Ellie?"

Eddie paused. "No, that was me. She didn't like it at first. She wanted to seem more worldly back then, but it sort of stuck."

Maggie turned back toward him. "And?"

Eddie rose to open the window, his cigarette smoke wafting

on the breeze. "Your father asked me to keep an eye on Agnes. She was quite attractive then, and full of confidence. He was afraid she'd fall for someone else while he was gone."

"Did she?" Maggie asked.

Eddie smiled. "No. She didn't want to admit it then, but there would never be anyone for her but Kurt. I knew that." He paused. "But it didn't stop me from falling in love with her."

Maggie sighed, and they were both quiet for a moment. Maggie studied her uncle and found that he looked older, or perhaps it was only the shadows playing across his face. "Did Mother know?" Maggie asked.

"She knew, but she stayed true to Kurt. They married before the war ended while he was home on leave."

"Did my father know?"

"I don't think so."

Maggie went to Eddie, put her arm through his and lay her head on his shoulder. "I'm sorry, Uncle Eddie."

He patted her hand. "I'm not. It was a long time ago. Agnes and I understand each other and we want what's best for you."

Eddie stubbed out his cigarette on the windowsill. "Talk to your mother in the morning, Maggie. Don't let this fester."

"No matter what she says, I won't change my mind. I wish she could see how much our situations are alike. She could have married a perfectly wonderful man who loved her, but she waited for the man she loved. She says it wasn't the wrong decision for her, so how could it be for me?"

Eddie kissed her forehead. "Oh Maggie," he said. "You've grown up—and Agnes and I were too slow to accept that—but you still have so much to learn. Good-night, honey," he said, closing the door behind him.

Maggie sank down in front of her vanity and unpinned her hair. She studied her face, looking for a young woman called

Ellie, but saw none of her mother there. Agnes had always said she favored her father. She wished she could remember him, this man whom she'd known only through photographs and stories from Eddie's childhood, this man who had claimed her mother's stubborn heart and then broken it. She decided in that moment that no matter how things turned out, as long as Colin came home, she would never look back, never wonder what could have been. She'd take what was best about her mother—her determination—but not her bitterness. She would learn to live like Eddie, with no regrets. She would look ahead, not behind, and she'd believe in their future so strongly that no matter what Colin had been through, no matter how much he had suffered or changed, he'd see it too.

Gwen's newborn baby boy slept on Maggie's shoulder, his downy head against her cheek. The porch swing creaked as she rocked and hummed a lullaby, and a sparrow chirped from the young oak tree. It was an unusually warm day in mid-October, and Maggie was glad her mother had chosen to walk downtown to do some shopping.

William rounded the corner of the block, his eyes finding Maggie immediately, a smile spreading across his lean face. He strode up the walkway, removing his hat as he came up the porch steps to lay his hand on the baby's head.

"This is Gray Junior," Maggie said. "I'm watching him for a couple of hours. Isn't he beautiful?"

"He's a healthy-looking boy. Gray will be very proud. Have they heard from him lately?"

"Yes, Gwen got another letter a few days ago. He seems to be well. He even got the picture she sent. They must treat prisoners better in Germany, or maybe it's just that he's an officer."

Maggie stroked the baby's smooth cheek with her thumb, his warm breath tickling her skin. She kissed his head before rising and laying him gently in the old pram that Mrs. Finnely had used for Colin.

William sat down on the wide porch ledge and leaned against the round post. "You look . . . very pretty today," he said.

She saw him move his eyes quickly away from her legs. Perhaps selfishly, she'd wanted to look nice for him today and had donned her favorite green dress with the semi-fitted bodice, short sleeves, and narrow belt. She'd tied her hair back with a cream-colored ribbon and, at the last minute, clipped on the pearl earrings Eddie had given her last Christmas. She touched the earrings now, thinking that final touch had taken things too far.

For his part, William looked handsome, as always. His dark eyes shone, and he smiled with lips closed. His tan double-breasted jacket hung open, showing a starched grey-and-white striped shirt. He wore black leather shoes and a homburg, and Maggie felt a pang of loss remembering how Verna had told her once what a handsome couple she and William would make.

"How was Seattle?" she asked, surprised by how nervous she sounded.

"Fine. I had some business to take care of, but I never meant to be gone so long. I'm sorry I haven't called you since I've been back. Things have been . . . busy." He looked at Maggie, and they both smiled at his excuse. "So, what was so urgent you had to see me right away?" His words dragged, but there was a tinge of hopefulness to his voice.

She cleared her throat, fussing with the baby's blankets. "We heard Colin on the shortwave radio the night before last."

William's smile faded. He leaned forward from the post. "Are you sure it was him?"

"Yes. He said his name." She offered William the paper with the message, explaining Colin's meaning as he read. She waited for him to say something, but he only handed the paper back.

"Uncle Eddie says the program was broadcast from Japan, so he thinks Colin may have been moved."

"Really." William had stood and was buttoning his jacket. "Well, this is good news but . . . you shouldn't get your hopes too high. The war's not over yet. Anything could still happen. I don't want to see you get hurt, Maggie."

"That seems to be a concern of everyone these days," Maggie said, glancing across the street. She could see her uncle smoking his pipe, dipping in and out of view behind the screen door of his porch as he rocked in his rocking chair. "I suppose I've deserved to be treated like a child. Didn't you call me that once?"

"I never meant it that way."

She smiled. "I know. But you were right. I've relied too much on my uncle and my mother—and you. But I've given this a lot of thought, and I've never been so sure of what I want . . . I know Colin's coming home, Will. I can *feel* it in my heart. I've waited so long to feel that."

"Are you trying to say good-bye, Maggie? It's not like I haven't expected it."

He reached out to smooth her hair coming loose in the breeze but pulled his hand back. She wanted to touch him, too, but could see by the sharp rise and fall of his chest, the way his lips parted and his eyes bore into her, that he needed more—much more than she could give.

"What will you do now?" she asked.

"I don't know. Maybe go back to Seattle. My father would like that. He likes me up there keeping an eye on things."

He turned to leave. At the foot of the steps he paused, looking out across the withering lawns to the barren foothills. "I have to know, Maggie. If Colin doesn't come back . . . will you want me here?"

She moved to the edge of the porch. "He *is* coming home, Will."

He nodded slowly, set his hat on his head and tried to smile. "Will you still write to me?" He raised his hand to cut off her answer. "No, I know you can't."

On an impulse, she reached out to hug him, forgetting for the moment the neighbors and her uncle. Will held her tight.

"I've been unfair to you, Will," Maggie said. "I'm so very sorry."

"No. You've always been honest with me. I just haven't been honest with myself." He gently pushed her back. "Take care of yourself, Maggie." He turned quickly and walked away.

Eddie waited a moment before crossing the street. He stood looking at the baby sleeping in the pram, then glanced up at Maggie.

She smiled, and he came to stand beside her.

"I told him I couldn't see him anymore," Maggie said, staring at the corner William had turned.

Eddie put his arm around her shoulder and sighed. "Your mother will be very disappointed," was all he said.

Chapter 30

Japan, 1944

The harsh winter of 1944-45 was the hardest on the men. They'd languished in prison camps for three years, lived through starvation, dysentery, scurvy, heart problems, influenza, and pneumonia. They'd relived the recurring symptoms of beriberi, malaria, and colitis. Their skin ulcers and rat bites failed to heal, their intestines filled with roundworms, and they couldn't shake head colds and coughs. They endured mysterious illnesses that caused their testicles to swell painfully, the hair on their arms and legs to break off, their eyesight to falter. And, always, there was the hunger. Men who stood six feet tall, who'd weighed one hundred and eighty pounds on Wake, now weighed one hundred and ten—or less.

To see them was to get an x-ray view of the human skeleton. And there was nothing anyone could do. No medicines, no treatments, no extra rations for the sick. But the human body could endure so much more than Colin ever would have imagined. For those who didn't die, the body found ways to heal itself, or at least to keep itself alive.

Those who did die in their bunks or in the infirmary—the lice and fleas rushing from their bodies toward the nearest live host—were buried in shallow graves under porous dirt that failed to cover the stench.

Colin had only two thoughts to occupy his weary mind. He must find things to eat, and he must hold on, for all the men in camp knew the war was winding down. They'd heard it from the Koreans in the steelworks and from sympathetic *honchos*, Japanese civilians who rented prisoners for outside work details. They'd heard that Japan's conquered territories were slowly falling into the hands of the Allies.

It was one such *honcho* who saved Colin's life that horrible winter. Yamata was a tiny, sinewy man with a house full of children and a sickly wife. He ran a small lumberyard several miles from camp, and a few of the stronger men, if you could call them that, were chosen to help him. That was in late December. It snowed as the prisoners were driven in the military truck to the lumberyard. The third day on the job, Colin cried briefly for the first time since Frank died, tearless shudders brought on by a recollection of the hot, sunny day back on Wake when he'd loaded lumber with Red then driven to the construction site and joked with Chaplain. It was so strange to think now how they'd compared the island with the heat of hell, without knowing that the true hell lay before them. But Colin could not figure out why, after so much suffering, such a simple memory would make him cry, and that's what worried him most of all.

Yamata took pity on Colin, for what reason Colin could only guess. It might have had something to do with the question he'd asked Colin. "Christo?" the older man had said, pointing at

Colin, then showing him a small wooden cross he wore hidden beneath his wool shirt.

Colin nodded. "Yes, Christo."

Yamata told him in halting English, using gestures and sign language, to go to the south corner of the lumberyard each day to the fence post, and there he would find a rice ball. Yamata was true to his word, and each day Colin waited until the bored guards were dozing before sneaking to the fence. On Christmas Day there was something special: two rice balls and a piece of fish. The best Christmas dinner he'd had in years.

The work detail at the lumberyard ended after only four weeks, but the extra calories had a powerful effect on Colin's health. He felt stronger than he had in months, and his mind had cleared enough to give him the uneasy realization that he was now in debt to the enemy. He could piece together bits of news he heard from Patrick, who still worked at the steelworks, about the Americans fire-bombing the industrial cities of Japan, and the Navy fighting bloody battles in the Pacific in a push toward an invasion of Japan. Maybe this new sense of hope was also contributing to his returning strength.

A few weeks after he stopped working for Yamata, Colin was lying in the barracks, a cold wind slithering through the floorboards. It was Saturday night, and perhaps tomorrow they would be allowed to rest.

Patrick lay beside him on the narrow bunk. Like most of the men, Patrick barely spoke now but would wink from time to time to let Colin know he was okay. His hair had thinned, his beard was tinged with grey, his eyes glassy. Patrick's heart could sometimes be seen beating in his emaciated chest.

Colin pressed his tongue against the new gap where his bottom front tooth had fallen out. He was wearing all his clothes at once for warmth, though the holes in his work shirt and Japanese uniform jacket let in nearly as much cold air as the layers kept out. His left boot had split open along the inside seam by the sole, and the snow melted against his sockless foot. The braided string belts he'd worn in Woosung and Kiangwan had long since frayed away, but Yamata had given him a thin piece of rope for a belt, which he knotted only when his diarrhea was in submission, and he didn't need to move with speed. The rest of the time, he tied it in a loose bow that fell apart often, so he'd have to catch his pants before they slipped to the floor. Still, he and Patrick looked better than many of the men in camp. At least Colin thought so.

George Tanner hobbled over using a walking stick, a tree limb that Colin had found outside the gates of the lumberyard. "There's a new fella," George said, struggling to bring some excitement to his hoarse voice. "They just brought him in. A pilot. The Marines have claimed him as one of their own."

Colin looked at Patrick. "Let's go see."

"I'm not movin'."

"Come on. The walk will warm you up."

They struggled to their feet and followed George to the next barracks building. Several prisoners had clustered around the pilot, who wore the bruises of interrogation. He seemed to be in his mid-twenties, with a pretty, somewhat girlish face, thick dark hair and tan skin. He seemed unnerved by the way the men stared at him and reached out to touch his leather flight jacket or smell his disease-free body.

"Where you from?" the senior Marine officer asked.

"Ohio."

Pleased, the men nodded and muttered to one another as if they were all from Ohio.

"There's men outside tied up and kneeling with boards behind their knees," the pilot said. "They look dead."

"Not yet," said the officer.

"What'd they do?"

"One lost his head and swung at a guard at the steelworks. They got the other guy for sabotage. He was winding electrical coils backward. He'd been doing it for weeks, and the Japs finally caught him."

"Will they die like that? Out in the cold?"

The officer only shrugged, changing the subject. "Where's your crew?"

"I don't know. We were on a reconnaissance flight over Osaka when we were shot down. We bailed out. My chute caught in a tree, and the Japs found me. Guess the rest of my crew got away."

"They won't get far." The officer laughed dryly.

The pilot looked angry and confused. Colin could guess what was going through his mind. He could only be disgusted by the horrific creatures around him—men who looked nearly as dead as they did alive. Likely his impulse was to get as far from them as he could; instead they kept pressing toward him. But this was no nightmare from which the pilot could simply awaken. For some reason, seeing this healthy, arrogant boy suffering like the rest of them gave Colin a degree of satisfaction. He heard himself laugh too. The pilot glanced his direction before curling his chest inward and hunching over his crossed legs.

"What's the news?" someone asked. "Is it almost over?"

"You mean the war?"

"What the hell else would I mean?"

"We're closing in on Hitler. They should have him soon."

"Who gives a shit about Hitler," said a Marine. "What about us? Are they gettin' ready to invade?"

The pilot looked at the anxious faces of the prisoners. He seemed nervous, unsure of what to say. "Yeah. I'm sure they'll invade soon."

The men clapped each other's backs, talking excitedly as they slowly dispersed. George and Patrick rose to head back to their barracks. They motioned for Colin, but he waved them off. He sat staring at the pilot, transfixed by a slight tear in the boy's warm jacket.

"What do *you* want?" the pilot asked.

Colin was silent for a moment. "Who's your favorite actor?"

"What? I don't know . . . Gary Cooper, I guess."

"I like Spencer Tracy, but my girl, Maggie, can't get enough of Clark Gable. I don't see why. I mean those ears . . . Is he still making pictures?"

"Who?"

"Clark Gable."

The pilot nodded. "How long since you got caught?"

"Three years," Colin said.

"Have you lost many men?"

"Too many to count."

"I'm not gonna make it in here." The pilot sounded so young, so frightened.

"Yes, you will." Colin scooted closer and gathered his strength. "Don't spend time worrying about disease. Either it'll kill you or it won't. Do your work and mind your business. Watch out for Bull. He's real mean, the worst one here. Almost as bad as the interpreter at our last camp. If they beat you, try to cover your head. Don't trade your food for anything." Colin lay his forearms on the pilot's bunk. "My friend once told me they can control your body, but never let them control your mind. I let that happen once, and it nearly killed me."

He looked out across the room at the men huddling on their bunks. "It's the boredom that really gets to you, the feeling of being trapped, of *never* knowing when it's going to end. Will it go on like this forever?" He studied the pilot. "But you said yourself the war's almost over."

"What else was I supposed to say with all of them staring at me like that?" The pilot lowered his head. "Tojo's not going to be taken as easily as Hitler. I'm not sure how much longer the Pacific war will last. It could be months. God, it could be months."

Colin paused for a moment, then leaned in close. "Well, don't tell anyone else. You gave them hope today. It's all they've got left."

"I want to go home." The pilot lifted his head, and in his tear-filled eyes Colin saw such intense emotion it stopped his breath. No one in camp had been able to show such depth of feeling in months, especially not since the rice ration had been cut again. Not even the guards showed much life these days. They were growing thinner under their own reduced rations. The civilian men and women at the steelworks were no better, like sullen, voiceless machines.

Colin wiped his runny nose on the back of his hand and patted the pilot's shoulder. He pushed himself up and slumped toward the door, dreading the cold breeze that would hit him when he stepped outside. He couldn't remember the last time he'd laughed or felt fear or anger, or anything besides the odd, thrumming drive to live. But Clark Cable was still making pictures, and back home Maggie was still sitting in the red seats of the Ada Theater surrounded by the elaborate Egyptian decor and beneath the dangling chandelier—watching.

"They're gettin' ready to move us again," Patrick said a few days later.

"You sure?"

Patrick nodded. "I think they might separate us this time."

Colin put a hand on his friend's bony knee. "I doubt it. But even if they do, you'll be fine, Patrick. You've stayed pretty healthy, and you've managed to avoid any serious beatings. Most men in camp would give anything to be in your condition."

"Luck of the Irish," Patrick said.

Colin smiled, remembering the way his father used to say that. "Oh God." He stood.

"What?"

"I have to get to the steelworks."

"You're crazy. They've shut the camp down for the night."

"I have to get something."

"You mean this?" Patrick pulled Colin's watch from his pocket. "I had to carry it in my mouth to get it into camp. Always knew this big mouth of mine would come to some good."

"How'd you know about this?" Colin asked.

"I saw you hide it behind the machinery when we first got to camp. You're a stupid, stubborn ass, Colin, riskin' your life for a watch."

"What do you think you just did?"

Patrick grinned. "Guess I'm as big a sap as you."

Colin put a hand on his friend's shoulder. "Thank you."

Patrick shrugged. "I owed you one." He lay back on the bunk beside Colin and closed his eyes.

Colin looked at his friend, feeling his body warm with affection. Maybe it was just luck that had kept Patrick's body stronger than most of the men in camp and his mind free from the nightmares and moments of crippling despair. Or maybe it was that Patrick was a true survivor. He knew when the odds were for or against him, so he would risk retrieving a watch but not rush into battle as Chaplain had. He could fight off the diseases that had killed Frank and Arthur because he could not stand to be sick. He didn't waste energy on schemes, and he lacked the wit to outsmart the guards or the other prisoners. He balked against authority, but he knew how much he could get away with. He could smile at the guards and go along with their commands, but with a curse on his lips.

He'd smoke a cigarette when he wanted one, trade it when he needed extra food. He knew better than to ever be alone. He drew his strength from his friends, clung to them, but gave them back his devotion. He lived one day at a time, without thinking to the future or dwelling in the past. And he could talk about his life back home, without much doubt he could pick up where he left off, that the camps would be a thing of the past. Colin admired him and hoped for Patrick that the camps would someday fade from memory but, for himself, he had accepted they would remain a part of him forever.

He drew the blanket up over himself and his friend, cupping his hands beneath it to pop the watch open and stare at his father's initials. In his foggy mind, he could barely remember the day his father was brought home dead from the mountains, but he remembered his mother taking the watch from Fergus's pocket and handing it to Colin. "He would want you to have this," Laura had said. "It meant more to him than anything in the world, except you."

A flat-faced guard suddenly loomed above Colin. He was tall, close to six-feet, with large, rounded shoulders and a narrow waist. He walked with his head down and forward, his eyes menacing, hence his nickname, Bull. He always carried a bamboo stick and whacked indiscriminately at any prisoner he could reach without veering from his course.

"*Ki o tsuke!*" Bull roared, tearing the blanket away. Colin rose slowly, painfully. He lifted his eyes, acid churning in his empty stomach. Bull was eyeing his hand. Patrick made a low, soft sound, like an old dog straining against its leash. Colin bowed respectfully, but the guard yanked him upright. He jabbed Colin's chest with his stick and shouted in Japanese for him to show his hands. Colin turned his right palm upward. Bull slammed his stick into Colin's left elbow, smashing against the pieces of shrapnel Colin still carried from the Battle of Wake. Colin cried out, his left hand opening. The watch dropped to the floor, and Bull shoved him backward to pick it up.

Silently, the other prisoners looked away. Patrick rose to his feet as Bull turned the watch between his fingers, his crooked yellow teeth forming a smug smile.

Colin's hand gripped his throbbing elbow. He slouched forward, his mouth open, his eyes blinking at his father's watch— the gold surface looking old and dull against the guard's brown hand. Bull turned his back to Colin and raised the watch in his hand, chiding the prisoners for the ignorance of Americans.

Colin's left foot slid forward, then his right.

"It's just a watch, Colin," Patrick warned. "Not worth dyin' for."

"It's all I've got." Colin said. Bull turned to see Colin moving toward him and held the watch out, baiting. He raised his bamboo stick. Colin looked into the guard's smirking face and thought about his mother's words, the image of his dead father forming clearly now in his mind. He held his breath and made a desperate lunge for the watch as the bamboo stick swung down toward his head.

Chapter 31

Boise, 1945

Time had moved more quickly these last months of the war. Nearly two years had passed since Maggie heard Colin's voice on the radio and since then, there had seemed so much to do. She had started working alternate Friday nights at Reilly's in addition to her Saturday night shift and her day shift at Mountain Bell. She'd been saving scrupulously, watching the catalogs, planning again for things she'd need to set up a home. She'd noticed few houses for sale, but Uncle Eddie told her not to worry. He had a feeling the building industry would surge back to life after the demands of war were set aside. So Maggie had spoken to a banker about a loan—avoiding the bank owned by William's father.

She and Ellen had also renewed their attempt to get aid for the families of the contractors. They'd written to politicians, spoken to the heads of every local organization that could possibly help, even tried calling the White House again. Nothing had come from their efforts, but Maggie refused to let that get her down. She still had hope that if the men came home, someone—the government, the military, Morrison Knudsen—would reimburse them for the years of missed work and hardship.

The dark spot in these busy months had occurred four months earlier on April 12, when Franklin Roosevelt died suddenly at his summer home in Warm Springs, Georgia. Maggie had been working the phones that day when Miss Achurra walked quietly behind each girl and whispered the terrible news in her ear. The switchboards blazed with lights as everyone in the nation seemed to turn for comfort to friends at the other end of a phone line. For thirteen memorable years Franklin Roosevelt had seen the nation through the Depression and then the war. Maggie had always imagined he would shepherd them into peace. Like every other operator, Maggie manned her lines that day with a lump in her throat. Even now, it brought tears to her eyes to think of his death.

But she didn't dwell on this or on anything but the end of the war. Japan had surrendered today, August 14, and Boiseans had taken to the streets to celebrate. Confetti and streamers showered from second-story windows, car horns blared, people laughed and shouted and cried. They hugged strangers, kissed each other's cheeks. A group of elderly men sang "When Johnny Comes Marching Home Again," and boys tossed their hats into the air.

Maggie pushed through the crowd toward Reilly's Place. She knew the popular bar must be swarming with customers, and Verna would need her help—if she could just get through.

Mr. Reilly stood in the doorway of his establishment, waving his chubby hands back and forth to indicate no more room. His forehead was soaked in sweat, and his voice boomed as he fought back the revelers, but his eyes twinkled when he spotted Maggie, and he reached out to pull her through the crowd.

She maneuvered between two soldiers standing in the doorway and entered the noisy bar with a nod toward Hal, the bartender, whose flying hands were flipping tumblers onto the bar and splashing whiskey over their rims.

Verna came up behind Maggie and hugged her hard. "I'm so glad you're here!" she shouted. "It's crazy. I been walkin' on glass all afternoon."

"Poor Mr. Reilly. They're tearing this place apart."

"Oh, he don't care." Verna laughed. "They're throwin' money at Hal and me without even waiting for change."

"Was it like this on V-E Day?"

"Louder," Verna said.

"I would have liked to have seen that, but I had to watch the baby so Gwen could go out. V-E Day meant more to her than it did to me."

"Of course," Verna patted Maggie's arm. "But, hey, now *your* fella will be comin' home soon."

"I hope so."

"Ah, I know he will." She hugged Maggie again. "I better get back to work."

As Maggie was about to follow Verna she noticed Ellen fighting her way through the crowd.

"El! Over here!"

Ellen reached her and said something to Maggie, but her soft voice didn't carry over the noise.

"Let's go out back," Maggie suggested. "I can hardly hear myself think in here." She took Ellen's hand and led her through the bar to a back door that opened into the alley. A group of men drinking beer just outside the door nodded and stepped back gallantly.

Maggie leaned against the brick wall of Reilly's Place. "I had no idea it would be like this," she said, laughing as she indicated celebrants at both ends of the alley.

"How is Gray?" Ellen asked. "Did he make it home?"

"Yes, and he's hardly the worse for the wear. He's a good man, really. Gwen's so happy. She never doubted for a minute he'd come back."

One of the men in the alley tossed a beer bottle at the wall. It shattered, and Ellen jumped. Inside the bar, the crowd was thinning. People were too restless to stay in one place. Maggie put an arm around Ellen's shoulders and guided her back inside. She picked up a rag and started to wipe a table. "How is Mr. Gulley?" she asked.

"Better since the funeral. Poor Annie. She lived much longer than anyone expected. I think she wanted to see Patrick home again. She nearly did." Ellen pointed toward the rag. "Can I help?"

"You may not," Maggie said, looping her arm through Ellen's and leading her to a stool by the bar. "It's time you let someone take care of you. I'll get you a Coca-Cola."

Ellen leaned forward. "I saw your friend William on the street."

Maggie paused.

"Did he stop by here, Maggie?"

"No. I didn't even know he was in town. It's been two years since I spoke to him, Ellen."

They watched the celebrants for a moment, then Ellen spoke again.

"What will it be like for Patrick and Colin? So much has changed since they left. We've changed, Maggie. God only knows how our lives will turn out." She smiled gently. "But I'm glad you didn't choose William. Now I know whatever happens, we'll still be able to see each other through. You've been the best friend I've ever had."

Maggie hugged her tightly.

Ellen laughed. "I'm so very tired."

"Yes," Maggie agreed. "It's been a long war."

Chapter 32

Japan, 1945

Colin rested with his back against a tree, rubbing the knot on his head that had never completely disappeared. He knew he'd been lucky the beating had ended with that one blow. Bull could have easily taken him to the guardhouse, worked him over some more. Still, every time he felt the knot on his head, he felt his failure. Bull had kept his father's watch instead of trading it in the town for alcohol, food, or money. He knew this because, from time to time, Bull, who had also been transferred to this new camp with Colin, would take it from his pocket and open it in front of Colin, making a show of checking the time. If it was the last thing he ever did, Colin would get that watch back. But he'd learned his lesson the hard way. This time he would wait until the odds were in his favor.

He closed his eyes and took a deep breath of the pine-scented air. After so many years away from Idaho, it felt good to be in a forest again. He could see for miles beyond the green rolling hills, past Sendai—his camp for the last four months—across the open pit mines where most of the other prisoners toiled, out toward the Sea of Japan. Sometimes he was even sure he could see Russia far off on the horizon. Other times he imagined the American fleet sailing toward them.

But there was also something eerie about this Japanese hill. It was so still and quiet, he felt as though he were standing in a painting. He could find none of the creatures he had come to expect in the mountains back home. No squirrels, birds or even snakes—no animal life of any kind. He guessed the hungry peasants had killed them all for food. After the pounding chaos of the steelworks, Colin knew he should appreciate the silence but, in truth, he'd give his next ration to hear a bird sing.

If anyone ever asked Colin to describe Sendai, he figured he'd say, "It was just like any other camp, only worse." When they'd first arrived here, back in March, he'd been sure he'd die from the cold. Even now, in early August, the air was damp and chilled, and he almost wished for the steaming hot summers of his years in the China camps.

In addition to the hundred or so men who'd been transferred with him from Kawasaki, there were fifty Australian officers, and over a hundred Americans who had served in the Philippines. They kept to themselves, steering clear of the men from Wake, particularly the civilian contractors. That was fine with Colin. He'd come to accept partisanship over the years, though he still didn't fully understand it; after all, they were all on the same side, and all in the same mess.

Most of the prisoners who were able to walk had been put to work in the underground copper mine. Colin had labored there for several months, feeling the dampness in his bones, fearing the rumbling that sounded a cave-in, slaving to remove his quota of rock and soil each day. So when they'd called for volunteers for a detail cutting timber, he'd been quick to claim experience with a saw.

His guard on this new detail was no older than sixteen. They'd nicknamed him Johnny. He told Colin about America's victories in Okinawa and the Philippines, good news except Johnny said some of the Japanese officers wanted to kill the prisoners in retaliation. They would certainly do it if they lost the war, Johnny insisted. So Colin sat among the silent trees wondering if the haunting beauty of these woods would be the last thing he ever saw.

"I don't want to die in Japan," he said to George Tanner, who was sitting a few feet away.

"Did you just figure that out?"

"Course not. Not a day's gone by I haven't thought about it . . . I want to be buried near my father, back home where my family can come to my grave."

He waited for George to answer, but his friend was listening for Johnny. George's eyesight had grown steadily worse, and he relied more and more on his hearing and on Colin to guide him. Colin shifted the weight off his right buttock onto the mossy patch of grass beneath his left side. He was so thin that sitting on hard surfaces had become excruciating, and standing was hardly better. "I wish Patrick was here," he said.

"So you've said."

It was possible Patrick was still at Kawasaki, but unlikely. Johnny had told Colin the Americans had increased their fire-bombing campaign, and the industrial areas were hardest hit. The local populations had retreated to the countryside, and, with that work force scattered, the factories and shipping yards were shutting down. Most of the prisoners had been moved to remote camps, such as Sendai. Colin swatted at a mosquito, glancing up at patches of blue sky just beyond the branches of the "duration tree." He called it that because he intended for this tree to stand until the end of the war. He and George had begun sawing early this morning and had yet to reach an inch into the tree's thick trunk. They sawed only when the guard was around, for that was all the strength that remained in them, and as long as they were working when he came by, Johnny seemed to figure he'd done his job.

George cleared his throat, his signal that Johnny was coming. Colin struggled to his feet, hauling the long saw off the ground. He and George lifted it into place, but Johnny didn't even glance at the tree. Instead, he did something completely unexpected. He fell to his knees, bowing down to the ground before them. They dropped the saw and stared.

Johnny got to his feet, keeping his head low. "*Yasumi, Yasumi.* No work today."

"What's going on?" Colin asked.

Johnny threw his arms out in a wide arc, looking up with eyes filled with fear. "Many, many dead. *Pika don.* Big bomb. Hiroshima gone. Many thousand dead."

Colin took a cautious step forward. "You mean Americans bombed Hiroshima? B-29s dropped many bombs?"

The guard shook his head. "One bomb, *pika don.* Whole city gone."

"I don't understand."

"No work today. Go back camp." Johnny bowed again quickly and scurried away. They waited until he was out of earshot and huddled close, grabbing each other's arms for support.

"Could one bomb wipe out a city?" Colin asked George.

"None that I know of."

"But something's up. Maybe this is it, huh? The end of the war?" Colin said, thinking how strange it was to say those words, knowing they might really be true.

"Or this could be some kind of trick." George said.

They stared at each other for a moment. "We better get back." Colin reached for the saw.

"Leave it, Colin. If the war's over it can rust here for all eternity for all I care."

"No. It's not worth risking punishment. We have to take it back, George."

They shouldered the saw between them and stumbled under its weight as they headed down the hill, stopping often to rest.

On one such rest George said in his raspy voice, "I been wonderin' what it's gonna be like when we get home. I ain't spoken to a girl since we left Hawaii for Wake back in '41. I always thought someday I'd get married, have kids. But now, after all we've been through . . ." He grabbed his crotch. "Think there's any bullets left in the ol' gun?"

"I hope so," Colin said. He'd been worrying a lot about that lately. He couldn't imagine having enough strength to make love to a woman, much less comprehend how anyone would ever be able to find his bruised and emaciated body appealing. If Maggie had waited for him, as he so often prayed she had, would she want what he had become?

They rose without another word and walked the rest of the way in silence. When they reached the high wooden gate to camp, they kept their eyes on the guards in the sentry towers. Now, more than ever, Colin was determined not to die from a bullet in the back. Most of the men from the mines were already back in camp. They stood in small bunches, speaking in hushed tones, all asking the same questions. "You think it's true about the bomb? Think it's over yet? What if the guards decide to kill us all? What if our boys forget we're here?"

Most of the guards inside the camp had disappeared. But they returned after an hour, their faces no longer reflecting humility or fear, but anger. They called the prisoners to attention, and left them standing there for over an hour. Colin noticed Johnny, who had kowtowed before them only hours before, now pointing his gun at their chests. Beside him stood Bull.

Suddenly, an officer shouted an order. The guards raised their rifles to their shoulders and took aim. Behind Colin, someone whimpered, someone else cried out, but most of the men were too weak to make a sound. Colin, whose eyes were on Bull's pocket, felt George's fingers wrap tightly around his arm.

After a moment, the guards, just as suddenly, lowered their guns, and the camp commander released the prisoners, many of whom fell to their knees. A few of the guards stepped forward immediately and handed out their own cigarettes to the men.

"Look at those monkeys," George fumed. "Three and a half years in these goddamn camps and I still don't understand Japs. One minute they're gonna kill you, the next, they're giving you cigarettes."

Colin's eyes shifted back to Bull, who was standing in the doorway of the guardhouse. "They're not going to kill us," he said. "They don't have the guts. They know when our boys get here they'll have to pay for all they've done to us."

"You may be right," George answered. "But I don't aim to find out. I'm running first chance I get."

"How are you going to do that? You barely made it down from that mountain today. How far do you think you'd get?"

"I don't know, but it's better than getting shot."

"Tell you what, George. We'll give it a couple more days. After that, if we see a chance, we'll take it."

His attention was drawn to the sky as an American B-29 roared low over the camp. The guards scattered in fear, but the prisoners stood out in the open, stunned, gaping at the bomber until it disappeared over the mountains. Some began to cheer, others sank weakly to the ground, their heads bowed in thanks, a few looked defiantly at the guards, who were stepping cautiously out of the shadows.

"See," Colin said, his smile pulling his skin tight across the bones in his face. "It's just a matter of time now."

Chapter 33

Japan, 1945

A chance to escape never arrived. Colin and George had been taken off the timber detail, relegated back to the mines until the American fly-overs became more frequent; then all work stopped. Johnny told Colin about another bomb, this time at Nagasaki, and, within a few days, rations were increased. They began to find a few vegetables and an occasional piece of meat in their soup. The men wandered around camp wondering if this was only a lull in the war, and, if so, how long it would last. The guards wouldn't say. Then one day, they just disappeared. Colin woke to find them gone, the camp gate swung wide open.

The prisoners gathered cautiously inside the gate to stare at the road. They all talked about leaving, but it was hours before one man summoned the courage to step foot outside the camp. When nothing happened to him, others followed, and soon everyone was milling around outside the fence, some laughing, some crying, all shouting for joy. A Marine ran back to the barracks and produced a small American flag he'd made from scraps of fabric. The men raised it on the corner of a barracks and gathered around to sing "God Bless America," tears in their eyes.

Each day they'd roam a little farther from camp, scavenging in fields for food, testing freedom. Most would return to camp at night to rest and speak in unnecessary whispers about whether or not the war could truly be over.

"What if America won't take us back?" George asked. "We're all sick. Maybe they won't let us in."

Colin assured him that would never happen, but the more he thought about it, the more worried he became.

One day, some of the guards returned to protect the prisoners from the embittered Japanese civilians, they said. But the Japanese commander made it clear the camp Allied officers were in charge. A B-29 flew low over camp, the pilot waggling his wings to let them know he saw them, and the prisoners cheered. The next day, the B-29 returned, dropping leaflets which read, *"War's over, boys! Mark your camp and we'll drop supplies."*

The following day, two planes flew over, raining from their drop hatches crates and barrels of food and medicine, along with bales of clothing on pallets. They parachuted from the sky, bursting open upon impact with the ground. Colin ran for cover as drop packs with failed parachutes crashed through the roofs of the barracks and smashed wash racks. George was knocked unconscious by a falling can of fruit and, though Colin had been terrified his friend would never regain consciousness, they both found they were able to laugh about the accident later. But the next day, when a man was killed by a falling crate, no one saw any humor in it. The whole camp turned out to mourn his senseless death.

Inside the crates and barrels were leaflets warning *"Do not overeat or overmedicate,"* but few heeded the warning. After years of sticky rice, bland tea, and watery "Tojo Water," they could now feast on Spam, beef stew, soup, fresh bread, Pet milk, creamy butter, sweet jam, fruit cocktail, even ketchup. They could suck on hard candy, the sugar jump-starting their weak bodies. They could fit four American cigarettes in their mouths and smoke them all at once.

They ate until they were sick, gaining a pound a day in bloat, until a few were near death, their organs stressed by the sudden excess. Colin started to pace himself, rationing his food and giving away many of his cigarettes. He chose a new shirt, socks, a pair of trousers, and boots from the pile of air-dropped clothing. He held them for a moment before putting them on, marveling at their cleanness and running his fingers across the smooth, perfect fabric.

Three long weeks passed in the camp. It was now mid-September, and there was still no sign of American troops. The men were restless. They'd begun going to the village to loot the stores, hunt for prostitutes who wanted nothing to do with them, break windows, and steal bicycles.

George came up to Colin one day. "I'm leaving," he said. "Are you comin'?"

"Where do you figure on going?"

"Toward the coast. There must be American ships there."

Colin frowned. "The officers say we should stay put, wait for our troops to arrive with trucks."

"Since when do we listen to officers?"

"We don't know what's out there, George. There could be land mines, or Japs who don't know the war's over. They'd kill us on sight."

George shook a finger toward the gate. "No, we don't know

what's out there, but we know what's in here. And I'm not gonna be a part of it any longer."

Colin rubbed his palms together, considering. "I've come too far to get my head shot off now," he said, expecting George to be angry.

But George only held out his hand to Colin. "Then I'll look you up in the States."

Colin noticed how George's cheeks were filling out again around his large nose. He seemed to squint less, as if his eyesight was improving already, and he smiled often, as he had on Wake. "You know," Colin said, shaking his hand, "for a while there you were an ugly cuss."

George laughed, pulling Colin into a quick embrace. "Don't take any wooden nickels," he said.

Colin called out to him as he walked away. "Keep an eye out for Patrick, will you?"

"I will."

Colin watched George disappear into the barracks to collect his things. His mind was racing, wondering if he was doing the right thing. Then he saw a sight that stopped his heart. Bull was staggering, drunk, into camp, his uniform jacket open, his unbuttoned shirt stained with vomit. He held a bottle of American whiskey in one hand while his right hand rested on his hip where his sword once hung. He veered toward the guardhouse.

Colin's stomach burned, and his right hand curled into a fist. Someone said something to him, but he brushed past the man without a word. At the steps to the guardhouse he paused, blood rushing in his ears. He shoved the rough-planked door open and looked around. Leaning just inside the door was a bamboo stick. He picked it up, striking the stick against his open palm, remembering how many times he'd felt that sting on his back, arms, neck, head. He turned and closed the guardhouse door, and went to stand over Bull.

Bull sprawled on the floor, his back against the wall, the bottle of whiskey propped against his thigh. His breath was labored, and he muttered to himself in Japanese. In his right hand was a six-inch knife.

"You son of a bitch," Colin said, raising the stick. "I want my watch back."

Bull opened his eyes briefly to look at Colin and raised a hand. He reached into his pocket, withdrew the watch, and threw it at Colin.

Colin caught it, felt the familiar ticking in his hand. He lowered the stick to examine the watch, finding Bull had tried to scratch off his father's initials. He picked up the stick again, enraged, feeling another presence in the room. He could almost see Ishihara standing to the side, grinning, his boot on Arthur's bloated stomach. "Americans are so weak," the interpreter was saying. "You are race of insects, and Japan will crush you under her boot. Maybe not in this war," the interpreter seemed to whisper in Colin's ear. "But before a hundred years are over, whites will bow down to Japan."

The hatred Colin had suppressed for so many years rose to the surface. He gripped the stick in both hands, like a baseball bat, and rushed at Bull. He hit him twice about the head, opening a gash on the guard's forehead before Bull slumped to the side, and Colin noticed the knife plunged into his belly. He watched in horror as the guard, the gash spilling blood into his eye, righted himself and slowly drew the knife across his middle. Colin lowered the stick, his gaze fixed on the blood and guts spilling from Bull's open stomach.

Bull fell back against the wall, his eyes half closed, but he looked up at Colin—and smiled, crooked teeth glowing in the dark room. Colin dropped the stick and stumbled back against the wall. He fell to his knees, unable to breathe.

George pushed the door open, his eyes alight with excitement. He glanced at Colin. "Heard you came in here after Bull." He noticed the dying guard, walked over to him, staring at his open gut. He kicked Bull's leg. "You killed yourself, you son of a bitch." He traced a finger along a crooked white scar that ran across his jawline. "Goddammit, Colin," he said, pointing to Bull. "I wanted to do that."

Colin bent over and vomited. He held his head in his hands for a moment, and George walked over to help him up. "Let's get out of here." They walked into the sunlight, leaving Bull to gasp his final, ragged breath.

Colin wiped his mouth. "Think I'll come with you, George."

"Thought you wanted to stay here."

"Changed my mind." He rose, put his father's watch back in his pocket, and walked across the compound, past several prisoners who were rushing to see what had happened. Now he was anxious to get out of camp, away from the stench, the feel of death, the memories. He reached his top bunk and picked up the frayed linen sack he'd managed to keep with him all these years. He packed his Japanese army jacket and torn work shirt and took along his ruined work boots—just in case—but left the dungarees he'd worn throughout captivity. He'd never been able to rid them of the smell of shit.

He was too used to guarding his old mess kit to leave it behind, though he now had new utensils from the airdrop. He threw into the sack several cans of food, a couple packs of cigarettes, a bar of soap, a new razor, toothbrush, and American tooth powder. He cradled the sack in his arms like a baby, and climbed down, reaching for his old, fetid blanket. He stared at it for a moment, closed his eyes and told himself he could let it go now. He left it in a heap on the bunk.

He walked one last time between the rows of double bunk platforms, his new boots knocking hard against the floorboards, the air so heavy in the long, narrow room that it stuck in his nostrils. He realized he could no longer remember how it felt to sleep in a real bed or to wake to the smell of bacon frying or even to be in a room by himself. He vowed never to forget what had happened between the walls of this barracks building and the ones just like it in China and in Dispatch Camp, not just the beatings and starvation, but the power of the human spirit.

An emaciated man lying on a lower bunk watched him pass. He'd been unable to hold any food down, and Colin couldn't understand how he'd remained alive so long. "Do you need anything?" he asked.

"Water," the man replied.

Colin went to the end of the room, where a bucket had been placed. He brought back a dipper of water and fed it carefully to the man. The sick man gave him a thumbs up, and Colin smiled and patted his shoulder before stepping out of the barracks.

He stood in the doorway looking around the camp at the faded, leaning barracks, the galley, the *benjos*, the guard towers, the high wooden fence, the splintered remains of crates from the air drops, the hospital unit, and the shallow graves beside it. He realized a part of him had come to accept this place, if not as home, then as comforting in its familiarity. Seeing it with new eyes, he was surprised to notice how sparse it was, how sagging and rundown. It was sickening to think he could have lived in camps like this for so long when he should have been with Maggie, surrounded by the furniture he'd planned to build for their home, the curtains and tablecloths Maggie would have sewn, the doilies and afghans his mother would have crocheted.

His stomach tightened as his gaze continued past the

guardhouse where Bull lay in a puddle of his own blood and came to rest on George, squatting on his haunches, surveying the clouds that promised a late afternoon shower.

"You okay?" George asked as Colin approached.

Colin nodded. They walked quietly through the gate without a backward glance and turned east. As the camp fell farther and farther behind, Colin's steps lightened, and he felt a sensation he hadn't known in years, didn't even recognize at first: joy. He said nothing, though his eyes roved the countryside, taking in every tree, every hut, every rock. He even paused to pet a stray dog until it darted off into the bushes.

A group of women and young girls approached with short, quick steps. Colin and George stopped to marvel at their beautiful bodies, thin but healthy, their black hair shimmering. They seemed to glide over the road as they pressed close together, making a wide arc around the former prisoners and turning around a bend in the road.

George sighed, then asked. "Did the bastard say anything?"

"Who?"

"Bull, when he was splitting his guts open."

"No. He never made a sound. Just looked at me and smiled."

"What'd you go in there for?"

"This." He took out the watch. "It was my father's. Bull stole it."

"I thought you went in to kill him."

Colin looked over George's shoulder to the bend in the road where the young women had turned, and beyond to the hill where their "duration tree" still stood. He sat down on a rock and shook his head. "I almost did. I started to. God, what have I become?"

"Look, Colin, we've all done things we never thought we'd

do, things we'll have to live with the rest of our lives. Hell, I wanted to kill him myself. But we gotta put that behind us now. Those Japs aren't worth a second thought. Not after what they've done to us."

Colin blinked hard and rubbed his eyes. "You're right." He looked down the road. "I know you're right."

"Let's go home." George smiled and put his arm around Colin's shoulder. He tipped his head back, whooped and then started to laugh. "God Almighty," he said. "It's good to be free."

Chapter 34

Boise, 1945

"I went to the pictures with Mother last night," Maggie told Ellen as they walked together toward the room full of switchboards. "Mother thought I needed to get my mind off Colin. But the newsreel showed the troops coming home. There was a transport ship arriving under the Golden Gate Bridge with soldiers waving their hats from the decks. I couldn't watch. I had to go to the lobby."

"It doesn't do any good to talk about it," Ellen said.

"Well, it does for me. The war's been over for a month, and we've still had no word."

"I really don't want to talk about it." Ellen walked on ahead.

Annoyed, Maggie watched her walk away, then she went to her own switchboard. "Good morning, Mrs. Quintan," she said, glancing at the chair next to hers. "Ida's still not back?"

"She might not be coming back, dear."

Maggie sighed. "I hope she does."

"I didn't think you and Ida were friends."

"We're not, but it doesn't feel right without her here."

Maggie would never forget the day three weeks ago when the serious-looking man from Western Union had delivered the telegram. Almost every woman had held her breath when he came into the switchboard room, and when he walked down the row of switchboards right toward Maggie, she felt her heart beat wildly in her chest. She was later ashamed at her relief when he stopped at Ida's chair and not hers. He'd offered the telegram to Ida, but she did not take it.

Maggie had offered, "Should I open it, Ida?"

Ida looked at Maggie helplessly.

Maggie took the telegram and tore it open slowly, her eyes on Ida's ashen face. She read aloud how Ida's husband had died the day after the Japanese surrender when his jeep overturned in a ditch.

"I'm so sorry, Ida." Maggie said, but Ida only rose without a sound and walked stiffly past the switchboards, leaving her hat and handbag behind. She hadn't come back to work since.

"We all came through this war together," Maggie said to Mrs. Quintan, who had lost two of her three sons. "We've always helped each other get through the hard times. She should be here with us now."

Mrs. Quintan patted Maggie's arm somberly and left.

Maggie took her seat, grateful for this job. It kept her busy, kept her from wondering why day after day she received no news of Colin. She'd only been working a few minutes when Miss Achurra came to her.

"You have a call, Miss Braun."

Maggie stared at her supervisor. Operators were seldom allowed personal calls while on shift. "It must be my mother,"

Maggie said. Agnes was spending the day at the hospital with a sick friend.

"It's long distance," Miss Achurra said pointedly, and moved away.

Maggie rubbed the phone cord with her thumb and stared at the hole Miss Achurra had indicated, finally pushing in the cord. She forced herself to speak up. "This is Maggie." The line crackled. She gripped the mouthpiece in both hands, waiting.

"Your bad penny has returned," a voice said, with a nervous laugh.

She sat back hard in her chair and closed her eyes.

"Colin?"

"Yeah, it's me."

"Oh my God. Where are you?" She pressed the earphone hard against her ear, trying to hear through the static.

"Guam------They're fixing me up-------be home in a few weeks.

"Fixing you up? Are you all right?"

"Fine, Maggie. Don't worry. God, it's good to hear your voice."

Maggie glanced down the row of switchboards to where Ellen was sitting, waving frantically to get Ellen's attention. "Is Patrick with you?"

A long pause. "No-------separated several months back------don't know where he is."

"Oh." Maggie shook her head and Ellen slumped back in her chair. "Well, I'm sure he's fine."

"Yes-------sure he is," Colin said. "Did you hear what I said? I'm coming home."

"Yes. I can't wait to see you."

"Maggie, -----------"

She sat forward, pressing the headset hard against her ears. "I can't hear you, Colin."

"I said I'm ------------------"

She held her breath until she heard his voice again.

"Can't hear you, Maggie--------tell you everything when I get home------I'll see you soon."

"Colin!" she cried, but the line went dead.

Several women were looking at her now, including Ellen. In the back of her mind, Maggie knew the anguish Ellen must be feeling. But she knew it only as a fact, without any real compassion. She could only focus on one thing. Colin would be home soon.

She felt as though she needed to run, but held herself in her seat. "What's wrong with me?" she asked aloud. "I feel so mixed up."

Miss Achurra slipped up behind her. "Do you need to take a break, Miss Braun?"

Maggie nodded and slid out of her chair. As she crossed the room, she felt herself start to run. She ran from the building to the corner, stepping into the street to the sound of a car horn. She stumbled up on the curb, backing up against the wall of a drugstore and crossing her arms over her chest. Then she saw Eddie hurrying toward her down the sidewalk.

"You heard from Colin?" he gasped, out of breath.

Maggie reached for him and burst into tears. She cried for several minutes, the tension draining away.

"He's in Guam," she stammered. "He'll be home soon."

"I know. He called my house looking for you. I gave him the number to reach you at work." Eddie tugged a wrinkled handkerchief from his pocket and pressed it into her hand. "Are you all right?"

"He sounded different, not the way I remembered at all. I'm scared. Isn't that silly, Uncle Eddie?" She laughed. "All these years of waiting for him to come home, and now I'm afraid to see him."

"That's natural, Maggie. It's been a long time. A lot has happened."

She folded the handkerchief into a neat square. "I'll be fine. I just need a minute." She handed him back the handkerchief and straightened her skirt, but she still wasn't ready to go back. Her gaze wandered across the street to where a little boy walked hand in hand with his mother, a boy only slightly older than the child she might have had with Colin had he returned from Wake when he'd planned. Could so many years really have passed? Colin knew her only as the twenty-two-year-old he'd presented with an engagement ring so long ago. Would he recognize her now that the long hours of work and the late nights at Reilly's had left her exhausted, with dark circles under her eyes and little color in her cheeks? How she wished she could have spoken to him for only a few minutes longer. She had so much to tell him.

"Do you think I've changed much, Uncle Eddie?"

"I think you're beautiful."

Maggie smiled.

"Do you want me to go to the hospital and tell your mother, or would you rather tell her tonight?"

"You tell her, Uncle Eddie."

"Well, come on then." Eddie took her arm. "I'll walk you back."

Maggie made it through her shift, though she had trouble remembering the phone numbers, and she disconnected several callers. She went straight home after her shift, pausing only to hug Ellen and assure her that Patrick was alive and likely on his way home. Eddie and Agnes were sitting on the porch waiting for Maggie when she returned home that evening.

Agnes rushed down the steps to meet her. "I'm so glad to

hear he's coming home."

"Do you mean that, Mother?"

"Yes, of course."

Maggie hugged her mother for a long moment, weariness sweeping over her after so many nights of lying awake worrying.

Agnes pulled away and wiped a tear from her eye. "You come inside. I'll make tea and sandwiches."

Maggie went into the parlor and dropped down on the sofa. The windows were open, and a fan buzzed in the corner of the room. She lay down, turning her head toward the fan to feel the cool air on her face. She closed her eyes.

When she awoke it was dusk. Agnes was moving quietly about the dining room, setting out dishes and utensils at Maggie's place at the table. She heard Maggie stir and came to stand before her, putting her hand under Maggie's chin to look into her eyes. "Are you rested? You still look tired."

Maggie rose from the sofa. "I'm fine, Mother."

"Then come and eat. I kept your food warm."

"In a minute. I need to call Ellen."

"She came by while you were sleeping."

Maggie gripped her mother's hand. "Did she hear from Patrick?"

"No, Margaret. Not yet."

The front door opened, and Eddie came in. "Good, you're awake. How are you feeling?"

"Much better."

"I'm glad. Why don't you sit down, honey." He took out a cigarette and lit it, with a glance at Agnes. "I've just been to see William."

"Why?"

"He came to my house a couple of weeks ago to inquire

about Colin. He asked if I could let him know as soon as we heard anything."

Maggie smoothed her dress across her knees. "How is he?"

"He was very gracious. Quite the gentleman, as always. He thanked me for coming, though I could see he was disappointed." Eddie held out an envelope. "He asked me to give you this."

Maggie tensed.

"Don't worry. It's not a letter. It's a loan application from his father's bank. William signed it, so it's already approved. You have only to fill in an amount."

Maggie stared at the envelope, finally reaching up to take it. "He did this for me?"

"He knew you and Colin would need a house."

"He must have cared for you very much," Agnes said softly.

Maggie turned the envelope over in her hands. It felt wrong to feel so happy for herself when William must be hurting still. "How can I make this up to him?" she wondered aloud.

"I don't think he expects you to," Eddie said.

Maggie lay the envelope on the coffee table and rubbed her eyes. "This is all happening so fast." She laughed. "Doesn't that sound crazy after all these years? To think Colin and I might finally have a chance. To think we might really have a life together."

"You've earned it," Eddie said. "You've both been through so much. I'm proud of you, Maggie, and Colin."

Agnes glanced at Eddie and smiled. She took Maggie by the arm and pulled her to her feet. "Come on now and eat, Margaret. You've gotten entirely too thin. No man will find you attractive with so little meat on your bones."

"Oh Agnes," Eddie scolded, but Maggie only laughed and allowed her mother to lead her to the dining room table.

Chapter 35

Guam, 1945

Colin hung up the phone on the nurse's desk and leaned against the wall. Maggie had sounded just as he remembered, and he wondered if she looked the same. He hoped she hadn't cut her hair—hadn't changed anything about herself.

It was muggy in the white-walled room of the U.S. Navy hospital in Guam. Sick and wounded men in hospital gowns and healthy men in American uniforms wandered around the makeshift lobby. Colin went to a row of folding chairs against the wall and sat down. A dark Italian boy in uniform stopped to visit. But his eyes reminded Colin of Frank, and Colin found it hard to look at him. He stayed only a few minutes, and Colin was glad when he left.

It had been hard at first to be told he'd have to be treated at the medical facility before he could reenter the United States. After over eight months on Wake and forty-five months in Asia, it was funny that a couple more weeks could sound like an eternity.

He tried to focus on the bright side. At least he was looking better, feeling better, with each passing day. He'd filled out, and it was a healthier weight gain than the bloating that had occurred after the air drops. His wounds were finally healing, and his dysentery was clearing up. He'd had a haircut and a decent shave and had even had his teeth looked after. The dentist said when he got home he could get a manufactured tooth to replace the one he'd lost.

Now if he could just get his mind back to normal. After years of being surrounded by hundreds of men, he couldn't handle even a few moments alone. Most of the prisoners were being processed home through Guam, and he found himself searching them out, needing to be around people who understood what he'd been through. He'd come to avoid the pretty nurses who tried so hard to be sympathetic but could offer him no real comfort.

Most disturbingly, he found himself missing the camps, the routine, even the rice. Mostly he missed knowing what was expected of him. Out here, he felt confused and out of place. It seemed like everyone talked so fast—moved so fast. The American uniforms had changed, not to mention there were now women in the service. He didn't recognize many of the songs on the radio, couldn't accept that Glenn Miller was dead, couldn't believe Shirley Temple was all grown up. He'd never heard of penicillin, but they were administering it to everyone, for almost any ailment. The Marines from Wake weren't even called POWs anymore. Now they were RAMPs, Recovered Allied Military Personnel. Colin tried, but he couldn't seem to take it all in. He was scared he might never be able to.

"Still thinkin' too much?" someone asked.

Colin looked up to see Patrick leaning on crutches, staring

down at him. He bounded from his chair and threw his arms around his friend. Patrick thumped his back and laughed.

"It's so good to see you," Colin said. "I've been so worried."

"'Bout me? You didn't think I was gonna let you steal all the glory?"

"It's so good to see you."

Patrick grinned. "You said that."

"When'd you get in?"

"This mornin'."

"What happened to your foot?"

"I was walkin' with some fellas one night after the surrender. Fell into a ditch and hit my foot against a rock. It cracked just like that." He snapped his fingers.

"You're lucky you didn't break your neck." Colin laughed.

He sat down, feeling safe again. For several minutes, they said nothing, enjoying the comfortable silence between them.

"So," Colin said finally, his smile fading. "What happened to you, Patrick?"

Patrick paused. "I went to a camp up north. Real bad one, Colin. Worse than any we were in. Lots of fellas died." He waved away the memories, pulled a folding chair out in front of him and propped his injured foot on it.

"There were men there from the group we left behind on Wake," Patrick said. "And they told me what happened after we left. After the Japs took you and me off Wake in January, they shipped another three hundred fifty of our fellas out that September. They kept ninety-eight of our boys on Wake to finish the work . . . Red was one of 'em." He glanced at Colin, then continued.

"I met a sailor just before I left Japan that took quite an interest in us POWs. He made a phone call to his brother in D.C. as a favor and found out the Navy has reclaimed Wake, but he said all they found there was a bunch of half-starved Jap soldiers. They'd used up all their rations, and their navy never came by to resupply 'em.

"The Navy questioned the Jap commander on Wake about our boys, and he told him they marched them ninety-eight fellas out to the beach in October '43. Lined 'em up . . . shot 'em all."

Colin lowered his head, but he said nothing.

"You get what I'm sayin'?" Patrick asked. "If it's true, that means they killed Red."

"Yeah."

Patrick frowned. "I thought you'd be more upset."

"Guess I've known for a long time that he was dead. Ever since the nightmares started." Colin took a deep breath. "I think I might go see his parents."

"What for? The Navy will tell them what happened."

"I want to tell them what Red meant to me. That he saved my life." He turned to Patrick. "Ever since the war ended, I can't stop thinking about Chaplain, Frank, Arthur, Red. I've been wondering why I made it and they didn't."

"There you go again," Patrick said, feeling around his pockets for a cigarette.

"Here, have one of mine," Colin offered. "I've been saving them. I keep forgetting they're not worth anything out here."

"Thanks." Patrick lit up. "Where'd they take you?"

"Sendai."

"Hey, what about George?"

"He made it. He's still in Japan. Wanted to stay there and see some of the country."

"He what?"

"Yeah, crazy, huh? He said he didn't have any reason to get home, so he thought he'd just have a look around, see how we set up the occupation."

Patrick curled his lip. "He's off his nut. I couldn't wait to get outta there. Even now, it burns me up just seein' a Jap."

Colin sat up. "I know what you mean. They're all over this place, still wearing their uniforms, walking around free as birds after what they did to us."

Patrick gestured angrily. "I seen 'em lining up today right alongside Yanks to get lunch. Pilin' our food on their trays." He slammed his fist against his thigh. "I coulda smashed in all their faces."

His expression changed to an eerie smile, and he batted Colin's arm. "Hey, I gotta story for ya. After the war ended, our camp commandant ordered the guards to march us to meet the Yanks. So we get to this town and there's a battalion of Russian soldiers there. *Women* soldiers, and these dames was big." He spread his arms wide.

"Their lady captain asks if any of the guards mistreated us. So we all point to this one bastard, mean son of a bitch. He don't know what's goin' on. All's a sudden this big Russian dame is walkin' right toward him." Patrick squirmed in his seat, his voice rising.

"She pulls out her sword—and hacks his head clean off. There it is, layin' in the road—and all us guys with our mouths hangin' open." He shook his head in awe. "She wipes her sword on his body and turns around. 'Anyone else?' she asks, but there wasn't another guard in sight. Just swirls of dust where they'd been standin'." Patrick laughed. "What do you think of that?"

"I don't believe it."

"It's true. Swear to God."

Colin thought of Bull, remembering the weight of the bamboo stick in his hand. "What did you feel like when that happened?"

"What do you mean?"

"What was going through your mind?"

Patrick considered the question. "Well, it was kinda strange. I didn't feel nothin' really. Not sick, not glad—nothin'. Nobody cheered, nobody said a word. Just seemed like what was supposed to happen." He glanced at Colin. "That what you meant?"

"I guess so."

Patrick stretched. "I'm feelin' kinda beat. Think I'll go take a nap."

"Did you call home yet?"

"Nah. I'm thinkin' 'bout just showin' up. Surprisin' 'em."

"Are you gonna tell Ellen—everything?"

"Guess I will. Won't you tell Maggie?"

"I don't know. Maybe not."

Patrick stared across the room toward the phone on the desk. "You think I should call? My ma was sickly when I left, ya know? What if . . ."

"Sounds like maybe you should surprise them." Colin handed Patrick his crutches.

Patrick rose and lay a hand against Colin's chest. "Colin, you didn't ever see that big Swede in any of them nightmares, did ya?"

"Marty? No, I never did."

Patrick sighed. "Good. That's good."

Chapter 36

Home, 1945

It was sunny and mild on the day Colin was due home. The leaves had changed colors, a few now falling to the red brick platform of the Union Pacific depot. Across the train tracks, two boys chased each other in the tall grass. Their laughter was infectious. How different today felt from that cold, rainy day four and a half years ago when Colin left for Wake.

Maggie had arrived early to meet his train, but that had been a mistake. She'd been pacing for half an hour already. Her feet were beginning to ache, but she couldn't bring herself to sit down. Each time she tried, she thought she heard the train whistle and jumped to her feet. More people had arrived now, filling in the platform. She couldn't imagine where Colin's mother and sister could be. Agnes and Eddie had remained at home to give Maggie her moment, but she'd assumed Gwen and Mrs. Finnely would be here. She hadn't imagined waiting alone.

"I hear the train!" shouted one of the boys, who had his ear to the track. His mother called him back. He placed a penny on the rail and scrambled back onto the platform. Maggie stood on her toes, her heart racing. She could see nothing and hated the boy for lying. Then she heard the whistle. Her breath came in short pants. A young woman standing beside her chewed her nails.

"Are you waiting for someone?" Maggie asked.

"My husband. He's coming home from the war."

"So's my fiancé."

The young woman smiled. As the train approached, Maggie stepped closer to her. They locked arms as the train rolled to a stop, brakes hissing, smoke rolling across their feet. Porters rushed to place stools at the base of the steps to each car, and the first passengers disembarked.

The young woman cried out and broke away from Maggie to rush toward a sailor. He picked her up and swung her in his arms. Maggie felt a pang of jealousy, then her eyes darted from car to car until, gradually, the passengers stopped appearing. She shook her head and started pushing her way through the crowd. She walked up and down the platform calling for Colin, but soon the passengers had all marched through the arched doorways of the depot and she was alone.

Maggie searched the windows of each car, straining to see inside. She ran into the depot, thinking she might have somehow missed him, but the high wooden benches were nearly empty. She burst through the front doors, surveying the people getting into their cars.

A car stopped in front of her, and the young woman rolled down the window and held out her hand. "Did your fella miss the train?" she asked.

Maggie's voice was frail. She gripped the girl's hand. "I guess so."

"I could see when the next train's due," the girl's husband offered.

"No, thank you. You've been very kind. I hope everything goes well for you."

"He'll be home soon," the girl said.

"I've been telling myself that for four years."

Maggie stepped back to allow the car to pull away. Far off, at the other end of the boulevard, the Capitol Building seemed to lean against the foothills as the city of Boise came awake. If Ida's husband could die the day the war ended, Maggie reasoned, then something could have happened to Colin in the two days since he'd called from San Francisco. She put her hand over her stomach, feeling sick.

Behind the wheel of Eddie's car, she promised herself she would not cry. She dreaded going home to her mother and uncle without Colin. She parked the car in the alley behind Eddie's house and sat there for several minutes feeling sorry for herself. Finally she left the car and walked around the pathway to the front yard of Eddie's house. Across the street, she could see someone sitting on the top step of her porch, arms across his knees, head down. He looked up, and she saw his face. Her handbag fell from her fingers.

Colin rose from the step, and Maggie moved down Eddie's walkway until she stood across the street from her house, staring at Colin, her hand covering her mouth. For a moment, neither moved. Then, slowly, he began to walk toward her.

She ran across the street and into his arms, burying her face in his neck. The spicy smell of his cologne took her back to the days they'd danced at the Miramar, holding each other close. She could almost imagine the years had never passed.

A few houses away, a porch door slammed. Colin startled at

the noise, and Maggie pulled back to look at him. Only then did she fully realize the effects of time. She moved her hands along his thin chest up to a scar on his neck.

Gone was the broad smile that had first attracted her. Now his lips remained closed. His eyes had dimmed beyond the weariness she would expect from a long trip, and his right eye twitched. He took her hands and moved them from his chest, but she couldn't stop touching him. She toyed with a loose button on his shirt, keeping her eyes down, determined not to let him see her concern.

Colin stroked Maggie's hair, his pale, scarred skin contrasting with its rich darkness. When he'd first taken her in his arms, he'd felt only the warmth of her body against his and the way they fit so well together. He could have held her for hours, marveling at her beauty, so much more refined than he remembered. But then she'd pulled back, and he'd seen a shadow cross her face. He moved her hands away from him, smiling so she wouldn't guess there was anything wrong. He motioned toward the porch, taking her hand tentatively to lead her there. When he sat down on the swing he expected her to sit beside him, but she lingered by the steps.

"I went to the depot. I thought you'd missed the train," she said.

He wished she would keep talking. How he'd missed the sound of her voice, the slightly British way she pronounced her words, having grown up around Eddie and Agnes.

"I'm sorry I wasn't there. I caught the night train to surprise you," he explained. "I needed to freshen up when I got in. I wanted . . .to look my best for you," he smoothed his shirt nervously. "I meant to catch you here before you left, but I'm told I just missed you."

"So that's why your mother wasn't at the station. You could

have come to find me there."

"I had no car. And I thought, perhaps, it might be nicer to meet here." He saw her glance at the front window, probably looking for her mother, and wondered if she was disappointed he hadn't come to her as soon as he arrived or if she understood how scared he'd been for this moment. It bothered him he couldn't read her, couldn't tell for sure what she was thinking. He'd always known what the men in camp were thinking. They were thinking about food, about the cold, about survival.

"You look—good," she said.

He wanted so badly to be near her. He took a chance and went to sit on the porch ledge beside where she stood, but he didn't touch her, deciding to wait until she reached for him. He made sure to keep his lips closed when he smiled to hide the gap in his teeth. "I didn't think this would be so hard," he said.

She hesitated, then took his hand.

He held it to his cheek and closed his eyes. His voice shook. "I've thought about this moment so many times. It's what kept me alive."

"Are you really all right, Colin? Did they hurt you?"

He thought about the shrapnel in his arm, the knot on his head, the scars from beatings and work details, the missing tooth, the heart murmur they'd detected at the hospital in Guam, the many vitamins he'd been prescribed, along with medication for dysentery.

"I'm fine," he said.

"Can you tell me about it?"

"Sometime . . . but not today."

He let go of her hand, walked to the end of the porch. The rose garden lay below him. He took his father's watch from his pocket and laid it on the ledge. "I'm not the man I was when I left . . . I've been sick and hungry for too long. I have nightmares

every night about Wake and the camps. About friends that died."
He heard her come to stand behind him, longing to feel her arms
around him.

"There was a Jap interpreter, Ishihara, at my first two camps
that I can't forget. He was pure evil, Maggie. I heard the Allies
have captured him. They'll try him for war crimes, probably
hang him."

"Why was he so cruel?" Maggie asked.

"I don't know. I heard a rumor once that he spent a summer
in Hawaii before the war. That he was beaten up pretty bad by
three American sailors who didn't like the color of his skin. So
he hated all Americans. Others in camp said he wanted revenge
for the Japanese soldiers we killed on Wake."

He turned to face her. "I don't care what his reasons were.
I don't want him to die so easily. I want him to suffer. Like we
did." He slammed his hand against the porch post and regretted
it when he saw her step back.

He rubbed his palm and stared at her a moment, shaking.
"Do you still love me, Maggie? Because so many fellows got
Dear John letters from their girlfriends. A few even called home
from Guam to find their wives had remarried."

Her eyes filled with tears, but she looked at him steadily.
"Yes. I still love you."

His shoulders sagged, and he covered his eyes with his hand.

She led him back to the swing, pulled him down beside her
and lay his head on her shoulder. "You'll get stronger, Colin.
The nightmares will stop, you'll see."

The porch swing creaked as she rocked, the sound unnerving
him. He planted his feet to stop the noise.

"I'm sorry," she said. "Am I doing something wrong?"

"No. Nothing." They sat in silence for a moment. "I see you
still have the ring," he said, finally. "I thought the jeweler might

have taken it back when I was captured."

"He did. But he held it for me that summer. I paid it off with money from my jobs."

He raised his fingers to lift the gold locket from her chest. "I remember this."

She smiled. "I've worn it every day since the island was captured. It kept me close to you." She hesitated, and he lowered his hand.

"I have something to tell you," she said. "I had a good friend for a while. His name was William."

Colin felt something kick at his insides.

"He kept me company when I wasn't sure if you were alive. That's all."

"Did you love him?"

"No. I told you. He was a *friend*. You have to believe that."

He rose from the swing and turned his back on her.

"I wasn't going to tell you, Colin, but I was afraid you'd hear about him from someone else. I don't want you to get the wrong idea." She turned him around to face her and held his hands. "I've been faithful. Through all these years, I've only loved you. Please, tell me you believe that."

He knew he had to believe it, that he couldn't bear to think of her with another man. He nodded and sat down again on the porch ledge, feeling very tired. "So much has changed," he said. "The town, the country. I don't like this new music. My sister is married. She's a mother now." He shook his head. "Maggie, most of the money I'd saved for us is gone. My mother needed it for repairs on our house and to help Gwen while her husband was at war."

"It's all right, Colin. I have money. We'll get by."

"Nothing turned out the way I planned," he said.

"No." She gripped his hands. "But we're *lucky*. You're home

270

and we're together. Nothing else matters."

"It all matters, Maggie. I'm never going to forget what's happened. It's a part of me now." He touched her hair, shorter than he remembered. "And you've changed too."

"But what I've always wanted hasn't changed," she insisted. "To be with you."

He looked out across the lawn, past the trees with their colored leaves and the tidy two-story houses, far out toward the horizon. Out to where Wake Island lay isolated in a vast ocean, and beyond it, toward the ruins of the camps in China and Japan.

He turned to see her watching him closely and straightened up, determined not to weaken again. He'd survived all those years in the camps when so many others hadn't. And he'd survived for this. Surely he had the strength now to be the man she deserved.

"I've kept you waiting so long. But I'll be a good husband to you, Maggie. I promise."

She drew him to her and kissed him. He could feel her tears on his face, or maybe his own. Her body trembled with his. She lay her head against his shoulder and held him tightly. He closed his eyes, feeling her hair soft against his face.

Finally, he was home.

About the Author

Teresa R. Funke has a degree in history and has worked as a researcher for PBS and several museums. She has published dozens of articles, written a history column, and had short stories and essays appear in numerous magazines and anthologies. Two of her essays were listed as Notable Essays by *Best American Essays*. Teresa is also the author of *Dancing in Combat Boots: and Other Stories of American Women in WWII* and a series for young readers called the Home-Front Heroes about children in World War II. A popular presenter and writers' coach, Teresa is also the host of the video series *The Write Series*. Born and raised in Boise, Idaho, she now lives with her husband and three children in Colorado. Please visit her website at www.teresafunke.com

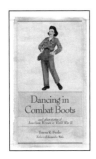

Also by Teresa R. Funke

Dancing in Combat Boots
and Other Stories of American
Women in World War II

ISBN 879-1-935571-09-4
162 pages • softcover • $12.95

Available at amazon.com, barnesandnoble.com and teresafunke.com.

"Women—free, independent, and self-motivated women—were essential to our victory in WWII. Dancing in Combat Boots beautifully recreates that time when American women's roles were evolving and their personal horizons expanding. Poignant and inspiring, these stories celebrate the contributions of America's other war heroes, the women of World War II."

— Doris Weatherford, author of *American Women and World War II*

When the going got tough during World War II, America's women got going. By the millions, housewives and mothers took off their aprons and stepped into factories, offices, hospitals—anywhere capable hands were needed to replace those of the husbands and sons now battling overseas.

The eleven fictional stories in this remarkable collection are based on real women whose experiences were at once typical and extraordinary. Irene bucks rivets in an aircraft factory while Doris learns to pilot military planes. Marjorie survives the Japanese attack on Pearl Harbor while Jean spends three years under guard in a Japanese internment camp. Lucy joins the segregated Women's Army Corp and Kathryn joins the Red Cross—shipping off to the front lines where she dances in combat boots with American GIs.

From the topsy-turvy days following Pearl Harbor, through four long years of hardship, to the post-war campaigns to put women back in their place, these stories reveal the many facets of women's lives as they gave their all for the war effort.

Also by Teresa R. Funke

Doing My Part

First in the Home-Front Heroes Series
for children ages 9 and up

ISBN 978-1-935571-10-0
144 pages • softcover • $7.95

Available at amazon.com, barnesandnoble.com and teresafunke.com.

Based on a true story . . .

Until World War II came along, fourteen-year-old Helen Marshall's biggest problem had been her height. Few men in Hayden's Valley, Illinois are as tall as Helen. But when Helen's mother is hurt and can't work and her favorite cousin ships off to fight, Helen must find a way to support both her family and her country. Along with her best friend, Janie, she takes a summer job at a war factory and discovers that not everyone welcomes her enthusiasm.

Determined to prove she can handle her new responsibilities, Helen must confront a lazy boss, two older women who try to slow down her work, and townspeople who gang up on one of their own. But when she answers the eerie cries of her mysterious German neighbor, Mrs. Osthoff, Helen learns the true sacrifice of war. And when she keeps a secret for a friend, she realizes that grown-up decisions sometimes have life-or-death consequences.